SOLEIL TANGIERE

By

Larry Bonner

ISBN 13: 9781492984986
ISBN: 1492984981
Library of Congress Control Number: 2013920023
CreateSpace Independent Publishing Platform
North Charleston, South Carolina

For Stephanie

A hush in the forest.

The bear stood on its hind legs, its nose quivering.

Twenty feet away the little girl was standing rock still.

Her scent was huge in the bear's world.

The bear fell back on all fours and walked straight up to her.

She stood still and straight as a pine.

He shook his massive head and smelled her.

Sniff. Her legs. Sniff. Her arms, her face.

Still and straight as a pine.

Her eyes narrowed. Then closed.

1

MONTANA BLUES

Francois Tangiere gripped the wheel of his truck as the snow whipped across the windshield. The cold, biting winters, which had been so much a part of his life since his birth in Quebec fifty-four years ago, were starting to get to him. He refused to write it off to aging—he was an active man with a young body and mind, and he had observed that when men started giving in to aging, they accelerated it.

Nevertheless, lately he found himself shivering at the first sign of snow.

He had always been a miner back in Canada, where he had lived within a fifty-mile radius of his birthplace for most of his life. But the mining business could be fickle to its employees, and when Frank was let go from his last job, he decided to make a move when he heard that there was a fresh opportunity in the States. He felt lucky to have gotten a job last year in Montana with Rapid River Mines: their discovery of a platinum "reef" in the foothills of the Rockies a few years back had opened up calls for experienced miners. The idea of being thousands of feet underground and taking outsize personal risks didn't faze him at all. He had rented a small house in a nearby town and moved in with his wife and youngest daughter.

He swerved to avoid a pile of snow. The newscaster on the truck radio was saying something about President Reagan holding a summit meeting with the Russians next month. Frank turned it off—he wasn't that interested.

"You drive like me." A voice from the passenger seat.

"*Non*. And if *you* drive like *me*, you're grounded. I don't care how old you are."

As the truck bounced along the icy road, Frank glanced at his youngest daughter in the passenger seat. Soleil had just turned nineteen, but looked younger. She had few of her father's physical attributes, and the local rumor mill had been busy since she was born. From under her green knit cap peeked a peaches-and-cream face with a small, straight nose, determined lips and sapphire-blue eyes, all framed by long, straight, blond hair that fell out over the shoulders of her insulated parka. A few strands of that hair were constantly in front of her face. She wasn't short, about five foot nine, and had the slim and athletic figure that active life in the outdoors bestows on young women. *Mon petite Heidi*, Frank would call her. His Swiss Miss. She was his sixth and last child, an afterthought and "another mouth to feed," as some of the Tangiere brood were wont to remind one another. And she was his secret favorite.

That favoritism resided within Frank alone. His wife, Jeanette, was too worn out and overworked to express much emotion, and his son and three other daughters had resented Soleil in differing degrees from the moment her pretty baby face made its unwanted entrance in the house. Only the oldest, Camille, didn't torment Soleil—the age difference was too wide—eleven years, so most of the time Camille was interested in other, more grown-up things. Her attitude toward Soleil was live and let live, even though the kid was slowly developing supermodel looks. Well, the world is big enough for two bombshells, she thought charitably. Most of the time.

Frank's second son, Kent, was killed at age twenty-two in a timber accident in Alberta. Of all her siblings, Kent was the only one who had clearly loved Soleil. She adored Kent and marveled at the breadth of his wide-ranging knowledge and interests—rare commodities growing up in a world of miners and loggers. With his passing, Soleil felt a profound sense of abandonment. Kent and I loved messing around in the snow, she thought. If he were here now, we would be having a blast rocketing through this little blizzard with Dad.

Since childhood, Soleil was out of the house at every chance, and the Canadian woods were her turf. She was afraid of nothing in the forest, and the forest gave back to her—gave her a healthy body, a clear and active mind, and a survivor's skill set.

When she was ten, her brother Kent built her a whole gym set out of scrap metal tubing he took home from a job site. It was like a free-form monkey bar and workout set, and Soleil quickly turned herself into an accomplished amateur gymnast. The rusting gym set still stood out in the yard. But Kent was gone.

On weekends when her older siblings would be involved in their own lives, Frank and Soleil would throw their bows and arrows in the back of the pickup and go out to shoot target. The local boys around here are becoming men, her father reasoned, which means they're becoming crazed sex maniacs, and I'm glad I taught her to shoot straight—she's going to need a ton of help keeping them off her. *Merde!*

Since Kent's passing, Soleil had grown much closer with her father. He had a quiet air about him that she understood— why use words when you can use your face or your eyes to tell people what you're thinking? Or hide things from them.

Frank peeked sideways at her profile as the truck bounced along. She was completely calm. What was in her mind? Soleil's mind was always working. When the weather gets warmer, I'll try to make some more time to shoot with her as we used to. Life's moving on, and soon time together will become rare.

And this was her first day on a new job. A job that she felt lucky to get—it allowed her to be up in the mountains again and to be with her father as well. It didn't get much better than that.

All through high school and summer vacations, Soleil had always worked part time—in stores, restaurants, and of course for some of the mine offices.

In Soleil's world, "college" was a word not even mentioned, let alone an actual consideration. This was a shame, as she had a sharp native intelligence. And being bilingual from birth, Soleil had that rare ability to listen to almost any language and start learning it at an astonishingly fast clip. Not that this was of much use here in the Montana mountains. The only French that the men at the Rapid River mine were familiar with were French fries or worse, and her father had ordered her to stay as far away from these roughnecks as possible. Soleil's effect on men was Frank's biggest fear, but she had other plans in life than to be an *objet du desir*.

As she grew through her teens, she was forced to learn a few necessary skills concerning the men her father was so worried about because Soleil Tangiere was just plain beautiful. By anyone's standards. No makeup, no improvements necessary. So, by necessity, she learned the fine art of saying no in a hundred disarming and non insulting ways.

Now, at nineteen, she was conservative but not prudish about sex, and she wasn't in heat twenty-four hours a day as the boatload of boys who couldn't stop thinking about her fantasized. There were plenty of hopefuls, but just a lucky guy or two once in a blue moon. Soleil didn't like to have her thinking done for her. Especially about that. It's my choice, after all, not the man's. When it comes down to it, I make my own decisions.

And now she was going to work at the mine, and if this new crop of men had to be taught their places right away, she was the one who had to do it. Soleil had natural street smarts and survival skills and knew how to cleverly use them to keep the boys at arm's length. Frank smiled to himself: she also kept a hunting knife with her all the time. He had given it to her on her last birthday. It had *S.* engraved on a small plaque set into its bone handle. It may have been an odd gift for a girl, but not for Soleil. She treasured it.

Soleil was lucky—the company, Rapid River Mines, needed someone to work in the office, which was really just a large trailer raised on blocks, with a few makeshift steps leading up to its metal door. The job was for a much-needed Girl Friday. Debbie, the current go-to gal, was in her ninth month, and the company needed a replacement to answer the phones, write the checks, and to be generally dumped on by just about everyone who could get away with it. It was a shrewd move on Frank's part to bring Soleil along when he approached Don Henderson, the mine manager, about the position—Soleil brought sunshine into a room, and to turn this eager and smart young girl down was not easy. Safety wasn't really an issue, as she wouldn't be in the mine itself, and her outgoing nature was a welcome plus. Besides, she would work for less than Debbie and was far, far more mobile.

Don Henderson, however, was no saint. He was a heavyset, chain-smoking, taciturn man who was not easy to be around. His eyes were always on the move as if he were being hunted. At least he kept a fair distance from Soleil.

Soleil's first week on the job consisted mostly of turning down advances, ignoring suggestive comments, and generally laying out the guidelines for the men vis-à-vis chances with her, which were zero. Once that was squared away, they seemed to return to their previous cooled-down state. She knew she was doing everyone a favor, including herself.

A few weeks into the job, on a windy and snowy day, Soleil was going over the time cards when the trailer door opened and Henderson came in accompanied by a police officer. The cop was massive, tall and with a heavy gut, and though he had a smile on his face, the back of his porcine eyes had a cast of animal violence. One look at Soleil, and her heart froze.

"Well, well, Donnie boy, what is *this*?" the cop stood before Soleil's small desk looking down at her. The man was around fifty and obviously comfortable in his intimidating persona. "Debbie's off today?" His barely disguised leer was unfortunately familiar to Soleil, and though she usually had half a dozen standard sarcastic or disarming replies for this kind of situation, the uniform and the heavy holstered gun in the belt threw her off. She said nothing.

"This is Soleil, Frank Tangiere's daughter," said Henderson reluctantly. "She's filling in while Debbie's off having her fifth kid." Soleil looked sideways and managed a short, silent wave of greeting.

"Well, young lady, So-*lay*, you be careful around these bully boys—they have no common sense and even less self-control when it comes to pretty little girls like yourself. Any one of them stallions gets out of hand, give old Bull Dorsey a call. My number's still 9-1-1." He stood close to her desk waiting for a response to this marvelous joke. "I *am* the chief, you know." He wasn't smiling while he waited for a reply. When none was forthcoming, he turned to Henderson.

"Get rid of the kid, Don, we have to talk." Henderson threw her a look, and Soleil straightened her papers, rose, and passed quickly by Dorsey on her way to the door.

Without bothering to look at her, his meaty hand reached out surprisingly fast and accurately and closed around her wrist.

"Remember, So-*lay*. 9-1-1." This last witticism was freighted with a threatening subtext. Soleil looked down. There was a crushing squeeze on her wrist, and the hand was released. She made her way quickly out the door. The cold air was freezing and welcome, but after one step, Soleil slipped on the makeshift steps and wound up sprawled on the cold ground. She shook her head and was about to stand up when she saw a small shape move quickly under the trailer. It was a cat, emaciated and obviously frightened. Soleil wiggled into the space below the trailer, but the cat was skittish and fled out the far side into the snowy yard. Soleil vowed to bring a bowl of food for the animal in the morning.

She was turning on hands and knees to get herself out of there when she heard voices coming from above through the floor. Normally, she would not try to hear what people were talking about, but the voices were harsh and angry, and Soleil was nervous. Henderson was speaking.

"Dorsey, there just ain't no more," he said with finality.

"Let me clue you in, Donnie boy. There's more, lots more, and you better step up production here if you don't want a problem: a problem from me, and a problem from Smythe's boys. The British are going to reevaluate my influence here, and I want them to stay nice and happy, savvy?"

"This is a platinum mine, Chief, not a gold dig," said Henderson. "You can't just 'step it up.' Platinum is hugely more difficult to mine than gold. It's not just lying around in riverbeds or in veins in the rock. This mine may be considered 'rich,' but we have to process over twelve tons of ore just to get a yield of thirty grams."

"Boo hoo, Nancy, now *I need more ounces!*" Dorsey growled. "Those limey pricks have been paying you off with gold coins forever, and now I need ten more a month than before. My expenses are growing, pal."

Inside the trailer, Henderson watched apprehensively as Dorsey paced liked a caged bear. "They pay you off, too! I'm mortally sick of being at the back end of this deal. It's bleeding me here."

"You'll cough 'em up and *now*, or I'll close this place down by sunset." Dorsey's anger boiled over. "Look at all these safety hazards." He went to the wall and pulled the fire extinguisher off. "Look at this! It needs a charge. That's a violation—a hundred-dollar violation!" He flung the extinguisher into a metal filing cabinet, where it made a hellacious crashing sound.

The wind reached under the trailer and brought snowflakes with it. Soleil flinched and was shivering, but kept listening intently.

"OK, OK, I have some extras," Henderson was saying. "Hold your horses." He crossed the room and went into the small bathroom, closing the door behind him. He reached carefully behind the toilet and pulled out a battered green container of bathroom cleanser. He twisted off a false bottom and looked in. Within glittered a small pile of one-ounce gold coins. He counted out five, carefully replaced the container, and walked back into the room.

"Here." He nearly threw the coins at Dorsey. "I'll have more next month."

Great hiding place, Dorsey laughed to himself. Then he exploded at Henderson, "You're goddam right you will! But by next *week*, by God! Don't mess with me, Donnie. I will for sure bring you and your ooh-la-la platinum mine down. We *both* know that you're digging on a dozen private land lots, and we *both* know what happened to the owners who found out and were going to make a stink. That can easily, *easily* happen to you, you little shit!" The two stood almost nose to nose, staring each other down.

"And there's this," Dorsey continued in a low, ominous tone. "Smythe's concluded that someone here is ready to spill everything to the federales. It's down to half a dozen men or so. I'm not sure who he thinks it is, but knowing that vicious Brit prick, anything and everything is on the table, including covering up his tracks if he gets too spooked. And you know what I mean by 'covering tracks,' Don."

The mine manager just stared at him.

After seeing that he wouldn't get much of a rise from Henderson, Dorsey broke the silence. "Now, I'm gonna go, Donnie, and I expect as always for you to keep your damn mouth shut about everything to everyone, or you and a lot of innocent people are going to suffer." He opened the door to leave. He took a step out and started to close it behind him, then thought better of it. He turned back into the room. "And speaking of innocent people: that new little lady you have working here. All this drama has got me in a real *jivey* mood, if you know what I mean. Me and So-*lay* could become real good friends." Under the trailer, Soleil's eyes went wide. "Her dear old dad, Frank, is on Smythe's short list of likely stool pigeons, by the way, so the situation appears to be getting hairier and hairier. Better keep a special eye on him, and I mean it." He turned and left before Henderson could stop him.

As the cop bounded heavily down the trailer steps, Soleil pushed herself as far back under the trailer as she could. Her heart was cold. This was awfully bad. A small voice inside her was warning that it would go from bad to worse, and soon. She couldn't help but shudder.

When she heard the squad car crunching away over the snow, she eased herself quickly out of her hiding place and went to look for her father. He was down in the mine, so she had no choice but to return to the trailer.

At 5:30 Soleil straightened up the papers on her little desk, got her few personal things out of the bottom drawer, and left. Henderson was nowhere to be seen. She walked down the hill to where the men parked their cars and waited in the passenger seat of the truck. In a few minutes, her father appeared.

He got in heavily, started the truck, and drove out of the complex of small huts and large drilling machines. He smelled like the earth, beneath which he had spent so much of his life. Soleil laid out what she had heard when she was under the trailer. She left out the part about Dorsey's plans to assault her, but Frank was smart enough to put two and two together.

After a mile or two Frank said to Soleil, "Now here's what's going to happen. You're gone from the job and from this worksite, and that's a pity, but there's nothing I can do about that. I don't know what 'short list' means, but I am sure that we might be looking at a world of trouble here. You and your mother are going to go down to Pinedale for a few weeks, and I'll have your brother Rolf drive you." Soleil's three sisters were out of the loop: Camille, Lana, and Nannette were scattered about the northern United States and Canada with their husbands or boyfriends.

"Come on, Dad, you're not going back there. You can't."

"Tomorrow I'm going in and telling Henderson that you got a touch of the flu. I'll act as if nothing else is wrong, but I've got to get a reading on this situation. I can't let it lie. And I can deal with a drunk or a miner with a nasty attitude, but a cop like this will likely find a way to have the law and its power on his side, no matter how bad he behaves."

Soleil sat looking straight ahead. The problem with the law was the people who were in charge of wielding it. If they were rotten, as plenty people naturally were, then the law became the sword, not the shield, and people like the Tangieres were often the targets.

Jeanette was exhausted when they came in the back door of the small rental house. Soleil's mother was a good woman, but back in Quebec, she had been the matriarch to an overcrowded house with little money, and on top of that, she had a habit of taking in stray family members, sometimes for years at a time. One day it just became too much, and Jeanette's motor just started running down.

Frank went in the bedroom to talk to his wife, but it was difficult, and she could scarcely be roused. Despite the urgency, Frank knew this conversation wouldn't happen now—it would have to wait until morning. He went into the kitchen, put the receiver from the wall phone to his ear, and dialed his son Rolf in Billings.

"Rolf's coming for you and your mother around six tomorrow night," he said to Soleil after hanging up. "I'm going to the mine in the morning." When she started to protest, he said, "No, don't interrupt me. I've made up my mind. You stay put until Rolf gets here in the evening."

Soleil knew it would be useless to argue. But she also held little faith in Rolf—her only surviving brother was a chronic no-show con man and couldn't be trusted to follow even the simplest instructions. She went into her small room, sat on the side of her bed, and stared into the middle distance. After a while, she quietly packed a few things in a canvas bag, knelt by the side of the bed, and reached under until she felt what she was looking for.

She went outside and carefully placed her compound bow and quiver in the back of the pickup. If there's one thing Dad taught me to do well, it's to shoot—arrows, rifles, guns— all of it. She looked at the bow and arrows on the truck bed. He might need these. I might need these.

Dorsey guided his squad car into the driveway of his impressive log home. He went around the side of the house and let himself in the back door. He hung his parka on the hook on the inside of the door and walked through the kitchen into his large living room.

Dorsey's wife had left him years ago, and he hadn't seen either his son or his daughter in over a year. Life's just so much crap, he repeated to himself on a regular basis, but he never blamed Madge—he drank and whored around and beat her so much, especially near the end, that if he were her, he would have left a lot sooner. Good thing I have beaucoup money now, he thought.

For some time now, Dorsey had been working on his "retirement plan." And this plan featured some surprising and very lucrative angles. Shortly after Rapid River Mines opened their platinum project in the next valley, a call came in for Dorsey at the station from a man named Smythe. Dorsey nearly hung up when he heard the British accent, but he was now vastly grateful that he had kept his cool and agreed to meet with the man here in the privacy of his own house.

Smythe turned out to be pale and tall, with thinning hair and a very serious demeanor, but his handshake was as firm as Dorsey's and he spoke with a measured and alien precision using some words that Dorsey didn't quite recognize. But the idea came across loud and clear.

Smythe outlined how his company in London had taken over the operations at the Rapid River mine and their studies indicated they would have to expand in a growing circle around five miles in diameter, starting from the center of the operation. Approaches to some of the local farmers and other residents to sign leases allowing for this activity were sadly and foolishly turned down, even with the promise of ample compensation. What can you do, Chief? How can you help us? We can help you. Are you familiar with gold?

Smythe, through obliquities and innuendo, outlined the plan. For each landowner Dorsey could "persuade" to sign off on a lease he would discover a satisfying packet of untraceable gold coins in his backyard, or in a train station locker, a post office box—wherever.

Dorsey was about to throw the cuffs on this Limey when he heard a dull jingle. Smythe's hand came out of his pocket holding a suede drawstring bag. He bent over Dorsey's wood coffee table and emptied the contents. Thirty one-ounce gold coins winked at Dorsey. He instantly liked those coins. Really liked them. And this was Dorsey's turf. At that point he decided that he had to frisk Smythe thoroughly and check for a wire. He came up clean. And he was singing Dorsey's song.

The chief of police settled back to hear the rest of Smythe's proposal. Each time a citizen could be persuaded to allow mining leases on his or her land, Dorsey would receive 250 of these coins. Each month another twenty would show up from their latest employee, Don Henderson down at the mine. Dorsey understood that the crisscross of payoffs between him and Henderson would ensure that they would all stay on the same path.

Dorsey had strong-armed his way up to chief over a dozen years in the police force due primarily to the fact that he had been a master of backstabbing, departmental glad-handing, and general butt kissing. Lately though, he had soured of it all, and Smythe had approached him at just the right juncture in his "retirement planning": Dorsey was in the process of getting his stash together to leave for sunnier climes. Lately he had dreams of being on a deserted beach with a brown girl. God save the queen, he thought, as he decided to go all in with the Limey bastard's proposition.

Now, two years, seven extortions, and three murders later, Dorsey sat in his large, two-story living room and contemplated the stuffed moose head hung way up high on the opposite wall.

This nice house of his and all his other goodies had come from slowly feeding some of his gold coins out into the market. Hell, some Jew from LA even comes by a few times a year to lay the cold, hard green on me in exchange for some of my coins. Dorsey had around a thousand of them hidden all over his property—some buried in the backyard, others in the basement, and most of them, over a hundred pounds of them, carefully stuffed in that fine moose head bolted way up near the sixteen-foot ceiling. The moose seemed to smile at him from way up there.

The chief had long ago resigned himself to the knowledge that he had degenerated mentally and physically, and he had given up any hope of the spiritual redemption that his mother had wailed about when he was a kid. He also decided that the moose would now be coming down and its treasure would head out, along with Dorsey, to Costa Rica. Screw the British, screw Henderson, screw everything. I'm a millionaire now, and it's time to saddle up.

But he didn't saddle up. He got heavily drunk and sprawled on the living room couch. Tomorrow will be my last visit to the mine, he thought before he passed out. I'll have a few words with Henderson, maybe pick up my new little girlfriend, and have one last Montana-sized party. Little fireflies were flitting around behind his eyes. Then all was black.

It was after noon when he finally hefted himself off the couch, got a beer out of the kitchen refrigerator, shrugged on his parka with the police patches on the arms, and headed out to his squad car.

Three emergency services vehicles and a fire truck were at the mine when Dorsey pulled up. He got out of his car and grabbed the closest man.

"What happened?" he asked. Oh crap.

"A cave-in in tunnel twelve. Six men trapped. It doesn't look good. Explosion of some kind, but there were no explosives supposed to be there." The air was almost impenetrable with a thick cloud of dust that was erupting from the mine and rapidly enveloping the mine site.

"You know who they are?"

"Jeffries, Murphy, the Johanssen brothers, Garrard, and Tangiere."

Dorsey let go of the man's arm. What? Did Henderson engineer this stunt? Impossible! It's too soon, totally unnecessary, and if what I think happened *has* happened, it's way too radical to be orchestrated by that prick of a mine manager, even if he is on Smythe's payroll. Henderson was far too much of a pansy to even think of such a thing. And my departure now is going to look way too coincidental. Damn it!

Suddenly there was another dull blast from the direction of the mine. Shouts and voices flew. The smoke got even thicker. What in hell is going on here?

As if in answer to the question, Henderson appeared through the fog. He saw Dorsey and froze. The cop strode up to him and whispered in his face, "Did you do this?"

Soleil had been at the edge of the mine elevator.

"Steve, have you seen my dad?" she asked an old miner she knew. The man nodded his head, pointed to the elevator, and indicated that her father was down in the mine. Soleil thought: I have to get him and myself as far away from here as I can, and right...

A loud roar blasted out of the mine. Soleil was thrown on her back by the force of the compressed air and sudden mini-earthquake beneath her feet. Then another blast tripped her as she was frantically pulling herself up. It took a few moments to orient herself, and then she was standing in a thick cloud.

She could barely see three feet in front of her. It was suddenly eerily quiet, a strange lull in the eye of a hurricane. Smoke laden with a heavy brown dust swirled around Soleil's head, around her eyes.

Slowly a figure loomed out of the smoke—a man in official-looking tan overalls. The letters MMSO were stitched in thick black letters on one of the pockets. "What's happening?" Soleil yelled.

Now the apparition was right in front of her. She stared at the weird grimace on his face—wild and unreadable. It almost looked like a grin. A sly, mocking, evil grin. He came within a foot or two of her, and then he was lost in the cloud of dust and soot. Shouting and screaming began all around her.

Soleil suddenly knew with a dark horror that there was no hope.

Henderson looked about to faint. "There was a guy from the Montana Mining Safety Office here this morning,

Dorsey, to conduct an inspection. He showed me papers, and it looked legit. Oddly enough, he asked if you were here."

Dorsey froze. Was it someone from England? Of course! These British bastards seemed able to read his mind. He said, "What did you tell him, you moron?" and instantly regretted it when it dawned on him that the trailer was likely bugged. Damn! Oh, damn, I'm being set up along with this idiot Henderson. We're going down for this! Rot in hell, Smythe!

Henderson was also at the breaking point. He stared at Dorsey for a minute and then exploded, "I said what I said to him, *Chief*! It all smelled like shit, and that's what you are, Dorsey. Maybe the evil bastard thought *you* were down the mine and wanted to do humanity a favor. The rest happened fast."

Crap, thought Dorsey, I'm outta here now. He pushed away from Henderson and strode to his squad car. Over his shoulder he lied: "I'll be back with more men." He got in the car, put it in gear, pulled a quick 180, and took off.

Henderson was almost apoplectic with dread and fear, and his eyes were barely registering his surroundings. Damn all this! As he debated whether or not to call Smythe now, a pickup truck roared by, snapping him out of it. He looked after it and could have sworn the driver had long blond hair.

Back at his house, Dorsey packed rapidly. He knew there was no way he could get the gold out of there on short notice, but most of it was safely buried in the basement and the backyard. No one will find it. I'll just get those coins out of the moose, pack them in three or four boxes, and forward them to my faggot half brother in Kalispell. He lives in the fear of me and the fear of God (in that order), so there won't be a problem.

Dorsey went to the shed in back of the house for his folding ladder, the one that he had been using to load handfuls of gold coins into the moose head each month. He got the ladder into the house, leaned it up against the living room wall, and climbed until he was near the ceiling of the two-story-high living room. That was when the phone rang. He climbed back down the ladder and picked up the phone hesitantly.

"Dorsey, it looks as if someone was about to squeal to your FBI about our little operation. Or maybe not, but why take the chance? Either way, everything worked out." It was that odd familiar voice.

"Smythe, you lousy prick! You better run all the way back to England! Don't even try to railroad me now—you murdered those people, not me!"

Smythe's laughter came over the phone. "I'm in England, you lout. I'm not in America."

"What do you mean, you're in England now?"

"I'm not the only one with interests at stake here, Dorsey. And I don't have to do the menial work."

"Who set those explosives?" Dorsey screamed into the phone. "Who was at the mine?" When only a high-pitched chuckle came through the phone, Dorsey exploded.

"You put me in this deep shit, and you're in *England*? No, Smythe, guess what? Better hide in some Yorkshire pudding, 'cause I'm catching the next plane to London and coming for your British ass..." Smythe had hung up. "Smythe! Smythe!"

Damn it.

Back up the ladder again, and he had removed two of the three bolts holding the moose head in place with a wrench when he heard her voice.

"You have to answer to *me*, now."

Dorsey froze. He turned his head slowly and looked down. Unbelievably, there, just inside the doorway to the kitchen, was the foxy girl, Tangiere's daughter. And if she thinks she's going to shoot me with that compound bow she's holding, she must be on crack.

He squinted at her and recognized her look, a look of barely controlled fury.

"You killed my father. And those other miners too. I want answers," she continued, holding the bow as if ready to let an arrow fly. "Who's Smythe? And who else is involved?" Her eyes blazed with fury.

Screw this, it's messing up my time line. She's gotta go.

"Sure, I iced them all," he lied. "Yeah, and it was a hoot. Especially blowing up your old man."

Soleil almost missed Dorsey's hand quickly pulling the gun from his belt holster. Her quick side step saved her life as a bullet blasted into the floor a few inches to her left. The noise was deafening. In the next second, she moved like a blur.

The arrow entered near Dorsey's navel, passed out his back, and stuck, quivering and red, in the wall a few feet under the massive moose head.

Shocked, he dropped the wrench and clung to the ladder, staring stupidly at his belly.

"I want answers," she was saying as she frantically reloaded the bow. "Who's Smythe? And who else is involved?" But she didn't take into account the determination and adrenaline overload that Dorsey was experiencing. It wasn't going to stop here. Oh no, this little bitch is going down and going down now. She'll pay for this.

Soleil was stunned by Dorsey's wild leap from the ladder straight at her. His massive body hit her in the shoulder feet first, and she fell hard. Her bow and arrows clattered across the floor and wound up behind the large couch that occupied the center of the room. Girl and cop rolled together violently across the floor.

Soleil was suddenly on her back. Dorsey's florid face and wild eyes were an inch from hers, his massive body an immovable weight. His hot whiskey breath gagged her. Blood seeped from his wound between them.

"Nice try, but you're done, girlie." Soleil couldn't move. Dorsey pushed his bulk off her a few inches then backhanded her across the face. Her lips split, and blood splattered her hair. "It's your funeral. For sure."

His gun suddenly jabbed against her forehead. It felt huge. It felt cold. Bleeding heavily from his belt area, he pushed himself up in a kneeling position over her and ripped at her parka. It opened, and he reached for her.

His hand impaled itself on the bone-handled hunting knife her father had given her for her birthday. Soleil had awkwardly pulled it from its sheath a moment before Dorsey slammed into her, and the tip of its naked blade had tangled in her shirt between her breasts. The finely honed steel went through his hand, and Dorsey yowled. For just an instant, the gun in his other hand wavered. Soleil snarled, and both her hands closed on Dorsey's gun hand and the weapon. She yelled and twisted the hand almost back on itself. The gun fired, and the roar deafened her and filled the room. Soleil felt a searing pain in her arm as the bullet blasted within a millimeter of her skin and blew a red-spewing chunk out of Dorsey's shoulder. Screaming, the policeman rolled off her.

He somehow held onto the gun and pushed himself like a crab on his back until his head came up against the wall at the base of the ladder, all the while howling with the insane pain. He tried to pull the hunting knife out of his hand with his teeth but saw that Soleil was already in motion. She dove behind the couch and disappeared. Dorsey lifted his head and fired twice into the couch, the thundering bullets kicking blossoming chunks of stuffing out of the cushions. Then his eyes flew wide as Soleil rose quickly from behind the couch, her bow notched and aimed at his chest. As he pointed his gun at her he heard her say, "Where's a good cop when you need one?"

The arrow crashed through his rib cage and stuck, pushing the man flat on his back. Dorsey's gun fired upward wildly, and the bullet smashed into the last bolt holding the heavy stuffed head high above on the wall. Dorsey's manic eyes looked upward as it broke free. "Oh shit," he managed to croak.

The moose head, packed tightly with 175 pounds of gold coins, zoomed down on Dorsey from its height of fifteen feet. The moose had a sideways grin on its thin lips as it crashed into Dorsey's face, breaking through the police-man's nose and most of his skull and shearing off his jaw, which rammed down into his neck, and the heads of both man and moose simultaneously exploded in a gory blast of fur, bone, hair, and glittering gold. Blood hosed out in all directions as the ruptured artery in Dorsey's neck drenched the body, the floor, the wall, and the gold coins in dark red. There was a clattering of coins, an antler crashed loudly through a glass coffee table, and Dorsey's body wrenched in a final twisting paroxysm. The coppery smell of blood mixed with that of gunpowder.

A sudden ringing silence.

A shaft of sunlight in the gun smoke air.

Soleil came around the couch and walked slowly over to what used to be the chief of police. She was unaware that the bow had dropped from her shaking hands, and she had to hold herself back from throwing up over everything. Her ears were loudly ringing, and her face and arm were bleeding.

The body was at the center of a gruesome pool of spreading blood and gold. Dorsey was an unidentifiable mass from the neck up, with an arrow sticking straight up from his chest. Soleil was sick and shaking. She leaned over the body and wrenched her hunting knife out of the bloody and still slightly twitching hand. She straightened up, wobbled to the door, took one more hard look, and left.

As Soleil walked away from the house, she knew that it would be very, very difficult from this point onward. They'll be coming after me right away—the police, probably the FBI, the owners of the mine, that guy Smythe, and anyone else involved.

She was moving in a dream: Dorsey's hand probably didn't physically set off that mine explosion—he wasn't there: I saw him drive up right after the explosions, and he probably wasn't clever enough to orchestrate all of it. And Smythe, whoever he is, is in England. He's responsible too. He killed Dad, too. She had overheard the whole phone conversation with Smythe at Dorsey's house. She had been in the kitchen listening in on another phone.

But Dorsey was beyond question responsible in part for the murder of her father and the other miners. She had been hoping to somehow scare, and if necessary, wound him enough to slow him down and somehow get him to confess. Face it, Soleil, she said to herself—somehow get revenge. He killed my dad, that fat disgrace to the human race.

She got in the pickup truck and drove it back to the small rental house. She left it in the back of the house but didn't go inside. There was no way she could go inside and speak to her mother about any of this now—it would kill her. So she just went out to the street and started walking.

Now the situation had come wildly unglued. Someone had used Dorsey for planning and executing the string of murders that had taken place in this area over the last couple of years. And he wasn't the only killer. The other killer or killers had yet to show themselves to the girl, and ironically she had done the one thing possible to embolden them—she wound up doing their dirty work by taking Dorsey out of the equation. Turning herself in now left her no exit strategy.

Even if she could evade Smythe, which seemed doubtful, Dorsey's cop friends would make sure that she would be murdered in jail in short order—cops have their own rules for cop killers.

Moreover, there was a major mass murder in which her father lost his life and she lost her only true friend left in the world. Someone will have to take the responsibility. As long as I'm alive, that is.

Dorsey was dead, and now she had to find her father's other killers.

And it's going to be at my own speed and on my own terms. It might take a long time, but I don't care. They didn't even give me a chance to say good-bye. Not a chance.

She wouldn't forget, and she wouldn't stop.

She had changed.

Forever.

The street crested, and snow began to fall. The figure of the girl in the parka got smaller and fainter the farther along the road she went.

And then she was gone.

2

THE STREET

Izzy's wife was a noodge. She was on him for every little thing every day. It was not enough that she was the undisputed master of their row-on-row house in Astoria, Queens, but since they worked together, her watchful eye was on him every minute and then some. But when I'm at work, forget the eyeballing already—at least I'm the boss in front of the customers.

Izzy Gutthelf was almost seventy, and the hair on his head had long ago taken a permanent vacation. He and Brenda had been married forty years, and their two daughters were both married now—one lived in Jersey, one in Brooklyn, and Izzy was proud that he had put them both through college and they were both betrothed to nice Jewish boys. Yet the Gutthelfs didn't understand why their daughters rarely came to visit. Certainly they were involved in their own lives, but they had become distant. Maybe those nice boys weren't that nice after all, Brenda often mused.

The Gutthelfs got on the train each weekday and traveled into Manhattan to their business. Gutthelf Fine Jewelry was a "booth" in a ground floor jewelry exchange on Forty-Seventh Street between Fifth and Sixth Avenues. Their booth, their entire business, measured ten feet on a side. The front was a glass counter, and at the back was a safe. Within the confines of the space, two chairs were jammed in with a small jeweler's repair bench, which doubled as a lunch table. There were over a hundred similar businesses in that one exchange.

It was there that Brenda Gutthelf sat, early on a Wednesday afternoon, quietly munching a pastrami on rye, while Izzy leaned over the glass counter, which contained his collection of rings, pendants, and bracelets. One eye was on the front of the jewelry exchange, another on the goings-on within a twenty-foot radius. Do I have what these lookers and buyers seek? Izzy's inner voice asked for the ten thousandth time. I wish this booth were closer to the door of the exchange—lookers have to pass by two dozen of my competitors just to wander by mine. It's not easy earning a living.

As he was leaning on the counter, he noticed a young girl coming slowly down the aisle looking casually into each showcase. Eventually she came to Gutthelf.

"So, young lady, what can I do you out of today?" Izzy had been using this same threadbare line for over half a century. It was kind of a trademark.

"Oh, just looking." Izzy could see the girl was not at all looking, and a small alarm inside him told him there was something wrong.

Something was different about her. Though she looked all of sixteen or seventeen, she was certainly not one of the raft of white street hustlers and "hos," as they were known today, who got off buses from Milwaukee and Omaha and cruised the exchanges for a variety of reasons, almost all illegal or immoral. This girl's face told Izzy that her troubles were greater than that.

She had the look of the hunted.

Brenda glanced up from her sandwich and saw the look too. She got up heavily.

"Darling, what's wrong?" she asked the girl.

"Oh," the girl said, "nothing, really," as she looked dully down toward the countertop. But as she tried to pull her worn and darkly stained parka closer around her, the Gutthelfs saw something even more frightening in her eyes—this girl was starving, and they both knew that could not be hidden. And the stains on the coat—that couldn't be dried blood. Could it?

With the Jewish mother's instinct of putting two and two together and coming up with five, Brenda said, "You have a place you're staying, no? Don't lie to me, please; your face can't lie."

"Could...could I sit down for just a minute?" Soleil had had it. Almost ten days of hellish travel, mostly by foot but also by hitching rides, had been punctuated by fending off innumerable men who tended to brook little restraint when they spotted the young blond hitchhiker. More than once her hunting knife had been the deciding equalizer that had kept her safe. She had literally walked over the George Washington Bridge last night and was now out of destinations and goals. She had reached New York, where she thought she might be able to disappear, but she had no further immediate plans. She knew she wasn't thinking clearly, and her head and stomach ached fiercely.

Izzy opened the wooden flap on the counter top that gave him access to the little space behind. As he took Soleil's elbow to help her, her knees gave way, and she collapsed in a heap.

Brenda went into action. She got on her knees and felt Soleil's pulse, which was weak, and she listened to her breathing.

"Benny!" she yelled across the aisle, "Bring over some of that soup!" The Armenian stone dealer rushed over with a steaming Styrofoam cup of what was up to that moment his lunch. A small crowd began to gather in front of the booth.

Soleil came up from her stupor, and Izzy got her onto one of the chairs. "OK, everyone, show's over," he said to the other jewelers. "She just couldn't stand the great deal I was giving her on some diamond earrings, and she keeled over. Good-bye. Shoo!" He made waving motions with his arms. The curious dealers returned to their little businesses.

Soleil took a tentative sip of the soup and then started to down it. "Easy, sweetheart," Brenda clucked and fussed, "you'll burn your gullet, and then what?"

"Th-thanks." Soleil was shaky and the soup was good, and these people seemed truly concerned.

Izzy stood looking at her and remembered how he had starved when he had been forced to walk out of Eastern Europe ahead of the Holocaust. He had been around her age, and like her, alone. He remembered how he had slept under trains, ate orts and leftovers from refuse heaps—how he had somehow survived. This girl was in trouble.

"Young lady." He cleared his throat. "What is your name?"

"Uh..."

"Please!" Izzy said with an unexpected urgency in his voice.

Soleil looked down. "Soleil."

Izzy felt suddenly old. "It's OK," he said gently. "I'm sorry. Your name is yours to have and not to give out just because someone asks." He looked at Brenda. "Brendeleh, come here," he said quietly. The two conferred in whispers for a minute or two.

Brenda faced Soleil.

"You have no money and no place to stay. We have an empty room in our house that needs to be used—it's been empty too long. Please come stay with us until you find work or can get back to your home. Whatever trouble you're in, you can't deal with it if you're dead or in jail."

She sighed and continued, "But if you say no, it'll be no. This is one offer, one time, take it or leave it." She crossed her arms in front of her.

Soleil looked at the woman: Brenda's face was doughy and worn, but kind. And Soleil was so tired. She nodded, reached for Brenda in a gesture of thanks, and once again passed out.

Soleil slowly regained her strength. On the third day, a Saturday afternoon, she walked the Queens neighborhood with Brenda for the first time. Brenda was intent on

Soleil's story of her childhood and her life but was not taken in by the flimsy story of leaving her home to look for a new life in New York and then running out of money. "No." Brenda shook her head as they walked near the elevated train. "Whatever happened to you was bad, very bad, and for whatever reason, you won't tell. Good! You're tough, and you're a survivor. Like me." She stopped on the sidewalk and appraised Soleil's face. "Impressive."

Soleil's body mended rapidly on a diet of boiled chicken, baked bread, chicken soup, steamed vegetables, and cold chicken. The Gutthelfs kept a kosher home, a concept unknown to Soleil, who had never met a Jew until she had met them. She liked the fact that no work was done on Saturdays, when Izzy went to the synagogue, or *shul* as he called it, and she and Brenda talked away the day. As a Catholic it seemed natural to honor God with a day of prayer and reflection—though since Montana, she felt that she herself was now beyond redemption.

She asked Brenda about that.

"Oy, Soleil, who knows? Redemption? God knows everything, and he is forgiving of the pure of heart and probably of the not-so-pure as well. Same goes for Jesus, I would imagine, but there I'm not an expert."

Soleil was deeply impressed with the order that these people imposed on their personal lives and how they cultivated their low profile as they went about their business. As she mended, she noticed that she had begun to crave neatness and order as well, and she reasoned that those qualities were a counterweight to the chaos of the real world.

That Monday she took the train with the Gutthelfs into New York and wandered about the jewelry exchange. Izzy gave her jobs to do, mostly messenger chores: pick up a repair job at a nearby jeweler; bring a topaz or some other stone to a dealer across the street. Soleil liked the easy interaction with these people and their business competitors, who seemed to be their friends, family even. And she was astounded that tiny jewels of great value were traded easily without written guarantees or contracts. A man's reputation was all that was needed. One day she watched as a dealer lent Izzy a beautiful, flawless, five-carat marquis diamond on consignment with just a handshake and an "I know you'll pay me." The stone was surely worth a small fortune. "Your name is everything, Solie," Izzy kept repeating to her at every opportunity.

But Soleil hated her name now, wished she had a different name. She toyed with the idea of changing it, but something inside insisted that such a move would be just a stall, that it would merely be postponing the inevitable. I'm leaving it as it is—what will be will be.

At the end of the week, Brenda asked Soleil if she wanted a real job.

"I can pay you off the books," said Izzy at the dinner table. "But please, you must come to terms with your past, whatever it was that put you into this misery, and overcome it. You are young, with everything to live for. Certainly it can be overcome." His eyes were tired.

Some weeks passed, and one day during lunch, Soleil walked a few blocks downtown and found herself standing on the corner of Fortieth Street across Fifth Avenue from the New York Public Library.

After hemming and hawing in her own mind for a little while and looking for excuses not to go inside, she crossed the busy avenue and went up the steps into the imposing building. She had decided to look for the whole story of the mine disaster in the library's microfiche files. She sat in front of the machine and scrolled through news clipping until, finally, she found it.

She found it but didn't understand it.

According to the newspapers, the explosion and cave-in at the Rapid River Mine in Montana had been determined to be an "industrial accident." Seven miners killed. Names withheld. The mine had been closed for an indefinite period of time.

She continued her scrolling, and then the headline she was searching for glared at her from the microfiche reader:

Chief of Police Slain in Bizarre Revenge Killing

Soleil's heart froze.
She read:

September 16, 1985: Blue Lodge, Montana: Lee "Bull" Dorsey, chief of police, was found slain in his home on Pine Forest Lane in what has been determined to be a revenge killing.

Police have concluded that Dorsey was the victim of an apparently irate and unstable acquaintance who had lent him money and had come to collect it. Dorsey's living room was the stage for what appeared to have been a desperate struggle with Don Henderson, field manager of the Rapid River Mine excavation north of the town.

What? Henderson?

Investigators have determined that Mr. Henderson entered Chief Dorsey's home, and what appeared to have been a ferocious struggle ensued, in which Henderson shot the policeman with arrows as well as bullets. Dorsey apparently tried to defend himself and shot Henderson, but not before he himself was felled by a final arrow to his chest. Henderson, himself mortally wounded, apparently pounded the chief with an unspecified taxidermy item before expiring himself from mortal gunshot wounds.

Local, federal, and other authorities have determined that the killing was financially and emotionally motivated, and evidence at Mr. Henderson's home and workplace, as well as at Chief Dorsey's home, positively verified the existence of a personal loan to the policeman by Mr. Henderson that was far in arrears and that undoubtedly set Mr. Henderson off on his rampage.

According to Mr. Henderson's wife, Helen, her husband's mental state was far from stable. "Don was very nervous and heading over the edge," she told reporters, "especially since the accident at the mine, which killed those miners. I think he blamed himself, you know. My life is ruined."

It hit Soleil like a hammer. Someone covered this up and threw Henderson into the mix when the mine was sabotaged so he couldn't talk. Who were those "other" authorities at the scene? Soleil thought she knew.

She stayed awake the whole night turning it over in her mind.

The next day she found herself on the corner opposite the library again. She pulled the metal handle of the phone booth open and stepped inside.

Life goes on, she thought as she stared at the pattern on the stamped metal floor for a minute or two. Then she put in the first quarter and dialed a number she knew by heart.

Clouds scudded across the Minnesota sky.

In one of the trailer homes on Rural Road 17, a phone was ringing.

Camille Tangiere Weston sat at her kitchen table and stared at the phone, a rag with ice cubes in it pressed against the swollen left side of her face. She was debating on whether or not to pick it up. Jake had stumbled out unsteadily about an hour ago, his hangover having been another excuse to whack his ex-wife one for good measure—a continuation of their loud fight that started when he had shown up earlier to mooch some money and that finally ended with a neighbor showing up with a shotgun. Cami had gotten in a lucky kick to her ex-husband's groin, so she considered it a draw. So why did she feel guilty about that?

Even with an angry bruise on her face, Camille fit anyone's definition of a beautiful woman. But her life had been a series of one bad man-decision after the next, which had worn down her native strengths.

The phone was insistent, and Cami glared at its fading brown plastic, its color a perfect match for the empty bottle of cheap whiskey that stood next to it. What the hell, she thought as she put the receiver to her ear.

"Hello?"

"Cami?"

Camille sat up straight in the chair, and the fog in her brain cleared instantly. Impossible. Wagon, I'm climbing on, right now. She held the receiver away from her face.

"Camille?" the voice said again.

No way.

Soleil was dead. At first she was considered missing, but then an eyewitness had said he saw her at the mine on the day of the disaster. When the victims were finally reached and removed from the shaft almost a week after the explosion, the remains of a girl's body were found. It had to have been Soleil. Like the other six victims, not only was the body crushed—it was blown to bits by the explosion first. There were no other women at the mine, so the assumption stuck. And Soleil had not shown up, had not called. The sad conclusion: It was she.

Frank and Soleil were given a double funeral. Camille had come west from Saint Cloud to make the arrangements. A handful of miners and their wives showed up. Her sister Nanette came but had to leave right after the service—she was driving down to Texas to look for a new life. No other Tangiere relatives. What a family, Cami thought bitterly.

The next day Jeanette's body was found in the small rental house, having passed quietly in her sleep. Her heart couldn't take it any more. Only Camille was around to make these last burial arrangements. It was a hard chore in a hard life.

Cami stood alone in the cold drizzle next to three graves asking the wind, "Where did everything go wrong?" Then she went back to Minnesota with its promise of gray clouds, a subpar ex-husband, and a bottle. Damn it.

But now this...

"Soleil?"

"I can't talk for long, Cami. Can you help me?"

"Soleil, it can't be true."

Suddenly it all came rushing out of Soleil:

"Well, it *is* true, and that damn cop killed Dad, or was at least a part of it, and I'd do it again if I had to, and there are other people involved too, and..."

"Wait! Wait, what? What are you talking about? What... where are you?"

Soleil came up short, and her voice stopped midsentence. I must be losing my mind, Soleil thought. What am I saying? It looks like Camille doesn't know I'm involved in Dorsey's death. At least, I don't think so.

Camille sagged in the chair. She could hardly hold the receiver against her ear.

"Soleil, everyone thought you were dead. We buried you with Dad. Or it least we thought it was you." Then, reasoning that she might as well get all the bad news out on the table now, she said, "Mama's gone too." She wiped away a tear and listened to the silence coming through the phone. Thank God you're alive, and at the same time damn you, damn you, damn you, Soleil, she thought crazily. Oh, damn everyone. Another tear rolled down her cheek.

A thousand miles to the east, the young girl looked left and right, up and down Fifth Avenue. People were everywhere, going about their business, climbing up and down the library steps, dodging cabs. Talking. Laughing. But it seemed as if she were watching a distant silent movie. In the middle of the midtown throng, the world had come to a halt for Soleil Tangiere.

"Cami," she said quietly into the phone. "Cami, I wasn't down in the mine. It was another girl."

Camille composed herself. "What they found was the body of a woman, but it was so messed up it could fit in a shoebox." She couldn't go on. God, do I need a drink.

Soleil began to breathe again, and her brain began to think. There were no young girls anywhere near that mine that day. No, now it only gets more puzzling. What's going on?

"Where are you?" Camille's voice came over the receiver.

At some point I'm going to have to risk it, Soleil thought desperately, but not this second. Besides, most of the damage is already done. She ignored the question.

The microfiche clipping was weeks old—Soleil had to find out if anything new had been uncovered about Dorsey's murder. "What about Dorsey?"

"Who?"

"The cop. You must have heard something. The chief of police who was murdered."

"Soleil, what are you talking about? What does the murder of that cop have to do with anything? What does Dorsey's killing have to do with you?" A neighbor's dog barked outside the open window.

Soleil realized that she had spoken too soon, so she backtracked. "Swear to me, Cami, swear to me that you won't tell anyone that I'm alive yet. Not your ex-husband. Not Nanette, not Lana, not Rolf, no one. Swear! I promise it will be just for a short time. Swear!"

They weren't that close, but they were the closest of the siblings, especially since Kent had died. The others were hopeless cases, and Rolf and Lana didn't even show up for their own mother's funeral. And Jake was as advertised— generally cheerful with a girl-killing smile, but ultimately useless. He showed up to drink and then mess things up just when they might be getting better. Sure, I'll keep my mouth shut—the kid sounds like she's been through hell. Well, welcome to the club.

"OK." Then, "How can I contact you?"

"You can't, Cami. Not yet. I'm not in Montana, and I have lots to straighten out. Just please trust me."

Camille felt strange. I guess it's the relief that Soleil's alive—that must be it. "I trust you. Why not? You're my kid sister. That's something, I guess."

"I'll call you soon. I love you. Bye for now." Soleil let her hand rest on the receiver for a moment after she hung up.

"I love you," Camille said to herself. Well, there's a novelty—I guess I'll take it where I can get it.

She set the receiver back in its cradle. Outside, beneath the open kitchen window, Jake Weston leaned against the trailer and smiled his famous smile.

As time went by, Soleil had taken to speaking with her oldest sister every few weeks or so, and Camille decided that since there were miracles in this world after all, it was a good time to make some headway in an attempt to conquer her alcohol problem. Soleil sensed that keeping a little distance might be best—her own life needed serious mending first. Besides, even if she wanted to see her, she had no way to gauge how safe she would be back west.

And Camille had connected with Soleil. While they were growing up, their age difference ensured that they were not very close. But now things were changing a little, and Camille decided to honor Soleil's request for silence very seriously. She never told anyone that Soleil was alive, not her brother nor her other two sisters. The hell with them, Camille thought bitterly. If they give a crap about anything, they sure have a lousy way of showing it.

As for the incident in Montana—silence for the next eighteen months.

No news stories.

No revelations.

No calls.

Silence.

It gave Soleil a chance to reset...

Soleil's fears and doubts from the past year and a half were beginning to change. She no longer awoke in a sweat of fear in the middle of the night. Her anxieties had taken on the form of a fine mist of caution that resided in the back of her subconscious. She had learned to live with that mist every day. But deep within her heart lay the mission: find those men who killed Dad. Bring them in, make them pay. One way or the other. Sometimes in the middle of the night, she hated herself for wanting revenge. But then she thought of her dad and what he would have done for her. He'd have done that and more, she thought.

With the willing help of the Gutthelfs and the other small business owners in the jewelry exchange, Soleil quickly became the go-to girl of the interesting gold and diamond world that she inhabited. While she sensed that it wasn't in her stars to make it her career, she was happy to have found a profession, or at least a body of knowledge, that she could fall back on. The Gutthelfs' little business had actually improved since her arrival—the Forty-Seventh Street world was one based on trust and personal contact, and a lot of the men enjoyed contact with Soleil—even a hello or a short, little innuendo-laden chat made their day.

At one point she even started toying with the idea of opening her own little booth in the exchange. Izzy liked to have her close by, but Brenda thought that it wasn't a good idea. She saw greater things for Soleil than the prospect of being stuck in a Forty-Seventh Street box for the rest of her life.

She gave Izzy a scornful look.

"What?" he said.

One Sunday morning Izzy knocked on her bedroom door.

"Solie! Come, get dressed!"

A few minutes later, she came into the kitchen, groggy and confused.

"Here, put on your coat. Come!"

Brenda smiled, but there wasn't much of a chance to ask questions—Izzy was on a roll.

They walked five or six blocks until they came to the Immaculate Conception Catholic Church. Izzy stopped and pointed at the redbrick building.

"Hurry, the mass starts at 7:30!"

Soleil nearly laughed out loud.

The two stood outside the church.

"Izzy, I don't believe you. How do you know when the mass starts, and how do you know whether I want to go to church or not?"

Izzy half closed his puffy eyes.

"Solie. It will be Christmas in a few weeks. Brenda and I see that you never go to church, but it seems like something you should do. Last Christmas came and went, and you refused to even acknowledge it. Solie, God probably misses you. I know I would." He took her shoulders and turned her to face the church. With a little push, he said, "Go, go. We'll have some breakfast after you get home."

She was touched. This was something her dad would have done. She walked up the steps and turned, but Izzy was already making his way home. Being reprimanded for not going to church by an Orthodox Jew. Only in New York...

And when she got home, hung her coat on the rack near the door, and walked into the living room, she was stunned.

There, standing on the floor right alongside the table where Brenda had displayed the family Chanukah Menorah, was a five-foot-tall Christmas tree, garlanded with tinsel and little bells, a star at the top. Gifts in Santa Claus wrap lay on the floor around it. They must have had all this hidden in one of the closets, she thought. She was speechless.

"Nu?" said Brenda, eyeing the tree critically. "Did we forget something?"

Soleil hugged her tight then went over to Izzy who was sitting on the couch and kissed the top of his head.

"No. No, it's perfect."

Brenda crossed her arms in triumph. "Good! There's a first time for everything! Now when my *yenta* friends come over for bridge on Wednesday night, oy! do we have something to talk about!"

Sometime during that year and half, Soleil had started to date.

It had taken her a long time to even think about being with someone of the opposite sex since her life had come unglued back in Montana. It was a natural reaction—the bad things that had begun happening in her life came from men pushing against her in every bad way. But as time passed, she felt that she could finally return to the normal world. Maybe I'm healing after all.

The world of the "Street," as the Forty-Seventh Street jewelry district was called, was a true United Nations of small business owners, jewelers, and diamond dealers as well as mobsters, runners, shills, and bagmen from every corner of the world. Soleil was never wanting for male attention in this heavily man-centric arena, and she had young American, European, Russian, and Middle Eastern men of all stripes after her—the girl with the natural blond hair and those arresting blue eyes. Soleil was no fool in this regard. She had an acute sensitivity to lies, and that served her well, especially when it came to the opposite sex. And in New York, lies were everywhere.

As for girlfriends, there were a few, but not many. Soleil never flaunted her looks, to women or men, and sometimes she wished she were plain or fat, but her face was her face and she had the ability to eat all day and never put on a pound. Some girls were put on the offensive by her looks. It made making female friends sometimes seem impossible.

But a girl around her age named Aimee who worked for a jewelry company across the street from Izzy's exchange did become her friend. Aimee was style-conscious and trendy and turned lots of heads every day with her rakish hairstyles, microscopic skirts, and an impressive stature made even taller in towering shoes.

One day she showed up at the Gutthelfs' booth with a piece of jewelry that her boss had repaired for Izzy. She struck up a conversation with Soleil, who was alone in the booth at the time. After work they went to a bar off Seventh Avenue, where they ate finger food and drank and talked until after midnight.

Aimee took the train in from Brooklyn every day and was an encyclopedia of guys: smart guys and dumb guys, hot guys and dorky guys, rich guys, poor guys and grifters: white guys, black guys, Asian guys, Chinese, Puerto Rican, Israeli and Bangladeshi guys. Soleil wondered where Aimee found the time for all these men.

"My TV's broken. I have a lot of time," she explained around a mouthful of Goldfish crackers. She had a classic Brooklyn accent that Soleil secretly thought was funny.

The two had taken to a sometime schedule of Saturday night club hopping. Inevitably Soleil would have to fend off a boatload of assorted guys, and inevitably it went nowhere with them. But Aimee reaped the benefits of Soleil's presence—the guy count increased exponentially after Soleil started accompanying her. Her already-crowded social calendar was reaching critical mass, and lately Aimee looked as if she was walking around half asleep. Her boss, Bruce, was not amused.

"What's the matter with you lately?" he finally had to ask in his cigarette-ruined voice. Bruce was a carbon copy of Izzy, but a little younger, like sixty. "You're a walking zombie, for God's sake."

"Club," she managed to say through heavy-lidded eyes. She was standing with Soleil on the other side of Bruce's counter.

"Do me a favor. Do yourself a favor. Lay off the clubbing. Try going to a movie. Go see the new *Batman* flick or something." The girls cracked up, and Soleil leaned over and whispered something in Aimee's ear.

The two women turned as one, and Aimee said loudly, "OK, bye, Bruce! See you back at the whorehouse!" And they went off arm in arm, secure in the knowledge that every male eye in the exchange was looking at them.

"Oh God," Bruce said to their receding derrieres, "God, please let me wake up tomorrow morning twenty-five years old again."

That evening they went to see *Batman*.

It was pretty good.

"He's sounds cute." Aimee was munching on a hamburger without the bun. In an effort to reduce her weight to emaciated from merely thin-as-a-stick, she had put herself on a trendy, high-protein "in" diet and could basically eat only meat, with a side dish of a hard-boiled egg. Soleil thought this was pretty silly—Aimee needed to gain weight, not lose it, and the only thing she might lose on this radical "diet" was a kidney or two.

"I don't like that word," Soleil said over her chicken salad sandwich. They were sitting in a deli on Forty-Sixth Street that was jammed with lunch customers.

"What's wrong with 'cute'?"

Soleil took a bite of her half-sour pickle. "Doesn't seem to apply to men. Or at least that's my view."

"How did you meet him again?" Aimee asked.

"He showed up at the place," Soleil said, referring to the Gutthelfs' jewelry booth. "He needed a new battery for his watch. It was a slow day and I was the only one there, so we struck up a little conversation. When he came by the next afternoon, he asked if he could treat me to a hot dog at the Sabrett's cart on the corner. I said sure."

"And then you slept with him."

Soleil threw the remains of the pickle at Aimee. "I didn't sleep with him."

"Oh c'mon, Ice Queen, I can see it in your face." Soleil was about to protest, but Aimee was unstoppable. "Why not? Sounds like he's tall, dark, and exotically handsome, and he has enough money to pay for a watch battery and a hot dog, which might or might not indicate he has a job. So, ipso facto, I hope you wrecked that man!"

Soleil couldn't help but smile. The fact was she *was* getting involved with this interesting guy. Tom was what Soleil thought of as a "world" person—someone whose vistas and possibilities extended past a small hometown or even a home country. That's pretty compelling to a backwoods girl like me, and besides, he's sweet in a way that the New York lounge lizards certainly are not.

And I lied to Aimee.

3

UPTOWN GIRL

It was raining as he unlocked the lobby door of the building at Madison and Eighty-Fourth Street. He opted to take the stairs to his third-floor apartment, as his trench coat was drenched and it wouldn't be fair to others to make the small elevator wet.

The building was a prewar beauty—small and immaculately maintained. Tom's apartment was large and airy, and he had owned it since the building went co-op five years ago. He had paid cash and was glad he did—it was one excellent investment. He thanked his stars that his business had been good to him.

He shrugged out of the coat before slipping the key in the lock. Once inside he was instantly attacked by Tango—the terrier mix puppy he had rescued from a kill shelter and who was now a pivot point in his home. It was as if Tango hadn't seen Tom in ten years, but it had only been five days.

Tom's neighbor came in three times a day to feed and walk the dog while he was away.

Tom kicked off his shoes and sat down to play with Tango for a little while. The rain made changing patterns of rivulets on the window...

Tom Patel was born in Chicago thirty-two years ago. His father had been a professor in the Art Department at Loyola University. His mother had died when he was twelve, and his father, who never married again, almost single-handedly raised him from that point onward.

After two years at Loyola, Tom dropped out. Mainstream education bored him, and his irrepressible energy pushed back against academia. His father was content to accept Tom as he was. Besides, Tom was a voracious reader and would consume books as if they were candies. As soon as he was old enough to get himself a passport, he traveled extensively on a shoestring budget, and had seen a lot of the world at a very young age. His dark complexion and exotic stature were alternately a blessing and a curse in his travels.

At twenty-two he got a job at the Chicago Mercantile Exchange, which at the time was the commodity-trading center of the universe. He found himself immersed in the whirlwind of the pit—standing eight hours a day in a seething mass of gesticulating, sweating men shouting orders and trading millions of dollars in contracts every hour. He loved it.

And not unsurprisingly, he got just too good at his job, and when two of his fellow traders approached him to go into business for themselves, he jumped in.

Their small firm grew rapidly, but after a year, one partner left unexpectedly and the other absconded with enough money to bring Tom to the edge of bankruptcy.

He fought back, though, and the experience only made him smarter and faster than most commodity firms that had been in business for decades. A Chicago grain trader named Kurt Ballas lent Tom $100,000, which provided the liquidity that he badly needed to rebuild.

That was six years ago.

As the years went by, Tom found himself sole owner of Patel + Co, a metals trading firm. He moved his office to New York. During this time he slowly became involved with many interesting businessmen and, more recently, a new cast of unsavory characters, the kind who inhabit the underbelly of the global commodity world.

"It's just business," rationalized Tom Patel.

One morning the phone rang at his office.

"How's it going, old shoe?" the now-familiar voice asked. It was a contact with an overseas firm, and Tom had done a number of deals with him already over the past several months. Those deals seemed a little odd and involved people and places that Tom felt a touch uncomfortable with, but "it's just business," he told himself at least once a day. If Tom had been a little more introspective, he would have recognized a certain elasticity of ethics growing in his psyche.

"Fine, and you?"

"Quite well indeed. We are very interested in your ideas to expand your business—our financial relationship will only benefit from them. Tom, our mutual backscratching is paving the way to both of our futures. Ha ha." Tom missed the patronizing tone. Maybe it was the English accent.

"Well," said Tom, "I can't move that fast. This takes time. I was considering a move into aluminum trading; it strikes me as—"

"No, no, Tom. I'm referring to expanding overseas physically. You know how anxious we are for you to grow—you grow, we grow." He sounded insistent.

"I'm not ready to open another office," Tom said without conviction.

"Rubbish. All you need is confidence. And money. That's where we come in." The voice paused and then finished in a slightly ominous tone: "Think about it, Tom. Carefully. We'll talk shortly."

The phone went dead, and though Tom felt he should be happy about the new business and an opportunity to open an office overseas, a small voice in his head told him to be wary. *Oh, just the usual uncertainty in my line of work. I'll think about this carefully, just like he said.*

And think about it he did. In fact, he was lost in thought that very afternoon when the truck ran him down on Madison Avenue.

The sound of blaring horns startled dozens of people on the sidewalk. A witness thought he had seen a bus pull out suddenly into traffic and ram a DHL delivery van, but no one could be certain.

The delivery van seemed to have lost control, and two pedestrians were pinned underneath it. A woman was lying near the rear axle crying—it seemed a rib was broken. And a man had his left arm stuck under a front tire.

One cop showed up in under a minute. He easily extracted the woman from under the van and with some help from a passerby placed her on the sidewalk to wait for EMS to arrive. Then the cop looked under the van again at the trapped man.

He straightened up and ran around to the driver's side. "Can you start the van?" he asked the driver. The driver tried the key, but the motor only grinded—wouldn't start. "Put it in neutral and get out. Quick," the cop ordered. The driver was a tall man; his hat had come off, and he ran a nervous hand through his thinning hair. He didn't say a word as he and the policeman pushed the van forward. The man beneath shouted in a pained voice, "OK, I'm free!"

The Emergency Medical Services vehicle bullied its way through the traffic mess, and two rescue workers jumped out. They were quick and efficient, and in a matter of just a few short minutes, Tom Patel and the woman were placed on stretchers and disappeared into the ambulance. The siren was turned on, flashing lights began turning on the roof, and the vehicle headed for the nearest emergency room.

But then the police realized they had a problem. The DHL driver, whom they needed to question and process, could not be found. No one had seen him leave the scene.

He had disappeared.

The now-familiar voice on the phone began with "How's your arm, Tom?"

Tom had just returned to his office after a few days of recuperating and was stunned by what he was hearing. He didn't reply. He touched the cast with his good hand.

The voice went on. "I hope you're considering the expansion we were speaking about. I hope we won't wait forever."

Tom gathered his thoughts. "When I'm ready," he said sternly.

"Listen, Tom." The voice had gone ice cold. "Listen closely. I'm going to read off a list of all the laws, both local and international, that you've broken recently. We're not an American company, Tom. We're allowed to deal with certain countries—you're not. You've been very bad. Now don't interrupt me until I'm done. We may just be compelled to report all of what you've been up to, you naughty boy. There are so many law enforcement agencies in the United States, after all." He started reading the list.

Tom's heart sank. He had hugely misjudged this man and his sleazy company. And he was in a lot of trouble. *I'd better not do anything rash or too quickly. How do I get out of this? Do I even* want *to get out of this? What was I thinking?*

The voice finished the list and now was droning on about something else. *Think, Tom, think—what do I do now?* Through his furious thinking he hardly heard what the voice was now saying: "Use any excuse you want. Tell her you need a watch battery or something."

What?

Tom interrupted him. He asked the voice to repeat the whole thing over again and wrote the details down.

"Keep me posted, Tom," the voice said, and then added, "How's your *other* arm, Tom? Still all right?" After a pregnant pause: "And the key. I do hope you're taking good care of the key for me." Tom shuddered involuntarily and held the receiver away from his face. Then he unceremoniously hung up.

Tom looked down at the strange information about a woman that he had just been given. What on earth did this girl have to do with anything? Then a voice inside him said do it, just do it.

He glanced out the window at the city.

"Soleil, it's for you!" Brenda shouted from the kitchen.

Soleil picked up the phone in her bedroom and reflected once again that it was way past the time to move out. Brenda and Izzy had tried to give her as much privacy as they could, but butting in seemed to be a genetic trait and was an annoying offshoot of their caring.

And even though it seemed that the Gutthelfs would have loved it if Soleil lived with them forever, they knew that she would need to spread her wings.

"Hi, Soleil." It was Tom.

"Hi."

"Can I pick you up at seven?"

"Pick me up?"

"Yes, pick you up. You know...I stop the car in front of the house, get out, come to the door, take you out to the car, drive away...you know, pick you up."

"I didn't know you had a car." The guy knows how to keep secrets. A plus or a minus? Don't know yet.

Tom had a Mustang that he stored in a garage a few blocks from his apartment. He drove up to the house in Queens at 7:00 in the evening and honked the horn a couple of times. The Gutthelfs were standing in the hallway by the front door.

Brenda said to Soleil, "When do we meet this fellow? You know we have to approve, don't you?"

Soleil started to laugh on the way out the door, but something in Brenda's eyes brought her up short. She turned and looked at the two of them, and then decided.

"Now. Come on." And the three of them went out the door and walked to the sidewalk. Tom got out of the silver two-door and walked around to the curb. He kissed Soleil's cheek.

"Hi, Tom. This is Brenda and Izzy, the people I told you about, my 'family,'" she said lightly, but her heart was conflicted and something seemed a tiny bit off. I'm not sure what, probably nothing, but I will think about it later when I'm alone.

Tom shook Izzy's and Brenda's hands, and Izzy looked over at the Mustang.

"Some car, Tom. Very nice." His face said other things.

Brenda: "Nice to meet you, Tom."

Soleil tilted her head a fraction as she watched the large woman.

A minute or two of chitchat, and then Tom held the passenger door open for Soleil, and in a moment, they had driven off. Brenda looked at Izzy.

"What?" he said.

Brenda thought something was wrong, and she knew Izzy felt it too. Putting it aside, she said, "You never picked *me* up in a sports car, you *momzer*."

Izzy snorted. Sports car.

Over the next month or two, Tom stepped up his entreaties for Soleil to move in with him. She was dead set against it at the beginning but was slowly being won over. She really liked him and decided to overlook the fact that he sometimes seemed to withhold things from her such as the fact that he had a car. To be honest, I would probably do the same. Why should I be the only one to have a trust issue with someone else?

And moving in was a giant step, not to be taken lightly. But she clearly saw that there could be a future with Tom, maybe even a marriage. Not now, not before she had finished what she had set out to do, but after that, if there was an "after that."

Besides, everyone seemed to be moving in with everyone else nowadays. It's 1987, for heaven's sake.

The day came when the three were sitting at the kitchen table, and she told Brenda and Izzy about her decision. Brenda's face stayed impassive. Finally she gave a little shrug.

"Go, Soleil," she said over the top of her teacup. "We didn't expect to have you here forever, as nice a thought as that might be. You're young, you know your way around New York now, and hopefully you've saved a little money. And besides, if anything happens, Izzy and I will be here— we're not going anywhere. Are we, Izzy?"

Izzy's eyes got a little misty as they studied Soleil. She had been with them for a year and a half, and now he found it hard to say good-bye. She would still be with them during the day at the business, but they had become comfortable with having a "daughter" in the house again. But it had to be. He went into his and Brenda's bedroom for a minute. When he came out, he handed Soleil a tiny chamois drawstring bag.

"Here, my Solie, keep these safe. Someday they may help you." He handed her the little pouch.

"And this too, Soleil." Brenda had gotten up to fetch a little box from the top shelf of a kitchen cabinet. Soleil took it and opened the hinged cover. A small platinum cross with tiny diamonds on a thin chain gleamed back at her. Soleil's throat choked up for a second. Pure Brenda and Izzy: this little gift said it all.

These people had saved her life and wanted nothing in return. She loved them, and she told them so.

Soleil's clothes and other possessions fit into the Mustang with little room to spare. Tom made a remark about women and their clothes, but Soleil told him his experience with women must be limited—this amount of clothes was negligible in comparison to most girls.

Hugs all around, and Soleil drove off with Tom.

Brenda and Izzy stood on the sidewalk and looked at each other.

Soleil sat in the passenger seat watching the iron-colored East River flow beneath them as they drove over the Fifty-Ninth Street Bridge into Manhattan. She patted the hem of her pea coat distractedly—it was where she had sewn in the little drawstring bag from Izzy. And in her pocket, resting in a neatly folded table napkin, lay the hunting knife with her initial that her father had given her.

Time passed.
Two years of it.
Two years of Tom.

The sound of a key in the lock, and the door opened.

"Soleil, are you home?" Tom had a clear voice with a slight Indian accent. Tango flew around a corner and attacked him with a barrage of licks and whines—where've you been, Dad? he tried to say in dog language.

"Soleil?" he said again. When no reply was forthcoming, he went to the small table where she had accumulated his mail. He wasn't surprised to find a certified letter for him that she had signed for from a New York State court. He opened and read it quickly, folded it in four, and stuffed it in his pants pocket.

"Hi" from behind him. He turned, and there she was in the still-open doorway. Beautiful, he thought for the thousandth time. They moved toward each other in unison.

The initial guilt that Tom had felt about the underhanded way they met had long ago evaporated from his conscience. I think I really love her, he had started to remind himself lately.

Later she asked what the letter was about. Tom's eyes seemed to get darker. He had been generally reticent about his business dealings when Soleil asked about them, but not to the extent that it seemed overly suspicious. When it's not about business, he's such a good guy. I have to try to distract him more, I guess.

"Oh, its just standard procedure when it comes to some of our oil deals overseas," he replied. "There seems to be some questions about correct billing jurisdictions that may have gotten crossed, and I may need to hire a professional consultant on international contracts."

Uh oh. "Why are you lying to me?" Soleil suddenly asked. Her antennas were up—there was that telltale tone in his voice and the tiny little twist in his lower lip that showed itself when he lied. For two years they had lived together, and Soleil had not only been Tom's friend and lover, but his staunchest cheerleader and advocate. By now, the cautious subterfuges that he was prone to should have come to an end. What's he hiding *now*?

Lately Tom had been traveling more than ever. When they were together, they lived well—it seemed as if Tom had more than enough money to burn, but Soleil paid no attention to it—she would take the bus to Forty-Seventh Street every day to earn her own money working for Izzy and Brenda. She had her money, and he had his. Very modern, she sometimes thought. But her sixth sense told her that this latest dodge of Tom's wasn't a money secret.

"Well?" She was adamant.

"Honey, see for yourself." He fished the folded summons out of his pocket. She looked it over and was barely mollified by its obtuse content. I'll let it drop for now, she thought. His smile didn't help either.

Tom was often away for a week or two at a time, and the social whirl had died out for Soleil. Now that she was with Tom, she didn't go clubbing with Aimee anymore. But they often met for drinks or sometimes dinner after work.

"So how's it going with Tom?" Aimee asked when they had finished ordering dinner at a restaurant on Fifty-Third Street. Aimee had met Tom a few times, but she never had an inclination to be a third wheel, and she was not a double dater. "Things OK? Any rings, babies, what?"

"No rings. No babies. Everything is fine."

After a minute Aimee said, "OK, you have a choice: either tell me about your sex life in intricate and lurid detail, or tell me what's bugging you about Tom."

"How about a third choice: let's talk about the Mets or something."

"Nope. Tom. Spill it, baby." She made a "come on" motion with her hand.

It was anathema to Soleil to discuss her private life, so she turned it neatly around. She put on a miffed face and said, "What about Tom is bugging you, Aimee?" Their appetizers showed up.

She looked at Soleil. "Nothing; it's just..."

"What?"

She hesitated. "I dunno, it's just that he's not like the men I'm used to—hunky, sports-orientated sex maniacs until they get drunk, which is when they become totally useless—you know, *normal* men."

Soleil laughed. "It is disconcerting that Tom likes books and art and things like that. I'm starting to adjust."

But under the humor, Soleil saw a bit of true concern on Aimee's face. She said, "Aimee, everything is fine."

They went to work on the food.

Not being one to sit around and watch TV when she was alone for weeks at a time, Soleil would try to be out from dawn to dusk on the weekends when Tom wasn't there. The three or four walks that Tango required every day just didn't cut it.

One block to the west of the apartment sprawled the Metropolitan Museum of Art, unquestionably one of the finest museums on Earth. Its vast and fabulous collections were startling and amazing to Soleil from the moment she first tentatively entered the building on one cool spring afternoon.

Since Tom traveled so much on business, Soleil had gotten hooked on spending the hours after work and the long weekends strolling the galleries with Monet and Matisse. She began to love art, great art, and then she discovered MOMA, the Museum of Modern Art on Fifty-Third Street. It was so close to work that she spent lunch hours there with Kandinsky and Picasso, and sometimes Aimee, who usually had some entertaining comments about this Giacometti nude sculpture or that Gauguin nude painting. "This art stuff is pretty cool," she said. Soleil agreed.

Soleil quickly acquired a discerning eye but didn't consciously realize it—she loved art without the pomp and phony verbiage that so many New Yorkers used to impress others. She felt sorry for people like that—great art was just beautiful. It didn't go much further than that.

On some afternoons and evenings Tom's friend Pradeep would accompany her on her museum wanderings. Pradeep was Indian as well, and his lilting voice and fey mannerisms suggested that he was gay. Soleil didn't care—this was 1988, old stereotypes and mores were fading away and being replaced by an era of social and political correctness. But truth be told, I don't really care much about *that* either, she reflected. There was something in Soleil Tangiere's psyche—or missing from it—that evaluated the world only from street level. People were people, responsible for themselves, and what mattered was how they treated others, that's all. What they did out of sight was none of her affair.

Tom's apartment was wall-to-wall books about art, among many other subjects. Tom had avoided mainstream education and considered himself a self-made Renaissance man when it came to art and literature. With time on her hands, Soleil became a walking encyclopedia about a lot of things in a very short time.

After trying to dope out a book on the work of the artist Paul Klee in its native German, Soleil tried her hand at learning the language. She enjoyed the puzzle of the convoluted grammar and sentence structure that stymied many English speakers, and she insisted that Brenda and Izzy speak to her in Yiddish as much as possible, which was really just a bastardized form of German. The Gutthelfs both knew German, and though they had sworn never to speak it since the Holocaust, they decided to help Soleil with it—her clear heart didn't carry any threats or agendas, so what would be the harm? "Oy, all right," Izzy had said. "For you, Solie, I'll make an exception."

One evening when Tom was off on another vaguely secret trip to Europe, Pradeep called Soleil at the apartment.

"I was wondering if you would like to come out with me tomorrow night?"

Soleil was nonplussed.

"What do you mean, Pradeep?"

"I so apologize, Soleil, but I need some female support, and you are one of my only friends."

"What female support?"

Pradeep hemmed and hawed for a minute or two and then finally blurted, "I've started taking dancing lessons at a place on Seventh-Fourth Street and need a partner to work with me. I asked Tom, and he said it's perfectly all right with him if you came along. Are you free, Soleil? It will, of course be my treat."

Perfectly all right with him? What does *that* mean?

She replied, "Pradeep, surely you know another girl who would go with you." Then she instantly regretted it.

"No. Not off the top of my head." He sounded dejected.

She thought for a moment. Well, since it's "perfectly all right" with Tom the plantation owner, then why not?

"Of course, Pradeep. I always wanted to really learn to dance the right way. Hitting the clubs with my girlfriend has always been an amateur hour for me when it comes to dancing."

"Great! Thanks, Soleil!"

So off and on for months, whenever Tom was away in Europe or wherever he said he went, Soleil and Pradeep would meet at the May I Have The Next Dance Studio on Seventy-Fourth Street. Soleil had a natural poise and could instantly memorize moves, and her skills quickly caught up with and surpassed Pradeep's. Soleil was surprised that he was into this, and when Tom explained to her that Pradeep was only doing this because he had his eye on Dave, the studio owner, Soleil didn't completely buy it.

One day Pradeep announced that he would be going to India for a year to live with his family. Soleil thought it was time to stop anyway, as she had gone as far as she wanted to with the dancing lessons, but she was grateful for the new skill.

Pradeep, Tom, and Soleil stood by the cab that was waiting to take him to the airport. Tom hugged him, and so did Soleil. She kissed his cheek, and he hugged her tighter and for a surprisingly long time. She felt something. Gay, huh? She gave Pradeep a look, wagged a scolding finger at him, and he got into the cab.

Once in a while Tom would bring some of his work home with him. And Soleil became his free office helper and advisor. Soon she had picked up a number of things about his commodity business.

His was a business of making deals to buy, transport, and sell metals—aluminum, zinc, nickel, gold, silver, and platinum.

Tom was making more and more deals in those metals, and when Soleil told him she knew a thing or two about platinum mining, he suddenly paid rapt attention.

He was fascinated by the story of Soleil's young life in a family headed by a miner. At first she was hesitant to tell him about the incident at the Rapid River Mine. Even after more than three years, the mist of uncertainty was unabated, especially at night. Early on in their relationship, Soleil had told Tom that her father was killed in an in industrial accident, but she was vague about it and he didn't press the issue. Now he was all ears.

"It was a cave-in. An explosion of some kind in the platinum mine."

"And there were others?"

"Five or six other miners were killed."

Tom listened with great care. Boy, he's really interested in this. I guess there are some things that can pull him away from that darn business of his.

She told him everything she knew about mining.

But she left out the part about Bull Dorsey.

Patel + Co was becoming established to a small degree in New York, but Soleil was seeing less and less of Tom. When he returned from trips to Europe, he was nervous and distracted. She finally confronted him.

"What do you have going overseas, Tommy? You tell me about a lot of meetings all over the world, but your plane tickets are almost always to Geneva. Is there a girl in Switzerland? A little Swiss Miss, eh? If so, come clean now— I'll be angrier with you if you lie. Just tell me about Heidi or whatever her name is."

Tom had been waiting for Soleil to ask about this. Just yesterday he had been instructed that now was the time to bring it up. "I do have a mistress in Switzerland; it's true." Soleil's face changed instantly. "She's in Europe, and her name is also Patel—Patel + Company AG. I spend all my time with her when I'm there." He smiled, but Soleil wasn't amused.

"You have another *company* in Switzerland? Another *business*?" she said, her cheeks beginning to redden with agitation. She stiffened and said to him, "You lied to me about the trips you've been taking."

"I've only omitted the part about my other office. It's really no big deal."

Soleil was incensed, and she was nobody's fool. It *was* a big deal. First of all, it confirmed that Tom was capable of bending and hiding the truth. She had known that he was comfortable with hiding harmless little things from time to time, but this was major, huge. How could I have missed this?

Also, she thought, there are few reasons to set up a company in Switzerland unless you're making chocolates or cuckoo clocks. Was he avoiding taxes? Or worse? Soleil felt a slight shift in her universe.

"Were you ever going to let me in on this? No, forget it, it's not my business—why should you have to tell me anything? In fact," she was up and on her way to the door, "I have some business of my own, and it's not any affair of yours. Not one bit." The slam of the door seemed especially loud.

Soleil didn't return for two days, and when she did, Tom's pleadings and excuses fell on deaf ears.

"Give me one reason why I shouldn't pack it all in now, Tommy. Well?"

"Here's one." Tom reached into his jacket pocket and brought out a small black jewelry box. Tango came over to sniff it.

Soleil wouldn't touch it as it rested on his hand, so he closed his fist around it and said, "Soleil, I'm sorry. Come to Switzerland with me, and do it as my fiancé."

He opened his hand, and she took the box. Inside was a diamond engagement ring—a pretty little emerald-cut stone set in platinum. Soleil's apprehensions eased, but just slightly. She looked up at him and gave him a tight smile.

"Don't ever, ever do anything like this again."

Tom felt a wave of relief. "I won't," he said with sincerity.

Soleil had to get a passport, and it was complicated. She was a Canadian citizen, and it was several weeks until the process was completed. And there was the constant worry in the back of her mind about the death of her father and the other people in Montana. When her passport arrived with no police officers accompanying it, Soleil breathed a sigh of cautious relief.

During that time Tom had been especially solicitous and caring of Soleil. She was ostensibly engaged to Tom, but their conversations about the future centered on doing more business and getting finances in order before they set a wedding date.

That didn't sit completely right with Soleil, but she was just twenty-three anyway, and there shouldn't be a rush, she rationalized. She gave Tom the benefit of the doubt. She felt that she loved him and that he loved her. But a small part of her kept a vigilant eye—trust yet verify.

"You're asking *me*? Sure, why not—I'm an expert in the art of picking honest men." Camille was sounding a lot better lately. And when her youngest sister tried sounding her out about her opinion on the upcoming trip, Camille offered the following: "Let me get this straight," she told Soleil over the phone. "Your boyfriend has a business of his own that brings in good money, has opened an office in Europe, has you living in an East Side apartment, doesn't have any action going on the side with the exception of working, gave you a diamond ring, and treats you like a princess. And you want me to give you an opinion about whether or not you're doing the right thing by going on a vacation to Switzerland with him? Did I miss anything?"

When you put it that way, it does sound kind of lame, doesn't it? Soleil said to herself. "No, you pretty much covered it." Then: "There's just this trust issue, Cami. There's this sneakiness that bugs the heck out of me."

"But he's not sneaking around with women. You're certain of that, right?"

"That's not a problem as far as I can see." But who knows? "No, he's fine and totally honest except when it comes to that business of his."

"This is the business that puts diamond rings on your fingers and surrounds you with luxury? Huh! I say let him lie about it. Who cares? It seems like he loves you."

"I care. A lot. I feel betrayed when he lies. About anything."

Camille looked out the small kitchen window at the other trailer homes. She knew her sister was right about that and sighed. "You're good at this, Soleil—good at gauging people. My advice, which you *did* ask for, by the way: go to Switzerland and have a good time. It's just for a couple of weeks. When you get back, see how you feel, and then we'll talk again."

She's right. "OK, thanks. When I get back, I'm coming out to see you. It's been too darn long."

"Watch your language," Camille admonished. They both laughed and hung up.

The last day on the job came around. Brenda and Izzy were busy closing up the little business for the weekend, which was simply a process of putting the contents of the glass counters—a few dozen trays of jewelry—into the safe. When they were done, they asked Soleil to wait around until they were ready to leave for the evening. Then the three of them stood in the booth and hugged. Tango slept under the jeweler's bench. The Gutthelfs had offered to take him in while Soleil was gone.

Soleil sensed their nervousness. "What's wrong?" she asked Brenda. "I'll only be gone for a couple of weeks."

Brenda looked at Izzy for a moment and said, "Honey, we only want the best for you. Please be careful in Europe."

Soleil looked at Brenda's face and said, "That's not all of it, is it Brenda? You're not certain about Tom, are you?"

"I don't know, Soleil." Her eyes had an odd look. "We hardly know him, and over the past two years, whenever you tried to bring him around or meet us for more than a quick hello, he always seemed to be either very distant or a no-show. Am I wrong?"

Soleil shook her head. Then, feeling the odd need to defend her man, she offered up, "You know how men can be."

Brenda looked at Izzy. "I know how a man can be, Soleil. I've had practice with one for forty years. A good one."

For some reason a sadness came over Soleil. She looked at Izzy. He saw into her and said, "Solie, my love, I think—just think, mind you—that your soul is burdened: that you need to talk to someone, and that someone is not us. Am I right?"

He was dead right, and Soleil's face couldn't hide it.

"OK," he said. "Here's what I think you should do..."

"Forgive me Father, for I have sinned."

The white-haired priest sat on one side of the small window. Soleil knelt on the other side, her face near the closed curtain.

"What are your sins, young lady?"

I can't believe that Izzy got me into this church again, she said to herself. But now that I'm here, it feels right.

"I haven't been to confession in, well, in many years."

"Many years? How old are you?" He had seen her come into the church and thought she was a new alter server or the daughter of one of the regulars. She looked very young.

"Twenty-three."

"Continue, please."

"I have lied. And I've spoken the Lord's name in vain."

"Go on."

"I've disrespected my parents, who are no longer alive. Now I can't tell them I'm sorry."

"Those are the wages of sin, young lady."

"I've had carnal knowledge outside the bonds of matrimony."

The priest sighed in boredom. Nothing new there. "Go on."

"I killed someone."

What did she say? "Pardon me?"

"Well, he certainly brought it on himself," she said. "I was just there as a kind of catalyst, I suppose." She paused. Did that sound all right? "I was in the process of trying to get revenge, I guess." No, that certainly *didn't* sound so good.

"That is terrible, a terrible mortal sin. And did you say 'revenge'?"

"Yes."

"Revenge is the provenance of the Lord, my dear. Not of mere mortals."

"Well, there're probably going to be some more sins coming up, then." She felt frustrated. "You see, my father's murderers are still living in the mortal world."

Well, I sure don't hear confessions like *this* every day, he thought. Finally something with a little meat on it!

"Your soul must feel lost," he said.

"It's been hard dealing with it."

"I'm sure it has."

After a moment or two, he said, "Is that it?"

"Isn't it enough?"

"Penance will be to say five Our Fathers, five Hail Marys, and an Act of Contrition."

She got off her knees to leave.

"One more thing, young lady," came the voice from the other side of the window.

"Good luck."

4

AIRPORT

It was the first time Soleil had been to a major airport or flown in a commercial airliner. Her father and a friend had taken her up in a small single-engine Cessna when she was fifteen, and she had loved the freedom of soaring over the hills and fields of Quebec. She promised herself that one day she would fly a plane herself.

She was silently disappointed in the chaotic melee that commercial air travel had devolved into. Between the nasty stop-and-go cab ride out to JFK Airport and the crowded and agitated terminal, she found herself amending her previous promise: one day she would not only fly a plane, she would own one.

They had just finished installing metal detectors and had started hiring bag checkers and installing x-ray machines at the major airports. Soleil didn't get it. What's the point? If someone wants to hijack an airplane, they could do it without a gun. And if you're afraid, don't fly. And if you have to fly, pray.

Waiting in the SwissAir gate area, Soleil had little to do to pass the time. She decided to just sit and evaluate her fellow passengers while Tom pored over the *Wall Street Journal*. She enjoyed silently giving strangers names and trying to guess what they did or what their lives were about. But while there were middle-aged couples and a few young people, most of the passengers seemed to be businessmen of all stripes. Two of these button-down types were sitting opposite them against a far wall. Soleil felt a slight shudder. She could swear they were watching her, studying her. She was usually immune to the looks and stares of men, but this was different. It almost looked as if they were taking this flight to keep tabs on her for some reason. Montana is catching up with me, she thought. She was very good at this—she knew that faces told more about people that their words ever would, and these guys' faces were those of hunters. No mistake about it.

Her stomach felt cold as the events in Montana kept rushing back into the forefront of her mind. I knew I shouldn't have applied for that passport. Well, here we are. Now what?

The plane ride was long, and although they were seated in first class, Soleil was agitated and fidgety. She didn't tell Tom anything about her suspicions, but she decided that when they reached Geneva, she and Tom would stay seated on the plane until the two suspicious-looking men, whom she had mentally nicknamed Clip and Clop, disembarked.

The flight seemed to last forever. Soleil toyed with the meal she was served and tried flipping through some magazines. Let's face it: I've got an attention disorder or something. Doing nothing is like torture to me. She spent most of the long hours looking out the window.

Night came very quickly as the plane flew east over the Atlantic. Soleil tried to sleep, but it just wasn't in the cards.

When the plane landed and the passengers were leaving, Soleil told Tom that she wanted to sit and wait until the plane emptied out. Tom was indifferent, but when Clip and Clop came up to their seats, Soleil was shocked—they didn't even look at Soleil. It was obvious that they were following *Tom*. Tom's face went white when he saw them glaring at him, and he became very nervous very fast. These guys are watching Tom, not me? What's going on?

They had taken only carry-on baggage, as Tom had clothes in Switzerland and Soleil wanted to travel light anyway. In that way they were able to avoid the crowded baggage-claim area. When they left the terminal, Tom almost ran to the taxi queue, pulling her along. Soleil said, "You'd better tell me what's going on, Tommy."

In the cab Tom settled down. "What do you mean? Nothing's going on."

"Those two men on the plane. When you saw them, you had a meltdown. Don't even think of telling me you don't know them. Who are they?"

"I thought I knew them from business, but I was wrong. Forget it." Soleil began to protest. "Please, Soleil, forget it; it's nothing."

Nothing.

Either Tom was lying—not impossible—or Clip and Clop were watching *me*. Nope. I didn't make a mistake: they were watching him, and something is very wrong.

The city of Geneva is located at the southern end of Lake Geneva and is surrounded by the Alps and the Jura mountains: on a clear day you can see Mont Blanc. Its temperate year-round climate is a major asset, and the lake, studded with pleasure boats and dominated by its tall and commanding fountain, the Jet d'Eau, is stunning. Geneva is a center for world organizations and the European pivot point for the UN.

And it is in a country that doesn't recognize the tax laws of any other country in the world.

Soleil was happy that French was Geneva's spoken language—she was raised on Quebecoise French as well as English and loved speaking it with anyone she came in contact with. There were at least four languages spoken in Switzerland, and here she would be able to work on her German a little as well. German was spoken in Zurich and Italian in Ticino. There was even a native hodgepodge language called Romansh. Switzerland certainly qualified as international in Soleil's book.

Tom had only a clumsy working knowledge of business French, so Soleil was happy to help him with it. He had rented a nice apartment close to the center of the city—very nice in fact. Soleil's initial impulse was to do a quick search for any leftovers of a female on the premises. She told herself the search would come up empty, but, well, a short toss wouldn't hurt. She was discreet about it.

The day after they arrived, he took her to his office, which he had rented on the seventh floor of a classic brick office building near the business district. They went down the hall, and he stopped at one of the office doors. The door had a brass plate:

PATEL + CO, AG
Tom Patel
Soleil Tangiere

Soleil took one look at her name and exploded.

"What the hell, Tommy? What is this?"

"What, I thought you would be happy! I told you about the business! You've helped me with business, and now you're officially a part of it."

Soleil reasoned that by putting her name on the door, Tom meant this to be a nice surprise, but she wouldn't let him get away with slowly tightening control over her life, even if he had done it with good intentions.

"I really want my name off that door. *You* created this company, it's your baby, and it has little to do with me. Damn it, why couldn't you have asked me first—it seems like you have all these things to hide."

Inside Tom was seething. For the two years I've been with Soleil, I still don't understand a lot of her moods. What at first seemed charming and unique about her—her strong independence and sense of self—is now oppressive and distracting. Things are getting complicated, and at this time I need to control as much around me as I can. At the beginning she was pliable, so easy to distract. Now Soleil needs to stay out of the way. If I hadn't gotten strict orders, I would never have told her about any of this or brought her to Europe.

"I have things to hide?" he said, "I'm trying to bring us together in everything in our lives, and you keep pushing back. This was a kind of gift—everything I have is yours now, and I wanted to make a statement."

Soleil gave him a look, opened the door, and went into the office. Well, there's no question about a female presence here—who's *this*? A well-dressed brunette in her thirties, her hair cut stylishly short, sat at a small reception desk. She smiled at Soleil and Tom and said, "Welcome back, M. Patel. Mademoiselle."

Tom introduced the woman as Yvonne, his secretary. None of this was working out as he had planned. Soleil smiled thinly, and then her face turned to stone as she walked into the other office.

Tom's desk was covered with neat piles of papers and ledgers, and in the center sat a large framed photo of him and Soleil on the steps of the Metropolitan Museum that Pradeep had snapped of them last year. Soleil thought that its prominent position in the room was a tad too obvious. Nothing was going to make her feel good about Tom at this moment anyway. He could have brought in the pope to swear to his love and veracity, and it would have helped not a bit.

"Come on, let me show you the city." It seemed the safest thing to do.

Sweeping back though the reception area past her desk, he said harshly to Yvonne, "Leave a list of calls on my desk. I can't be reached today," and strode out.

In the elevator Soleil said, "You didn't have to be brusque with the woman on the way out. She didn't do anything wrong, and you looked ridiculous to her and suspicious to me. Why don't you go look at the city yourself, while I go about my own affairs."

"Please, Soleil, I'm sorry, OK? Can't we just enjoy ourselves, two people in love in this beautiful place? Please?"

Pathetic, she thought, but men are men, she told herself. There's nothing that can be done about that. But I can do something about our relationship if I have to. They strolled down toward the lake.

Clip and Clop stalked them from a distance.

Soleil and her fiancé had just returned from breakfast at Le Chat-Botte in the Beau Rivage Hotel when the phone rang. Tom had been nervous throughout the meal, and when the phone rang, he almost jumped. Soleil watched him pick up the phone and just listen for at least a minute.

"Must have been a wrong number," he mumbled, his eyes all over the place. He hung up the receiver.

One heartbeat of silence, then: "That's it, Tommy!" Soleil had reached the end of her rope, and her mind was made up. "Come clean with all of it, or I'm leaving you here and now. And don't make the mistake of thinking I'm an innocent, incompetent little girl alone and far from home. Don't even go there. Now, for the last time, what's happening?"

Tom sat down heavily.

"All right."

Soleil stood looking down at him.

"I'm not sure we can go back to the US. At least not soon."

Soleil waited.

"I've been doing business with a company that operates in restricted countries. A restricted country is a country that the United States prohibits trade with. One of my overseas partners in some of our deals has been trading with them. I never knew I was breaking laws, but I guess that's what's been happening. When I finally realized what was going on, I confronted him, but he convinced me that government edicts on trade only served to punish innocent people, and besides, if we had a Swiss company, we would be outside the laws of the US and could trade with anyone we wanted.

"At the time it all made sense. I had been thinking of opening an office overseas anyway, was mesmerized by the prospect of huge growth..."

"Greed, you mean."

"...and opened this company in Switzerland, where the government stays out of peoples' financial affairs."

"And my name on the door?"

Tom went on as if he hadn't heard. "We had suddenly become a player in the metals trading game with some of those sanctioned states on the forbidden list." He smiled weakly. "You probably never even heard of some of these countries."

"Don't tell me what I probably heard or didn't hear of."

"The dollars were so huge and blindingly tempting that we started using payoffs to the leaders of some small and very unstable countries in order to win mining concessions and contracts. That's the way all business is done in those places. If it weren't us doing those deals, it would be simply someone else. And a lot of money was involved. Once we were an offshore company, money seemed to fall from the sky as we became more involved with the larger players in the game. I was entranced. But it turned out to be the biggest mistake of my life."

It hit Soleil what this little snake she was engaged to had done. The government wasn't going to sit back and let him hide in Geneva. Now it was clear that the court order that she had signed for was just a piece of a larger case building against him. He was a US citizen. If he wasn't a fugitive now, he would be shortly. And she...*oh no.*

"My name on the door." Soleil turned colder than ice. "You made me an officer of the company because I'm a Canadian citizen." It was a statement, not a question. "They couldn't touch me or your money, eh?"

Tom stared at her nervously.

"And then what—you would convince your loving wife— me—that we had to move to Europe for more business reasons, all the while evading the cops, and, and—who else is in this mix, Tom—some other 'angels' throwing money at you from heaven, maybe? God knows what kind of gutter scum *they* are! And you tossed me into this cesspool while lying to me around every turn? Knowing that if the heat really turned up, I would be the one thrown to the wolves." Rage barely covered what Soleil was feeling. She had nailed it—Tom's face said it all.

"You don't know right from wrong, do you, Tom?"

The question hung in the air, and for a brief second, everything froze in time.

Then the apartment door exploded inward.

Clip and Clop were suddenly in the room. So were their guns.

The Renault pulled up outside a plain industrial building on the periphery of the Geneva airport. Soleil was in the back seat with Jeffries (Clip), the handcuffs biting into her wrists behind her back. Tom was in a similar position in the front passenger seat while Wallace (Clop) drove. Wallace's gun was handy in his jacket pocket.

Their arrest had been quick and brutal, the two men allowing them only to put on coats before slapping handcuffs on them. Documents that were waved in front of them were supposedly notifications that they were to be extradited to the United States to stand trial for breaking trade laws and fleeing arrest and prosecution. Soleil had studied up on Switzerland in the days leading up to their trip. She knew from the start that this behavior could not have been legal in Switzerland: a US law-enforcement agency was prohibited from arresting anyone on Swiss soil.

No, these two were hired help, probably a couple of private eyes working for a hyped-up prosecutor who had overstepped his authority. Or it could be something worse. This was bad.

Not a word had been spoken in the car.

Soleil was snookered into a dangerous corner and had no options. If these people were who they said they were, and if she were actually returned to New York, she would be appointed an attorney, plead innocent, and hope for the best. But she knew this was risky; she knew she would be incarcerated for a very long time as the wheels of justice ground along, and she was completely unsure and highly dubious of the outcome.

Also, a gung-ho prosecutor could make a name for himself by turning this into a high-visibility case. I can see the fifth-page headline in the *New York Post* now: "Rogue trader and his female Canadian accomplice trading with the enemy while evading the IRS." Just great. Unless...

Unless this is something else entirely.

They were shepherded through a side door of the building and into a small room with a table and some chairs. Suddenly Tom and Soleil were alone.

A man's voice with a slightly familiar British accent on a hidden loudspeaker: "Sit down."

The cloak-and-dagger bothered Soleil. Something—no, everything—was very wrong.

"Mr. Patel," the voice continued, "in order to avoid the unpleasant task of returning you to the United States, where the heavy arm of justice awaits you, we have a proposition."

Soleil froze, and it hit her that she was close to being a dead woman. This wasn't an arrest—it was a kidnapping. If this were even the slightest bit kosher, any deals would have to be made in the United States, not here.

The voice continued. "We have been commissioned by the CIA to make you this offer, and make it just once. If you refuse, you will be returned to the United States and stand trial, and since this has become a serious international incident, you will likely be faced with decades of jail time, or worse. You are, after all, Mr. Patel, considered a traitor and could face the ultimate penalty. And your actions, Ms. Tangiere, are dangerously complicit."

Baloney. I don't buy this. And I see Tom is looking everywhere but at me.

The voice continued. "This is your only way out. Listen carefully. You and your fiancé will travel to the Soviet Union to negotiate a deal for purchasing a large quantity of platinum with funding from a certain metals consortium using your company, Patel + Co, as a cover name. The true identity of that consortium remains no concern of yours.

"You will leave for Moscow on an Aeroflot flight in two hours, on which you will be briefed about all the details. We expect you to complete this deal within a few days. You will perform this flawlessly, be backed by all the funds needed, and then be allowed back in the US. When you do return to the United States, you will then be charged on far lesser civil tax matters, maybe face a fine and perhaps a suspended jail sentence. If you refuse, life incarceration, maybe even execution, awaits you. You will be briefed on the flight.

"And this must be accomplished immediately. You see, Mr. Patel, the Soviet Union is disintegrating. We must move fast."

Tom was immobilized, his eyes glazed over with fear. His face told a story—a story that revealed that he knew volumes about this and had hidden it all from Soleil. He slumped farther into his chair.

"Sorry, Tom, that it had to come to this," the voice suddenly continued. "We just had a feeling that a little push was necessary."

Tom slumped in a chair and stared at the floor, beaten. But Soleil, still standing, was shocked by something else: the one word, *platinum*. Her heart thumped in her chest. Who are you? she wondered at the voice. Why does this seem so familiar? And it's *me*, isn't it? Tom yes, but me as well. Who are these people?

"And Ms. Tangiere," the voice ended up, "you should welcome this opportunity to do good, to clear your soul of your past sins. Do you understand?"

There.

Now it was clear as crystal—the final piece of the puzzle.

Her blood ran cold as she stared into the face of the answer to her questions about the death of her father and those other miners. And the death of Dorsey as well. She was a pawn who had fallen onto these peoples' game board like a gift from heaven. And these people would stop at nothing, including murder. She knew that for a fact.

Smythe. It had to be. That British voice.

But the way she met Tom—was that an accident, or was it by design? There was no way *that* was a setup. Or was it?

Then something occurred to her: there was something that Brenda had said a long time ago. They were talking about Tom and how they met: the whole watch battery thing. Brenda had asked what seemed a silly question at the time: "Did you put the new battery in his watch?" and now I remember telling her, "No. His watch was still working." I didn't think much of it at the time and thought it was just a way for him to talk to me. But it was a blind, a trick.

The first of many, I know now.

"We're not criminals," she said out loud. "We don't need handcuffs."

Wallace and Jeffries came in the room. The cuffs came off, but the guns still ostentatiously bulged in their jacket pockets. Soleil thought that while these two men were morons, they were dangerous ones. "Don't think you're smart. These cuffs had to come off anyway," said Jeffries.

The four piled into the Renault, and they drove the remaining distance to the airport. They made a left onto a service road, and Soleil saw that they would be generally avoiding the terminals.

The road was a series of switchbacks complicated by concrete barriers on either side that made it difficult for Soleil to see the route they were taking. Tom was frozen in what looked like sullen fear. Sorry, Tom, Soleil thought briefly, but you brought this down on yourself and me, and now we're both in mortal danger. Yes, we'll be going to Russia, but we'll never come back. Do you get it now?

Soleil was able to glance back—a dark Audi sedan was closely following them.

An Aeroflot Tupolev TU-154 was being refueled at one of the gates. The silver jet was a medium-sized commercial plane carrying passengers on the Geneva-to-Moscow route. A Jetway had been wheeled up against the open door of the plane, attaching it to the terminal. The car came to a stop near one of the terminal's access doors at ground level.

The passenger door of the Audi opened, and a tall, ascetic-looking man in a dark raincoat emerged and began walking toward the access door. As he walked by the

Renault with his driver, he turned toward her, and Soleil did a double take—she knew this man, or at least had seen him before.

Then the man grinned.

Where have I seen him? She wracked her brain.

No, I never saw this man, but I saw someone who looks a lot like him. Who? Where? I have to figure this out, and fast.

Then she looked at Tom and nearly threw up. *His* face said it all: Tom *knows* this man.

Tom's lies have been building up like a pyramid.

Now what?

At the access door to the service level of the terminal, the tall man pressed a code on the wall-mounted keypad, and his driver held the door for him as he disappeared inside. A moment later he reappeared and signaled the men in Soleil's car to come ahead—it was safe.

The four got out of the Renault and walked toward the access door slowly, Wallace and Jeffries making a big show that any false move would be fatal. But Soleil's thoughts were far ahead, and she realized there was a chance: *they were all going into the terminal.* That meant that they were planning to board her and Tom on the Tupolev through the same gate as the rest of the passengers. Good.

Up a flight of stairs, through another door, and they were suddenly in the bustle and crush of the gate area with dozens of people in the throes of plane-boarding emotion. French, Russian, and English swirled in a verbal stew around them. They were well past the area of the metal detectors—surprisingly close to the entrance to the Jetway that led into the plane. So were their guns.

As they approached the gate door to the Jetway, the tall man walked ahead with his driver. It was now or never, she realized as her inner tension soared.

"Smythe," she called out in a moderated tone. The tall man stopped short. He turned slowly and brought the full force of his pale stare on her. She's figured this out, eh? How does she know who I am? Well, no matter—nothing changes.

"Who I am means nothing to you," he said archly. "You may know my name, but it is of little—"

"You killed my father."

A smirk began to form on Smythe's lips, but it was cut short, and his face froze when he saw the look on the girl's face—it wasn't cold, no, it was past cold—it was controlled fury and, what else? Yes, there was a vicious determination buried in there as well.

Wallace was walking close in to Soleil's left side. Suddenly she seemed to lose her balance and reached for Wallace's arm for support.

Switzerland had just finished equipping its major airports with sophisticated camera and detection equipment. There were no audio features on the cameras, but the quality of the videos was exceptional and the abundance of cameras covered every square inch of the airport. Little did the installations team expect that just forty-eight hours after the system was made operational, they would have a video the police would eagerly pore over for weeks:

Airport Interior Surveillance Camera Group 6T-62 recorded incident 789035 as follows:

20:08:21 Two men approached the Aeroflot boarding podium: one taller than average and wearing a raincoat. Immediately behind, a group of four—three men and a woman—followed closely.

20:09:02 The tall man in the raincoat stopped short and turned around to face the woman.

20:09:10 The woman looked at him for a moment and seemed to swoon. She placed her arm through that of her escort.

20:09:17 The man walking beside the tall man seemed to spin on his heel and then fell to the ground.

(20:09:22 Police lip readers confirm that at that point the woman screamed: "Help me!")

20:09:41 The man who seemed to be dancing with the woman turned, and a second man in his group went down as he finally lost balance and fell to the floor.

20:10:01 The last man, apparently of Indian or Pakistani descent, began running through the agitated crowd away from the scene.

20:10:43 The tall man disappeared through access door 32-HZ.

20:11:03 The woman followed.

20:11:52 The last uninjured man at the scene picked himself off the floor and followed the first two.

Stupid to keep your gun in the pocket closest to me, Wallace, thought Soleil. I just have to dip in your pocket... like...this! OK, good-bye, Smythe—burn in hell!

To anyone caring to look, it seemed as if she had lost her balance and slipped her arm through Wallace's for support.

In actuality, her hand had closed on his hand in his pocket—the hand that had been clutching the gun with his finger on the trigger. She shoved his hand and the gun forward and squeezed hard, and Wallace fired through his pocket. Smythe's driver went down.

She didn't see the man drop to the floor because she was falling on Wallace. The two twisted as they stumbled, and a second shot blasted through the coat pocket and caught Jeffries squarely in his chest. The man twirled once and then crumpled.

Wallace was off balance, teetering on one foot, and appeared to be doing a samba with Soleil, whose arms were tangled with his and whose hand was stuck in his pocket.

The gunshots sounded like sonic booms in the terminal. For an instant there was silence, and then the airport erupted in pandemonium around Soleil. People fell over one another scrambling to get clear and find a way out of danger.

Looking quickly around for Tom, she finally yelled, "Help me!"

But Tom Patel had taken off. She had a brief glimpse of the back of his head in the melee, and then he was gone.

Soleil realized that in another second Wallace would regain his balance. The chaos around her was intensifying. She spotted the Renault's keys, which had fallen on the floor next to Wallace. She quickly bent to grab them and out of the corner of her eye saw Smythe disappearing through the same access door they had just entered.

Soleil took a quick deep breath, threw her body against Wallace, finally causing him to completely lose his balance and fall, and in a moment she was out the door after Smythe, keys in her hand.

Wallace hit the ground heavily, but in seconds was up and running after Soleil.

Airport External Surveillance Camera Group 2R-14, incident 794922:

20:13:10 The tall man emerged from ground access door 32-HZ.

20:13:16 He proceeded rapidly to a dark Audi sedan parked 50 meters from the terminal.

20:14:20 The woman emerged from the same door and began to run toward the car.

20:14:48 The third man, believed to be the killer, emerged from the door immediately behind the woman and overpowered her on the tarmac.

20:16:12 After a moment the woman lay motionless on the runway as the man stood up beside her prone body and aimed his gun at her.

Smythe burst out the access door onto the tarmac and sprinted to the Audi. He got in heavily behind the wheel. He had his Sturm Ruger automatic in his hand now. *The Tangiere girl has to die right now! Too bad: this gives our Russian deal a bit of a setback. Now I'll have to round up Patel, and he'll have to handle it alone. Damn her!*

Soleil came out the door, ran a few steps, and then saw Smythe in the Audi—he was aiming his gun out the window. But before she could react, the roar of the gun filled the air at the same instant that Wallace plowed into her from behind, knocking her to the ground. He fell on her heavily.

For a moment Wallace thought he had just tripped. His gun was in his hand. This will be a messy affair, he thought, but I'll bluff my way out of it when it's over.

But suddenly he started to slide off the girl's body. What? Yechh, what's this? He kneeled and wiped his hand across the front of his shirt. It came away red.

Smythe's bullet had missed its intended victim and had found another target: Wallace's aorta.

Wallace, shocked, clambered to his feet, his gun pointed down at Soleil. But his eyes suddenly lost focus and rolled up in their sockets, and he pitched over sideways. He was dead before he hit the ground.

"Damn that girl," Smythe thought grimly from behind the wheel of the Audi as he watched this tableau unfold on the tarmac. He aimed carefully out the driver's window and fired at her. But the gun just clicked. He had used his last bullet on Wallace. Deciding quickly, he gunned the Audi.

Airport External Surveillance Camera Group 3R-09 incident 800781:

20:18:06 The dark Audi sedan accelerated and appeared to collide with the woman's prone body.

20:18:13 Four maintenance personnel were rapidly approaching the remains.

20:18:30 The automobile sped off along Runway A-2.

20:19:55 The maintenance personnel huddled over the apparently deceased woman.

She rolled to the right at the last possible second, the Audi's tires missing her by inches. A moment later, four men in overalls were hovering over her.

"Can you get up? Don't move! Be still!" they implored nervously in French.

She breathed deeply for a moment, forced a smile, rolled onto her stomach, and pushed herself upright. She looked around. The Renault sat quietly fifteen yards away.

"Please, water..." she said weakly but sweetly in quaintly accented French. "Can one of you men get me some water?"

The four men fell all over one another to run and do this beautiful, helpless, injured girl's bidding, and in the confusion she took the opportunity to jump up and sprint for the Renault. A moment later she was behind the wheel. The four men were stunned at her surprising speed, especially in her apparent condition of distress, but the car was off before they could react.

The Audi's engine roared. Smythe was bent over the wheel, the empty Ruger on the seat next to him. Somehow he had to stop and put in a fresh clip. He blasted the car down the curving service road searching for the route out of the airport, all the while narrowly avoiding construction barriers on either side of the road.

Did I hit the girl? This is getting worse by the second. I need to get back into Geneva and...

The Renault with Soleil behind the wheel crashed loudly into one of the rear quarter panels of the Audi as Smythe was about to maneuver through a tight curve at high speed.

The Audi was pushed off course, and the tires squealed in protest. The car fishtailed wildly, climbed a short concrete barricade, flipped over, and spun to a halt on its roof, blocking both directions of traffic.

The airbag, which had inflated, covered Smythe's face and chest. He was disoriented and slipped and crumpled onto what was once the ceiling of the car's interior, now its floor.

The Renault rocked to a halt a few yards away, and Soleil jumped out and quickly ran to the Audi. She knelt down and turned her face to Smythe. Smythe felt blindly around for his gun. Soleil reached in and pulled the crumpled airbag off the man's face.

"Creep," she said bitterly, and then saw that his body was apparently pinned into the car. The pale face smirked: "Help," said Smythe. He seemed unnaturally calm, thought Soleil. He's completely helpless and feels confident that I'll save him, or at least leave him to his own devices.

Here's the big decision: Now, *right this moment*, one of my Dad's killers, probably the mastermind of the multiple murders, is right where I want him. But what should I do now? Strangle him? Save him? What?

"Get me out of here, Soleil," he said, and his mouth parted in a devilish grin. There's that face, that grin, she thought. Where have I seen that? "If I die now," he continued, "my son will come for you, and no one can stop *him*."

Soleil couldn't stand him saying her name, and hated him for doing this to her. What son? What now—do I turn him in? What do I do?

She reached into the car to see if Smythe could somehow be freed, and he began to squirm his upper body through the driver's window.

Then fate showed up. Hearing a familiar sound growing rapidly in volume, Soleil stood up to look over the road barriers, and instantly saw that everything was about to change. She took three desperate strides and dove behind the Renault to safety.

A police car with its siren wailing flashed around the bend from the opposite direction. Soleil had seen that it was moving way too fast and was far too late to avoid the upside-down Audi. It crashed full tilt into the car's passenger side with the sound of a bomb going off.

Smythe's body was exactly half way out of the Audi when the police car struck. The car was loudly and violently pushed up on its driver's side, and it messily cut the Englishman in half. Soleil lifted her head to see around the fender of the Renault and watched as the two policemen extricated themselves from their patrol car. Then they approached the ruin of the Audi, froze momentarily, and then began to back off quickly. What are they...?

The Audi's engine erupted in a mini firestorm, and then its gas tank, mangled beyond its ability to hold itself together, exploded. The car tore itself to pieces—metal and glass whizzed and crashed in all directions, showering the road, the Renault, and the patrol car. What was left of the Audi was wrapped in flames in a matter of seconds. A blast of heat enveloped Soleil, and for a moment she thought she too would catch fire. She didn't want to think about what finally became of Smythe.

Two down, Dad, she thought bitterly.

She stepped out from behind the Renault and walked shakily over to stand by the two cops. Sirens wailed in the distance. Smythe's funeral pyre burned brightly in the road.

5

OFFICE

The questioning at the police station lasted two hours. Soleil told the investigators everything as it happened—she had little to hide about the facts of the last hour. After all, it was Wallace's hand that pulled the trigger killing Smythe's driver and Jeffries. Hair splitting? No, not really. *I* didn't kidnap anyone or force innocent people at gunpoint. You reap what you sow.

Though she couldn't have known it now, airport cameras would later confirm that Wallace was the murderer of Smythe's driver and Jeffries. Soleil felt a twinge of guilt for maybe a minute but knew that Wallace wouldn't care now. She could still claim self-defense and would probably beat the state's accusations, but time was of the essence. She feigned ignorance of the identity of her abductors, her suspicions of their motives, and anything she knew or suspected about Smythe.

The head investigator of this unusual incident was Henri Deshautels: midforties, unruly black hair, heavily lidded eyes. He was a chief inspector, and he carefully listened to Soleil and watched her face as her story unfolded. Soleil thankfully realized that Deshautels was open to her story, and the squad of detectives that accompanied him seemed to be of the same bent. After her exhaustive and quite voluntary monologue in her rough Quebecoise French that left the small crowd of leering investigators speechless, silently derisive of Canadian French in general, and a little randy, Deshautels was left with the conviction that she was the innocent victim of a frightful kidnapping and a love affair gone bad.

"Your fiancé abandoned you at the scene?" I wouldn't have abandoned this one—not in a million years, Deshautels thought. In fact, if I were only ten years younger...

Soleil saw his thoughts in his face. "It appears that way, Inspector."

Vive l'amour, she said to herself.

As a Canadian national, Soleil had few rights, but the Swiss were nothing if not reasonable, and the airport cameras confirmed her story to a *T*.

"I need to speak to your fiancé, mademoiselle. He obviously is the key to this series of sad events." Deshautels had great sympathy in his voice and his face. Soleil knew she was lucky that it was he who was in charge of the inquiry. A woman investigator would likely have kept her overnight or even for days in police custody. Deshautels was going to let her go.

"*S'il vous plait*, M. Deshautels," Soleil said, looking at the card he had handed her with his office phone printed on it and another, private number written on the back in ink. "I'll call you later when I discover his location. I am free to go, *oui*?"

"*Bien sur*, Soleil. I can call you Soleil?"

"*D'accord*."

"*Merci, mademoiselle*. Call me as soon as you know Mr. Patel's location. And be careful." Then as an afterthought, "May we call you a cab?"

"*Merci*."

Tom had sent Yvonne home, and now he was frantically packing the last of his files in some cardboard boxes. His shirt was limp with sweat, and his thick black hair hung over his frantic eyes. His brain was short-circuiting with fear and the imperative to flee. Gripped in near panic, he was oblivious to his surroundings.

"Where are you going?" said a voice from behind him. Tom had been bent over a cardboard carton. Now his heart skipped two beats.

"Back to the good old USA, Tommy? Or maybe Cuba or something like that?"

He stood up and turned. Soleil stood in the doorway. She had a bandage on her forehead, and it looked as though a small patch of her hair had been burned. There was darkness around her eyes, and her pea coat was torn.

"This the evidence you're going to ditch, Tommy?" She waved at the cardboard boxes. "Or is this all the stuff fingering *me* in your clever little business? Shipping it all off to your pals, whoever they are? I'll bet my signatures are all over it, eh? Why didn't you get a rubber stamp made: 'Soleil Tangiere, Vice-President and Chief Patsy'? Ah, you probably did."

Summoning whatever courage he had, Tom stared her down. "I didn't think it would come to this."

"No, why should it 'come to this'? Just string me along for a year or two, take advantage of the little ol' country gal with her valuable Canadian citizenship and her naïve and innocent outlook on the world. Just use me in every way, and brother, do I mean *every* way, and then let me take the rap for your crimes. What was next on the menu, Tom—your disappearing act followed by a knock on the door and me being led away by another set of goons?" Her eyes blazed.

Tom came to a decision: to hell with her. "That's the way the cookie crumbles, Soleil. There's nothing you can do now to make the situation any better, or any worse for that matter, or change it in any way." Suddenly a long steel letter opener was in his hand. His face told her he meant business. OK, she thought, this engagement is officially over.

Tom never expected what happened next. Instead of backing off, Soleil crossed the short space between them, balled her fist, and let fly a roundhouse left that caught Tom in his right temple. He was almost knocked off his feet. Soleil's hand felt as if it were nearly broken. The letter opener clattered away harmlessly.

"I can just see you now, you creep, cowering in some backwater slum until it all blows over—until I'm behind bars, or worse." Her face glowed with suppressed fury.

Her voice lowered: "Were you going to go off with your friend Smythe?" Tom blinked rapidly. "Don't plan to do that anytime soon. They needed *two* body bags after what I did to him."

Tom shook his head and backed up a step. Something finally snapped in his brain, and he charged at her. She ducked, pivoted, and as the man careened past her, she used his body's momentum to shove him into the wall. The sound his head made was surprisingly loud. He fell to his knees, shook his head, and turned his face to her.

"Here's a little sentimental token to take you down memory lane," she said. She grabbed the large frame off his desk, the one displaying the picture of the two of them so happy and in love, and backhanded it into his face. His nose crunched as the glass disintegrated and his face came away with a dozen small cuts. From the back of his throat came a growl that grew into a scream.

He charged her again, fast this time, wrapping his arms around her waist, and the two bodies crashed into a closed window. A snowstorm of glass swirled loudly around them, cutting them both, and Soleil found herself being pushed out through the ragged frame. As she twisted, she saw the street seven stories below. And she saw something else, too.

"This is your fault!" Tom screamed. "I'll kill you!" He had lost all control and was now nothing more than a dangerous rabid animal. Soleil reached out and grabbed the sides of the window frame and pulled with all her strength. They both rocketed out the window, but Soleil had had a glimpse at that something else—a sturdy TV antenna cluster a few feet to the right bolted into the bricks of the wall. As they came out the window, she twisted and with one hand grabbed the sturdy metal lattice and swung away, her feet dangling over thin air. Tom slipped quickly downward, and his hand grabbed one of her ankles.

Tom hung on to Soleil for a few desperate seconds, and then he yelled her name as his fingers let go.

Hans Petzenfelder loved his new BMW. It was parked on the street outside the building's entrance. Hans was coming out of the building and he just *had* to stop on the sidewalk to admire it for the tenth time that day. *Ja, das is a sweet car. Ja*, look at those lines, what a beauty. And so perfect. I love perfect.

A split second later, Tom Patel slammed into the car. The entire roof crunched down to the tops of the seats, every window including the windshield exploded outward, the passenger door was ripped off the car, and both pedestrians and passing cars were hit with a storm of broken glass. The car's alarm began whooping. Hans just stood there. He stared at the remains of his car and its new occupant with disbelief.

Then he looked up to see a woman seven stories up on the side of the wall swinging by one arm. He gasped out loud as he saw the metal antenna grid she was holding onto tear off the side of the building.

Soleil knew she was finished, and she almost welcomed the oblivion that was seconds away. She never wanted or expected to have this kind of a life—a life that seemed to be getting more vicious and insane, but neither would she sit by and let others lead that life for her. OK, see you in a minute, Dad.

But something had grabbed her wrist, and she swung wildly. The antenna grid, freed from its mooring, tumbled away toward the accelerating mayhem on the street below.

She looked up to see a man half out the window.

"Do not panic," he said in French. "Let me do the pulling, mademoiselle."

"*Merci*," said Soleil Tangiere.

Henri Deshautels was surprisingly strong.

Deshautels had pushed his way into the office when he heard the commotion and was just in time to hear the crash of the window and Tom yell "I'll kill you!" Without hesitation he crossed the room was able to reach Soleil without an inch or a second to spare.

Now, back inside the office, Soleil sat down immediately on a chair near the desk. Her eyes seemed to lose their focus, and she leaned over and threw up into one of the cardboard boxes of documents. Deshautels paced around the office for a minute or two, politely looking anywhere but at Soleil. He was secretly proud of his life-saving grab. After a short time, she had composed herself.

"When you are up to it, it's back to the station for the two of us," he finally said.

She looked at him and nodded. Her eyes were tired but amazingly calm.

"Did you see what happened?" she asked quietly.

"Yes."

After all was said and done, and after the boys at the police station had a few more hours of ogling this apparently dangerous, disheveled, and striking woman, Soleil was left with a gentle warning from Deshautels: stay close by. Be accessible. Soleil had no intention of disobeying this order—she was exhausted. At least for now.

This man Deshautels had saved her life, and she appreciated it immensely and thanked him again. With words. That's all I can offer, Inspector.

It was evening when she returned to the apartment. The broken door would not lock, but she was too tired to care. And she didn't think about Tom at all.

She lay down on the bed in her clothes and was instantly asleep.

Over the next week, Deshautels called her at least once a day. Mostly it was to question her about details of what happened, and it soon took on the tone of what Soleil had begun to fear—Deshautels was a man at a dangerous age, and having saved Soleil's life, he was subject to feelings and fantasies that could do neither him nor Soleil any long-term good. He was almost twice the girl's age, apparently in a loveless marriage, and Soleil was determined to avoid any more mistakes with men—for as long as possible.

When Deshautels finally asked her to meet him for dinner (his wife conveniently visiting relatives in France, of course), Soleil refused but was wary.

"I'm sorry, M. Deshautels, but please, I will be happy to come down to the station again to speak with you about anything, anytime you want." She waited on high alert for his reply.

There was a short silence.

"That is all right, Mlle Tangiere. Whatever it is will wait." Now it was back to 'Mlle Tangiere' again.

"Thank you so much, monsieur," Soleil said into the phone in a strong tone of good-natured finality. They said their good-byes, and Soleil leaned against the wall with the phone in her hand. Her eyes were thoughtful and stared at the opposite wall.

I have to figure out what to do.

When Soleil walked up to the building, there were still some signs of the accident and the wreck of the car that Tom had hit—some fading chalk marks in the street, tiny bits of glass on the edge of the sidewalk, a dark stain or two. She stood on the sidewalk for a moment and silently cursed the events at the airport that had led up to this. And she cursed herself.

This is my fault for not seeing who Tom was. I had a hundred little hints right in front of me and chose to either ignore or excuse them. Never again. I'm tired, but more of these people are going to keep coming, so there's no time for the luxury of a rest. I'll rest after it's all over, whatever that means.

She carefully placed the small bouquet of Alpine wildflowers that she had purchased from a nearby store against the wall of the building opposite the exact spot where Tom had died. She stood looking down at it for a minute. Then she crossed herself, looked up at the sky, and said a last good-bye to Tom Patel.

When she went upstairs to the office, she found a note scotch-taped to the door. It was a bill for the repair of the office window. Soleil sat down at Yvonne's desk looking at it absently and tried to sort out the future. That was when the brunette secretary came through the door.

Soleil smiled at her. "Sit down, Yvonne, please," Soleil said in French. The older woman had her defenses up and was as nervous as a cat. It looked as if the Canadian girl had been in a bad accident. Yvonne sat down in a chair against the wall.

"I want to give you your final paycheck, Yvonne. Certainly Tom owed you some money."

Yvonne was taken aback. She began to stutter a protest, but Soleil put up a hand. She held Yvonne with her open, steady gaze. In a moment she said in French, "You can tell me, Yvonne—tell me what trouble Tom was in. You don't owe it to me, but maybe you can see how I feel."

She continued, "I lived with the man for two years, and during that time he became a thorough sneak and a liar, if he wasn't one before. He fooled me completely. I didn't think that I was such a blind and naïve person, but I guess I was. Maybe you can understand how I feel about being lied to for two years and then being almost killed by a man I loved and who professed to love me. Please. What was really going on here?" Soleil said quietly.

Yvonne's eyes moved around the room. Then: "Lately he had become a different person, and nervous and uptight. It began when some very bad people started to come here, Ms. Tangiere—"

"Soleil, please call me Soleil."

"All right, Soleil. In the last few months, some men had begun coming here, speaking in English. My English is not very good, but it didn't matter—Mr. Patel would always escort them out of the office to talk. Most often when he returned to the office, he would be very nervous." Yvonne fidgeted. A pigeon alighted on the ledge outside the new window, walked along it, and flew off.

"It's OK if you call him Tom, Yvonne. Was one of them a tall man with a British accent?"

"Oh, oui! I believe Tom called him Smith or something like that. I didn't like him, not one bit."

"Smythe. Why?"

Yvonne hesitated as if she were looking for the right words. "He was, how should I say, antipathetic. When he came into the room, it felt as if he had brought a devil in with him as his companion. Sometimes he *would* bring a younger man with him—almost like a young duplicate of himself. Brrr—that one, he made my blood run cold. Perhaps *he* was indeed the devil—he was more repellant than Smythe."

"What was he called?"

"I think I heard him being addressed as John, but I'm not sure."

"What else about this John?"

"He came with Smythe often and rarely spoke, but he seemed to be very close with him—he even looked like him, only shorter."

Soleil felt the same way she did hiding back under the trailer at the Montana mine—disoriented and disconnected, yet aware that something terribly bad was coming at her in the future. Could this have been Smythe's son? Why not?

After a moment, Soleil shifted gears. "Yvonne, what do you know about the way business was done here?"

Yvonne seemed a little relieved that the conversation had changed direction.

"Well, Tom was in and out of the office, when he was in Geneva at all, and he left it to me to create the occasional bill and write the occasional check." Yvonne looked at the floor. "Some of those checks were large."

"What do you mean?"

"Well, some of the checks were for hundreds of thousands of francs, or dollars, sometimes to metals or mining companies and sometimes to individuals with strange, foreign names." She slid her foot back and forth on the floor.

She's holding back on something else, Soleil thought.

"What, Yvonne? What's wrong?"

"I saw how he signed the checks. He signed your name." The woman seemed to collapse inside. Soleil wasn't surprised. What a crumb you are...*were*, Tom. Now what do I do?

After a moment Soleil said, "Yvonne, would you like to work for me for a little while?"

A double take. "What?"

"Well if my name has been on the checks all this time, and I seem to be a partner and my name is on the door, well then, I guess your job is still intact—as long as I remain solvent, out of jail, and still breathing, that is." Soleil smiled. "But as soon as possible, I want to get out of Geneva. I won't completely leave Switzerland now; I can't, but I want to get out of this city." She looked at Yvonne. "Where's the checkbook?"

The police had ransacked the office pretty well and had taken the boxes of books and documents that Tom had been frantically trying to pack. Certainly if there had been checkbooks, they were gone.

Surprisingly, Yvonne got up and went over to Tom's mahogany desk, now devoid of papers or paraphernalia.

"Here," she said as she bent down and slipped her hand under the desk. There was a muffled click. She straightened and pulled up on the top of the desk. The whole top was hinged, and it lifted to reveal a shallow depression. In it were some soft-covered ledgers, a small, single-entry checkbook, and in a little open-ended envelope, a key. Soleil was amazed and then looked at the secretary.

He really trusted this Yvonne, Soleil thought, throwing her a direct gaze. Might have slept with her too. Isn't that great. "You know you're in trouble too, Yvonne. Tom seems to have had a way of involving the mademoiselles in his messes. I'll bet you've signed my name and his name and who the hell else too on checks and whatever, eh?"

Yvonne blanched.

"Don't worry. Let's see what we have to work with."

Soleil picked up the checkbook. The first check, number 001, was still there. There was no indicated opening balance. She was about to put it in her pocket when she noticed a small photo was scotch-taped on the leatherette back of the checkbook. It was a picture of Tango, their dog. I guess Tom had some genuine love for someone.

"How much is in this account?"

Yvonne said she didn't know, and Soleil believed her.

"How much do we owe, Yvonne?"

"I don't think very much, Soleil. Most of his bills he paid from another checkbook, and that account was up to date. The police must have that one—it was in a little safe that is no longer here. I think this checkbook was his 'emergency fund.'"

Well.

Maybe, just maybe, if she was very careful and was extremely lucky, she would get out of this unscathed. But she didn't want her name dragged through the Swiss financial mud and wanted to pay any debts that had her name on them, even if she had nothing to do with how they got started. This was Switzerland, her home for the time being. Her future rested on her financial, as well as her personal, reputation.

She looked at the checkbook. The account was drawn on the Zurcher Suisse Bank, Bahnhofstrasse 8, Zurich.

She thought for a moment and then said, "OK, Yvonne, I'll be going to Zurich. I may try my hand at this commodity business. Would you like to come there and help me out for a while? I'll try to make it attractive financially." She outlined her idea and offered to pay Yvonne as long as she could. Yvonne agreed to come to Zurich the next week and stay until Soleil got settled.

"I'll also be changing the company name as soon as possible, Yvonne. Patel + Company is out as of now. How does Tangiere International sound to you?"

Yvonne smiled. *Bon.*

The envelope arrived with the rest of the mail. Brenda noticed that it had a Swiss stamp on it. She smiled and opened it. A picture post card of the Alps fell out along with a folded handwritten note:

Dear Brenda and Izzy,

I hope you are both well and happy.

I'm in Geneva but am now heading to Zurich. Switzerland is a beautiful and interesting country, and my German's coming along real well—thanks again for that!

Guess what! I fell into a real good opportunity here and may stay for a long time. So I guess you'll need to find someone else to take over my job at the business. You know (and like, I hope!) Aimee. She would probably love to work for you part time. Before I left she told me it would be no problem. Ask her—she'll say yes!

You were right about Tom. He's no longer in the picture, and I could kick myself for being a fool and not seeing who he really was. Anyway, it's certainly over, and one day I'll give you all the details.

I don't have a permanent address yet, but when I do, I'll let you know.

Be safe and happy, and kiss Tango for me.

Soleil

PS: Thanks for being my 'parents.' I love you.

6

FUNERAL

Highgate Cemetery lay in a shroud of wet misery as a cold rain fell on the crowd of mourners.

A few dozen interments still took place in this famous landmark north of London each year. Philip Clooney's was one of them.

His body had arrived in England three days previously from Switzerland. It was a difficult case for the mortuary. The fact that the body was crushed into two pieces was not the major issue—it could be reassembled. The bigger problem was that it was also burned to a crisp. That would be hard to disguise.

The burden of the funeral decisions rested on his son, John. In spite of the gentle entreaties of the mortuary, John insisted that his father's wrecked body not be cremated. It was left to the experts to fix Philip up as best as possible. Eventually even John agreed to a closed-coffin wake.

Philip Clooney, who had called himself Smythe for so much of his professional life, was waked for two days. While he had few personal friends and fewer close family members, some executives from his company showed up at the funeral home to pay their respects. Among those were the largest shareholder and four or five members of the company's board of partners.

As for family, the crowd was thin, to say the least. His much-abused wife, Sheryl Clooney, had left him when their only son, John, was thirteen. One day when Philip returned from work, she was just gone. John was in the kitchen slicing a salami.

"Where's your mum?" Philip asked. The boy popped a hunk of meat in his mouth with the end of the blade.

"Ummph, mmph, mmph," said the salami mouth.

"Come on, John!"

John looked at his father, raised one eyebrow, said, "Ask me no questions, I'll tell you no lies, Father," and touched the tip of the knife to his greasy thumb. Sheryl had gone. Philip suspected (but didn't at all fear) the worst, and almost a year later, he heard a rumor that she had taken up with a tennis pro in Ireland. Philip didn't care; he was too busy molding his acolyte and heir apparent. Like father like son, he sighed to himself.

And that rumor turned out to be just that: a rumor. Sheryl Clooney never made it to Ireland and was never heard from again.

John Clooney, now senior vice president of the company his father had helped to build, was enjoying his life at the tender age of twenty-eight. Though almost a head shorter, he showed the strong features of his father, especially the eyes that had by now developed their own cast of low cunning and deeply buried madness. He resembled his father in other ways as well, in the important and necessary ways: he had become ruthless and pitiless, with a limitless flexibility of morality on all levels. He was also quite capable of murder.

John's company, Carrington Metals, or CM, as it was known in the trade, dealt in platinum on a fairly large scale, and they did it in less-than-savory fashion. Most of the free world's platinum came from African countries where CM had ongoing shadowy relationships with government officials, crooked mine bosses, and illegal organizations. Needless to say, according to CM's unwritten policies, business trumped human rights. And sometimes human life.

Aside from John, the only other family member present was John's grandmother Delores. Delores was the largest shareholder and the power behind the throne at CM. She was a tiny, wizened ninety-two-year-old prune of a woman, holding viciously on to life and power from her seat in a wheelchair—a wheelchair that was more of a mission control than a chair. The motorized mount bristled with tubes and monitors, enabling Delores's body to breathe and function effortlessly, to be independently mobile and even achieve bursts of speed up to fifteen miles an hour when necessary. John stood by her as people paid their respects at the casket.

"Who's responsible?" It was a dry, soft question from the wheelchair. The voice sounded like the breath of a corpse.

John knew what his grandma was asking.

"I know who it was. I know who did it. It was the woman." He scowled at the air in front of his face.

"The woman? Ah, yes, yes, the Canadian girl." The dry as dust voice again.

"It should never have gotten this far. Had Father taken care of the problem the correct way years ago, he would still be alive."

"The same could be said for you, boy." Was that a dry chuckle?

"Father always said that he would need the woman in the future, and look where it got him."

There was a minute or two of silence. Then she said, "Do nothing, Johnny-boy. Your Dada was only following my advice."

John was startled. "What do you mean?" A conservatively dressed couple walked up somberly to shake John's hand and mutter a few words of consolation. When they had passed, John continued.

"What do you mean?"

"What I mean isn't part of this discussion. I said she lives until I say so," the voice a thin wind blowing across a sand dune.

"Do nothing? Are you daft, Grandma?"

From the chair, the old prune swung her purse with surprising strength, landing a blow on John's groin area. He grunted in surprise—what did she have in that purse, her rock collection?

"Don't you dare speak to me that way, you vile whelp! I said for you to do nothing to that girl, and nothing it shall be." Sahara wind. "The woman will have her uses in the future, and mark my words, she will pay with more than her life. She burned up my son, your dada, into a crumpet—there's almost nothing left to bury, and more's the pity. But you must wait, Johnny boy."

John was certain his grandmother was barmy, but a shudder ran through him nevertheless. "I cannot keep her alive, you know, if fate intervenes."

"That's not what I said. You will need her in the future." She gave him a dose of squinty eyes set in leathery folds of skin. "You may also find a good use for my shares of the company. Let's see, if I remember, considering the additional shares that Philip bequeathed to me, I now control the company completely. So be smart. Revenge will come sooner or later. Let Soleil Tangiere craft her own demise." A pause. "It's far more satisfying. You just keep a very wary eye on her, my boy." A dry, dry cackle.

John marveled at his grandmother. This virago was born before the turn of the century—they really turned them out tough then, he thought. Real tough.

And now the rain was falling, and the crowd, in their macs and hats, were dripping and impatient. Some words were forthcoming from the minister, and then the coffin was lowered into the ground.

John stood by while the crowd slowly filed past one last time. People disbursed down the gray, oak-lined lane to a group of cars. Finally he was alone, except for one other.

Back from the gravesite, a woman in black with a black hat whose wide brim fell over most of her face leaned against an oak tree. It was John's fiancé, Fiona Dyche. She looked over at him calmly.

Fiona was almost as tall as John, around five foot nine, and the same age, twenty-eight. She was trim with an almost military posture and poise. Her straight blue-black hair framed her pale, perfect face. Her most arresting feature was her eyes—large with glittering mahogany pupils. Her nose was straight, her lips full and lipsticked a deep burgundy.

No one knew exactly where Fiona had come from, but she had told John that she was born in the Netherlands and was sent to England at an early age when her alcoholic parents split up and neither of them wanted the burden of raising her.

She was reared in different foster homes, but her general sullen attitudes and underlying vicious nature forged a lifestyle that wasn't "mainstream," as she would refer to it. She was good at getting things, especially from men. And her taste in men ran from the rough to the horrendous. Those gents did little to contribute to her growth as a sterling member of society.

The net effect was not a good one: In a clinical setting, Fiona Dyche would easily be diagnosed borderline insane.

But this was not a clinical setting.

They had met in a pub two blocks from the offices of Carrington Metals. He was surprised when Fiona approached him that night—it was annoyingly obvious that every man in the bar was either trying to buy her a drink or imagining what it would be like to be with her. She was dressed in an iridescent top and a tiny skirt, and her shiny black hair fell in a severe arc down one side of her face. That Fiona had done a little preliminary research on John's financial standing never occurred to him.

John heard someone clearing her throat and looked up to see her sitting next to him at the bar.

"What are you drinking?" she asked in her surprisingly deep voice.

"G-Gin and tonic." John almost gagged on his words. For all his bluster and braggadocio about the opposite sex, he wasn't really successful with women—it was always an uphill battle. Girls didn't generally like him first off, and it usually got worse after that. He had to work at it and toss money at any female in the vicinity. Prostitutes were the major features of his love landscape. So when he was approached by this dark-eyed beauty, he found himself a tad speechless.

After he bought Fiona a few gin and tonics, it was incredibly easy sledding: His stylish London apartment, sex, phone calls, dinners, sex, weekends away, drinks, pot, sex—he had achieved relationship nirvana. In spite of the fact that he threw money around with abandon, he sensed that Fiona had started to love him for who he was. Well, most of the time, and what really was the difference in the big scheme of things anyway? He was an important man and deserved a knockout on his arm.

That was a year ago. Now they were engaged, and Fiona had to be circumspect with her cheating on him. Did he really believe that theirs was going to be a closed marriage? No—she needed to be with a man with other, er, assets from time to time. Johnny may have a big financial future, but that was the only big thing about the sad blighter.

But when he gets nasty, like his dad, well, all I *do* need is him, thought Fiona Dyche. Blind aggression and pointless, testosterone-triggered violence were her aphrodisiacs, and John Clooney, when the mood struck him, could deliver.

She pushed off from the tree and came up to him, her slim hips doing that swishing thing he liked.

"Damn, Grandma," he spat and explained the situation to Fiona. The girl took out a cigarette, put it between her lips, and waited while John cupped his hands around his lighter and lit it for her.

"What's her name again?" Fiona asked, two thin jets of smoke coming from her nostrils.

"Soleil. Soleil Tangiere." John's eyes were dark.

A pause. "How old is she?"

"Young. She must be in her early twenties."

"That young? Impressive. What does she look like?"

"Smashing, some would say," John said and instantly regretted it. "But no one comes close to you, luv."

Fiona threw a stony look at him: that's not going to work, John, but I'll let it slide this time.

"Where is she?" she asked.

"As far as I can tell, she's in Switzerland. At last count she was still in Geneva, where she murdered my father."

Fiona looked at him. "Why? Why did she do it?"

John contemplated telling Fiona the details about what had happened in America four years ago and about last week's aborted plan to recruit Tom Patel and Soleil as the patsies in a totally illegal deal with the Russians.

But instead he said, "I'm not sure. What it probably boils down to is one of two things: either it was a case of mistaken identity—she mistook Father for someone else, or she was just off her rocker, crazy." He gave a watered-down version of what happened on the airport road and what the police had told him.

"But the Swiss police called it an accident," she said. "This Soleil person really just showed up at the scene of the crime and, according to them, may have even tried to help your father out of that car."

John looked at her with obvious scorn. "Trust me, luv, she killed him in cold blood."

Fiona thought about that for a minute. If that's true—if she could do such a thing—well, I should like to meet this Tangiere girl, I would.

"Your grandmother said you should do nothing and use this girl in some way or other. But she didn't say anything about *me* doing something, did she?"

John looked at her from beneath angry brows. Fiona is certainly one of a kind. If Grandma hadn't issued strict orders she could go the distance with the girl, he thought, eyeing her critically. Knock her off, as they say in the States, given the smallest of encouragements. Of course she could.

And look what I'm doing for *her*. She's here at my feet, me, a powerful man in a powerful company. I can command her if I so choose. Her cupidity has her trapped.

His eyes looked off into the distance for a moment. Do I let her off her leash to go after Soleil or not? I can't, at least for the moment. But heaven knows I would love to see what my fiancé is really capable of.

He said, "Carrington Metals has to keep an eye on Soleil Tangiere at this time, that's all. Would you want that job, Fiona?"

"I've never been to Switzerland, Johnny." Her smile dripped menace.

He looked down at her.

"Fiona, what are you doing?"

"I have an itch."

"That's disgusting. Cut it out."

"Sorry, Johnny."

Then he said, "Bring her back alive, luv."

Fiona dropped the cigarette in the wet grass. She used the very pointed toe of her shoe to stub it out, but it wasn't really necessary.

7

MONEY AND SEX

ZSB, the Zurcher Suisse Bank, was housed in a modern, bronze-fronted, nine-story building at the edge of the business district in Zurich, close to the Baur au Lac Hotel and Zurichsee, the lovely lake that graced the city of money. It was a cool, pretty day, and small puff clouds dotted the Swiss sky.

Soleil Tangiere stood across the street from the bank.

In her hotel room the night before, she had carefully cut open the lining of her pea coat and removed the small chamois bag that Izzy had given her those few years back. She shook out the contents on the little hotel desk. Five round diamonds, about one carat each, twinkled back at her. They were beautiful and worth enough money to keep Soleil going for at least a few months, even here in Zurich, one of the most expensive cities in the world.

As she set the little cloth bag down next to the stones, she felt one last bump. She worked her fingers into the bag.

Her eyes opened wide as her thumb and forefinger pulled out the last stone: a marquis-cut diamond that must have weighed at least five carats. It was splendid, totally colorless, and its broad table facet revealed no flaws, at least to Soleil's naked eye.

She was breathless. One day I'll thank you properly, Brenda and Izzy. I promise.

Now she stood there in the Bahnhofstrasse in a long, deep-gray cloth coat, its collar high against the back of her neck and its tapering cut accenting her trim body, made even taller by a new pair of black shoes with high heels. The light wind tossed her straight hair, and men walking by tended to turn and sneak a quick appraising glance before their wives or girlfriends walking with them smacked them with an elbow or a withering stare—no fondue for you tonight, pal!

Soleil crossed the street and entered the bank.

It was 10:59 a.m. precisely. On the sixth floor of the Zurcher Suisse Bank, Menschel stood up behind his desk and tugged his vest.

Through the glass door to the reception area, he had seen that his next appointment had just arrived and was speaking with the receptionist. *Gut!* Punctuality is the ultimate compliment and reflection of one's character. It showcases the seriousness with which one takes his life experience. Or in this case, hers. And *ach!* Hold all calls!

Through the glass he saw the young woman presenting ID to the receptionist—standard operating procedure in the bank. Can't be too careful when it comes to money.

Herr Oscar Menschel, forty-two years old, was proud of the fact that he cut the trim form of a classic Swiss banker: dark-gray three-piece suit with a barely noticeable pinstripe. Starched white shirt and muted claret tie. Reading glasses perpetually on the end of his thin nose. An almost military crew cut to his plain brown hair.

Menschel was also proud of the deadpan demeanor that he presented to everyone—his superiors, his inferiors, his clients, his wife. *My view of the world is wide, yes it is. I observe it from heights most others cannot hope to climb. But who is that woman?* He squinted through the glass.

Eleven on the dot. He touched the intercom button with a thin, manicured finger and said, "Please send the lady in." He came around the desk to hold open the door.

Soleil had shed the long coat in the reception room and stepped into Menschel's office wearing a European-cut suit of oatmeal-colored gabardine over a red blouse. Her little diamond cross winked at Menschel. She smiled.

Menschel took her hand and held it lightly in lieu of a handshake. "*Guten morgen*, Frau Tangiere. I am Oscar Menschel." He was suddenly a little off his stride. *Ach*, what a looker. And punctual. For some reason his deadpan demeanor appeared to have taken a siesta.

"*Guten morgen*, Herr Menschel," she said dryly, sensing a small and familiar personality shift in the man, even though she had known him for all of five seconds. *Well, this is all business, Oscar, so cool your jets.*

"*Bitte setzen Sie sich*," as he gestured to a chair. Then: "Would it help if we spoke in English, Ms. Tangiere? I talk English quite well."

Soleil smiled as she sat down. "That would be a help, Herr Menschel, but I do know some German. *Ein wenig.*"

Menschel laughed a touch too loud. *"Ach, gut!* English it is."

He sat down in his desk chair, opened a ledger in front of him, shuffled some printouts, and seemed to peruse it all for a moment down his nose and through those reading glasses.

"Yes, you are Tom Patel's, er, partner?" It came out as a twisted question, not a statement, dripping with some indecipherable innuendo. Soleil shrugged inside. A bit of a stuffed shirt.

"Yes."

"And how can I help you?" He closed the ledger and sat back in his chair.

Soleil gathered herself for a moment.

"First, Herr Menschel, there is some disturbing news of which you must be made aware. I am afraid that Tom Patel is dead."

Soleil's eyes watched Menschel's carefully. His reaction, a fraction of a second of defocusing and then the slight widening of the eyes, appeared to her as if he was truly taken by surprise. She couldn't be sure, but she would have to go with her gut—Menschel was hearing this for the first time.

"Gott im Himmel! Such a young man! What has happened?" This really was news to Menschel, she concluded.

"He fell from his office window in Geneva. The police are baffled—accident, suicide..." her voice trailed off.

Menschel was quiet for a moment. It seemed to Soleil as if he were doing calculations in his head. Then, "My deepest regrets, Frau Tangiere. I am so sorry."

"Thank you. I will be moving our company here to Zurich soon, and am looking for the proper banking relationship. Since we are currently doing business with the ZSB, you of course are my first stop."

Back to business: Menschel felt confident. This stunning woman, how old? Twenty-five? So impressive. "Ah, *zehr gut!* Of course. We value your business highly and will be happy to help you with your move. With financing, locating an office, an apartment if you don't already have one..." Menschel paused for a second. "I can help with many things, Frau Tangiere," with a look.

Without skipping a beat, Soleil said, "Hopefully with many *financial* matters, Herr Menschel. What is a good bank for if not for its expertise and focus on the business of money?"

Putting his mind back in its proper place, Menschel continued. The discourse was too short for him to be crestfallen. Besides, I will be here for a long time. Hopefully she will, too. "Where should we begin?"

"Our accounts. I need to verify balances."

"I have them right here." He pushed the little glasses a millimeter up his nose as he perused the ledger. "It seems as if you have just the two accounts, the trading account and the reserve account." He glanced up. Soleil was impassive. He continued.

"Hmm. The trading account shows a positive balance of 1,198 francs. Since there appears to have been little activity in the account in the last month, unless there are checks outstanding, that is accurate. And as you may or may not know, this is well below our minimum balance requirements. Shall we close the account, or do you wish to replenish it?"

"I will be replenishing it," she said, not knowing exactly where the money would come from. "What about the reserve account?" Soleil looked at Menschel, who was anticipating the question.

"It is slightly embarrassing, but in order for even you to access information about this account, I need to ask for verification."

Soleil felt a chill. She pulled out the checkbook that she had found in Tom's desk drawer and flipped it open. "This account," she said, sliding it across the desk in front of Menschel.

He looked at it archly and said, "Of course." He sniffed. "The verbal password, please."

He stared blandly at Soleil. She stared back and then remembered the little photo stuck to the checkbook.

"Tango."

Menschel checked his ledger, lifted his chin a fraction of millimeter in satisfaction, and announced: "The balance in your reserve account at the present time is 15,475,925 francs."

Oh.

Menschel looked at her and tilted his head a fraction. "Frau Tangiere?"

At the exchange rate, that would be around ten million dollars, she quickly figured in her head.

What on earth was Tom up to?

He slid a computer printout across the desk. No checks written yet. A dozen or so large deposits were listed, different amounts. Soleil had an intuition that now was not the time to ask who the originators of the checks were. She would find that out later, in private. I'm not completely sure about this man or whether he had any involvement with Tom outside of banking.

"When was the last deposit made?"

Menschel looked at her and then down at his ledger. "Around two months ago. From an account in the UK," he offered. After a pause, "Would you like an origination history of the deposits?"

"If you would be so kind."

Menschel spoke briefly into his desk phone.

"It will be brought to you in a moment."

Soleil sat quite still and tried to organize her thoughts. A minute later a secretary came in and handed Soleil the paperwork.

Finally: "Thank you for your courtesy, Herr Menschel. The sudden loss of Mr. Patel was not expected. I was not present in our Geneva offices for a long period of time prior to that unexpected event, so this recap has been very helpful. I'm sure that ultimately I will continue doing business with ZSB."

She stood, and so did Menschel.

"May I schedule another appointment to discuss your many favored options with our bank?"

Soleil looked at him. "All right. Please call me in two weeks." She gave him a number, which he quickly scribbled on a pad. "I suspect we will have more to discuss."

He followed her into the reception room and helped her with her coat.

"Until we meet again," Menschel said clumsily. He took her hand briefly.

"*Auf wiedersehen*, Herr Menschel." A smile, and then she was gone.

Menschel went back in his office feeling light and classy, already planning which suit to wear to the appointment two weeks in the future.

On the street Soleil paused to catch her breath. It was good to be out in the fresh air. Why didn't I ask him? she pondered. Why didn't I ask him about this key? She stood looking at the key that she had taken from her pocket and was now in her palm. Was it a safe deposit box key, most likely from this bank? Or was it something else? Something told her not to show it to this banker. She slipped the key into her pocket and went back into the lobby of the bank to cash a check.

She was, after all, on her last franc.

Small puffs of white smoke came from its landing gear as Flight 723's wheels touched down at Geneva Airport in the clear twilight. Fiona Dyche sat calmly in her business-class seat and breathed a sigh of relief when the boor planted in the seat next to her stood up and prepared to leave the plane. Fiona hated men like him who clumsily tried to hijack her privacy by chatting her up. This one was particularly annoying—unresponsive to her lack of interest and finally even to her direct rebuke. American, she quickly deduced from the repellant accent and loud prattle. And the cherry on top: "Can I have your number, baby?" Awful.

She retrieved her suitcase from the baggage carousel, hailed a cab, and instructed the driver to take her straight to the Beau Rivage on Quai du Mont Blanc. John had the company reserve a suite with a view of Lake Geneva on the fourth floor for her. The room was large and opulent and must be costing CM a pretty penny. But who cares? she thought.

She looked over the room-service menu and called down for a large salad and a Riesling. By the time the busman brought it up, she was already in a hotel robe, having showered off the grime of the flight. She settled on the couch, her food and wine on the coffee table, slit open a large white envelope with a butter knife, and extracted a manila file. Written on the file: Patel + Co.

She turned over the file, and two photos slipped onto the coffee table.

Fiona concentrated. She read the short history in front of her.

Born in a semirural area of Quebec, her father was killed in a platinum mine explosion when she was nineteen. Her mother died a day or two later.

There was precious little information on her life before that incident: two brothers, three sisters. High school. Rube and rural. That was about it.

She turned up in New York a short time after her parents' death and lived with a Jewish couple in the borough of Queens. That's odd.

After a period of time, she took up with Tom Patel and became his houseguest and lover for two years. Lived in a nice building "uptown," which Fiona deduced was something desirable, having never been to New York. She picked up the photo of Tom Patel and looked at him. Handsome dummy, what? But obviously weak.

She read on: their sweet little romance went on for two years. Patel had been secretly working with some of John and his father's associates for the entire time, and when he finally brought his patsy girlfriend to Switzerland, she somehow subverted the good thing that he had going with CM, and somehow he wound up dead.

Along with John's father and three other men.

Cute.

Maybe this little tart had gotten extremely lucky. No—that's flawed and dangerous thinking. More often than not, luck has nothing to do with murder.

She turned over the other picture. It was a clear shot of a young girl, her straight blond hair blowing around a perfect face, a snowcapped mountain range behind. She was obviously slim and very healthy, and face it, a natural beauty. Fiona scowled.

No, beautiful she may be, but more importantly, she's competent and smart—I have to think that way to complete my little task.

"And to survive," a small voice said in the back of her mind.

Exciting.

Ten minutes later she was dressed and headed for a toney bar on the next block. Something had to be done to calm her down. She'd have a few drinks, and then surely she would meet that something at the bar. Boy, girl—doesn't matter.

The next afternoon she knocked lightly on the Patel + Co office door and came in before she heard a reply. Yvonne was behind her desk when Fiona came through the door, turned, and quickly closed it behind her. The French woman was immediately on alert.

"*Bonjour*. How can I help you?" with a barely concealed edge of suspicion.

Fiona's mahogany eyes looked down her nose at Yvonne. She had come dressed in a painfully tight black skirt and matching black silk blouse. A scarlet Hermes scarf was looped carelessly around her neck. Viciously steep heels. Hard scent of sandalwood. Very red lips.

In English she said, "Is Soleil Tangiere here?"

Yvonne knew this was so very wrong. I should run past her and out of the building. But Fiona stood with her back against the closed door.

Yvonne answered in English: "She is not here, Ms...."

"Demarary. Violet Demarary," she repeated. "I am a friend of hers. Are you expecting her later on today?"

"*Non*. She will not be retur—" Yvonne didn't finish the sentence. Her whole body was convulsing violently. She had no control of her muscles, and she jerked out of her office chair onto the floor. Two thin wires stretched from her chest to what looked like a thick black wand in Fiona's outstretched hand. Fiona grinned.

Suddenly Yvonne's body sagged. The power surge was shut off.

"Surprise, luv!" Fiona was grimly satisfied. "Truth, please!" Another bolt shot through Yvonne for a second or two and then was shut off again. Yvonne's eyes were almost shut. She tried to pull herself up but fell back to the floor. Fiona towered above.

"An adaptation of the classic cattle prod. Like it?" Fiona rolled the ugly wand in her hand. "My fiancé came up with the idea in his spare time.

"Now. Where is Soleil Tangiere?" Fiona held the make-shift Taser before Yvonne's face.

"I don't know."

Zzzap!

"Zu-Zurich." Yvonne wasn't fooled. This *putain* was obviously a follow-up to the English devils. I'm in trouble. Bad trouble.

"And where in Zurich?" The hated cattle prod floating before her.

"I, I don't know. She said she would call me with her address."

Fiona grinned. "Why? Why there?"

"I don't—" Another horrible zap. The three seconds felt like an hour.

"Hurry, bitch. Why is she in Zurich? Who else is there?"

"I swear I don't know. Why do you think I would protect her?" Yvonne was about to throw up. Fiona looked at her carefully.

"Oh, you can't protect her." Fiona wheeled an office chair in front of Yvonne, switched on the cattle prod, sat down, and draped a leg over one arm of the chair, lit a cigarette, and got all the information she needed.

On the way out of the building, Fiona paused and peered up at the seventh-floor windows.

She shook her head thoughtfully.

Later that day the emergency room staff saved Yvonne's life, but it was doubtful that she would ever speak again.

"I'll take it," said Soleil.

The apartment was small, but light came through the large windows. The décor was modern even though the building was fifty years old. Here she would be close to the center of the city and the action. The Zurich real estate agent was pleased that the apartment search was quick and ecstatic that Soleil had given him a check for six months rent up front. She was obviously not a native: most Swiss would pay each payment precisely on the first of the month, but never before that.

"Office space," she told him on the way out. "I am looking for a small office near here. Nothing fancy. When can we meet?" Tomorrow would be fine. He smiled in anticipation of another few hours with her and with her checkbook.

That afternoon she rented a suite of furniture, which would be delivered in two days. She didn't want to commit to her own furniture at this time: this apartment was a temporary home. She gave herself six months.

Clothes. She shopped for a few hours at some of the pricier stores and felt not at all guilty about doing so. She paid cash and had the stores hold the outfits, which fit her off the racks, until she was in the apartment. Then she would pick them up.

The next day, after renting a furnished office not far from the ZSB, she returned to her empty apartment to find the phone service had already been there. A plain black phone sat on a packing box under a window.

I need to get Yvonne here. She called her a few times over the next several hours, but she kept getting no answer. I'll try tonight or tomorrow, she thought, but a small voice inside her said that something seemed not quite right.

Old Emil Fritzhof adjusted the magnifying lens on his glasses. He studied the key in his hand. On the other side of the counter, the young woman watched him.

"*Ja,*" he said in German, "this is certainly a type of safe deposit key, but a very rare one, Miss. I don't think I've ever seen anything precisely like it." He turned it this way and that under the light.

Soleil had passed his locksmith shop on the way home from her new office and now had returned with Tom's key. She had to know more about it.

Emil peered at it closely, mumbling in German to himself. Finally: "Russia. The box this opens is in Russia, or was in Russia, but it definitely is a key to a Russian safe deposit box. Here, look at the way the denticles..." he was off on a technical tour of the key, which Soleil listened to carefully, but it was very arcane and her mind was already steps ahead.

When Soleil had entered his little shop, he had been quick to regale her with his life story of opening locks all over Europe. Light bounced off his bald head—he was shorter than Soleil and looked to be eighty years old. At least I won't get hit on in here, she thought. Thank God. The button-down Swiss didn't fool her anymore—they could be as randy as tipsy Italians when given half the chance.

"Can you make me a copy?"

Emil harrumphed and cleared his throat. "I would love to oblige you, young lady, but look here." He put the key up to Soleil's face. "These small letters in Russian. They say that the key is state property. And what is even stranger: I used a high-powered jeweler's loupe and found what look like two long lines on the edge of the key and a long list of symbols and numbers. I can't read them, and I don't want to.

"Also, the blank used is of a convoluted style that I have never seen. Short of fabricating a new mold and a new die, this key cannot and should not be copied."

Soleil was disappointed but said, "Thank you, Herr Fritzhof. How much do I owe you for your analysis?"

"Oh, no, young lady. It was my pleasure."

"Well, then, thank you. *Guten tag.*"

As Soleil was pushing the door open, she heard his voice behind her: "If you would like me to show you around Zurich, I am free tonight. And single."

Soleil smiled and left the shop.

The following day she tried several times to get ahold of Yvonne, but her efforts remained in vain, and the day after that, Friday, Soleil found herself in her office, as a workman in overalls was adding the finishing touches to the sign on her frosted glass door:

Tangiere International

When he had gone, she walked up the hall, turned around, and approached the door. She liked the look and the idea. If you had been different, Tom, maybe this could have worked out. But you were who you were, and that was a very bad thing.

Inside the office a second workman was installing the phones.

She felt uneasy, and that night she decided to have a solitary dinner at an expensive bar-restaurant near her office. Inevitably, a man at the bar made a move. He was handsome, around thirty, she figured. After he made a few somewhat silly pantomimes of drinking and eating, she said to herself, oh what the heck, and waved to him to come on over.

"May I join you?" A white-toothed smile in a mild face. First in German, but he switched easily to English. He and his drink sat down opposite her at the small table.

His name was Rupert, he worked for a bank (no surprise there), and after a few minutes, Soleil felt he was a safe bet. He was not that assertive and seemed a little out of his comfort zone making this move, and she liked that.

She acquiesced, as she felt a strong need for the company of someone who was not in her loop, out of the circle of events that now dominated her life. And she felt another need—strong and surprisingly demanding. After a minute or two of careful consideration, she decided she would probably give in to it. And after an hour or so of the cleverest chatter Rupert could drag out of his limited repertoire, and after some quiet and polite attention to him by her, she allowed him to pick up the check. And pick her up, too.

Rupert lived a few blocks from the bar. They walked and chatted, and neither of them noticed the dark Mercedes, which passed them several times.

They stepped out of the elevator and walked side by side up the corridor to his door. He unlocked it, and she stepped in. "Sorry about the mess," he said.

It wasn't messy at all. He flipped the light switch at the door, and the apartment was bathed in indirect lighting. Another switch, and there was soft music. Kind of cliché, Soleil thought, but so what.

She walked across the room, slid open a glass door, and stepped out onto the patio. Below, the city of Zurich was a crazy quilt of lights. She snugged her light coat around her. In a moment his arms were around her waist—he stood close behind her. Then her voice softly: "It's nice here."

Rupert wondered if he was dreaming. She let him turn her around to face him. Though he was a bit taller than she, the kiss wasn't awkward. From back inside the living room came the juicy contralto of Sarah Vaughan.

She ended the kiss in a few seconds, pulled away a foot or so from him, gave him a look that said, "I'll consider it," and stepped back into the apartment from the patio.

She slipped out of her coat, reminded herself that her hunting knife reposed in one of its pockets, draped the garment neatly over the back of a chair, and sat on one of the low couches. He stood across from her. He lifted his left hand and mimed the question "Drink?" by extending his thumb and pinky and wagging the hand once or twice, while tilting his head and arching his eyebrows.

She thought for a moment, and then she said, "A Kir Royale, *s'il vous plait*." Let him work for it. What's got into me? Am I trying to soothe the anger I have for Tom? Is it just hormones? Is this too much introspection?

He smiled and without missing a beat went to the kitchen, as if a Kir Royale were a drink he mixed every day. He ripped open a drawer, grabbed his mixology book, and quickly looked up the drink. Clever choice it was, he thought: "Kir Royale is an aperitif always served before a meal, yet requiring champagne in place of the usual white wine." Celebrating something? Hmm.

Not only that, but that choice assumes I have champagne on ice, which I do, which might indicate to her at the very least that I am an urbane and suave individual used to the finer things. Oh hell, I think I'm losing my mind—I've never, she's so beautiful...

He made one for himself as well, substituting raspberry liquor for the required blackcurrant. He brought the drinks into the living room.

They sat opposite each other and air-toasted across a low coffee table. She took a small sip, rolled her eyes slightly, smiled, and waited. He: "I was out of blackcurrant—finished it off at breakfast." She: "No problem."

After a moment he put his glass on the table, got up, and began pacing the room. She sat with her drink in her hand and calmly watched him pace. She smiled inside. Pace, pace. Back, forth. Then, "Soleil..." she looked at him quietly as his voice ran out.

Finally he stopped near her. He reached down for her glass, which she relinquished without a struggle. He placed it on the table.

He bent and gently took both her shoulders in his hands. She stood slowly, not taking her eyes off him.

His face was inches from hers. Their eyes locked. Hers narrowed slightly. His were clear, and for all the suavity, quite uncertain. Then both pairs of eyes closed.

The kiss was deep and long and satisfying. She smiled inside. All right, tonight. This night is for me. Just this one time...

The sun streamed in, and with it a bright chill of reality and the nagging feeling that boy, I probably just made a mistake.

Soleil's thoughts weren't harsh, they just were this: the night was very nice. That was it. Her body and her libido needed it badly, but it was over.

She knew that the hour of disentanglement was at hand: the night had been just a physical and psychic necessity. But this nice man was not necessarily a good man, not a man for her, and men get stupid very fast after a nice night.

Fortunately he gave her an out: after the obligatory "tell me about your life" jabber that came afterward, he had the lack of tact to try to learn more about her only long relationship—not something that she was proud of—and then tried to own it.

"What a fool," he said, coming out of the bathroom with a towel tied around his waist.

"Me?"

"Your ex. The commodity guy."

She stared at the ceiling. Inside she sighed with the inevitability: the best of men will blow it when they start talking. Especially afterward.

"Why did it end? He must have been an idiot."

"Not a good fit. He fell for the wrong woman."

"He must have been devastated when it ended."

She looked over at him. "It just killed him. Can we change the subject?"

"You obviously dumped him, not the other way around."

The sheet was pulled up to her chin. She wanted to get dressed.

"I won't make his mistakes, you know," he said. There it was—the key phrase, implying a future might exist for the two of them.

Soleil sat up on the edge of the bed, wrapped the sheet around her, and on the way to bathroom grabbed her clothes off a chair. She said, "I didn't realize how late it is." The bathroom door closed before he could say anything.

When she came out, she was dressed, and she found him wearing a pout. Modern Man. This familiar irritating little scene irked her. What I have do for a little sex, she thought. She knew what had to be done. She knew who she was. She liked him, but he wasn't for her. Take care of it now, don't drag it along, she told herself. Nice doesn't work well in this situation.

When he started in with the "is everything OK" chatter, she caught him up.

"Last night was terrific and you're very sweet, but I told you from the beginning, I'm not seriously dating anyone. Sorry, Rupert, that includes you."

He pouted some more. She didn't feel at all guilty, but she was wary. Even the nicest man could have an ugly side, as I've found out in spades.

A moment or two, and then the face-saving: "Well, the same goes for me, Soleil. Let's face it, we were just horny (Soleil hated that word), and we found each other (she wasn't much for clichés, either, but just waited it out). Fine. OK. Well, I'll see you around, I guess. At least let me walk you out."

She didn't bother giving him an "It'll be OK" look or telling him she would call because she knew she wouldn't, and she had never given him her number. Just a kiss on the cheek, and he walked her to the elevator. On the way down she thought, that was a dumb move. The problem is mine, I guess. If I have no real passion with someone, then why prolong the inevitable? Casual sex. Is it worth it? I feel a little cheap, but that's my doing. One day things will settle down, and I'll start to sort myself out in this department.

Or until I get that feeling again...

It was a mile or so walk to her new apartment. No problem. But this time she *did* notice the gray Mercedes that kept appearing every few blocks. When the driver realized that Soleil might have seen her, she finally drove off. Soleil stood on the sidewalk as the car turned a corner and disappeared. For a brief second she had had a perfect of view of a woman's face framed with straight black hair and dark, blazing, mahogany eyes.

Rupert couldn't believe his luck.

Two days ago he had experienced a night of ecstasy with the wonderful but fickle and therefore unstable Canadian girl, and now he was obviously on a streak. Same bar, same restaurant, only tonight a stunning woman, blue-black hair cut rakishly to one side and with large, mahogany-colored eyes had approached him at the bar.

The difference was that this time *she* was the aggressor. After belting back a few straight-up vodkas and daring him to match her drink for drink, she almost dragged him out of the restaurant.

At his apartment, there was no time for seductive background music, lingering glances, or tentative touches. Afraid he might be unresponsive or even comatose from too much alcohol, Fiona ripped off his clothes, pushed him onto the bed, ground a couple of methamphetamines in her teeth, and attacked him.

Rupert was stunned, borderline drunk, and he could hardly keep up. On his back, with Fiona bouncing up and down above him and moaning and growling with what appeared to be either unfettered lust or incipient insanity, Rupert felt as if he were being mauled. When she started screaming and slapping his face, the term "man rape" came to mind.

After it was over, they lay on the bed, and Rupert stared at the ceiling.

"Was she your girlfriend?" Fiona asked suddenly, anger swirling beneath the surface of her words.

"What, who, what?" Rupert was barely conscious, this encounter having caused a raft of emotions in his banker's mind—a raft featuring excitement, confusion, release, and a clawing component of dawning terror.

"Oh, spare me the blarney, Rupert. I was in that restaurant two nights ago and saw you leave with that tramp." A pause, then: "Is she your wife?" Fiona's eyes shot daggers.

Shocking. Scary. "No! No, of course not. I had never seen her before. It was a one-night stand, as they say."

Raw skepticism caused her to snort, and her large eyes narrowed to black slits. "Her name was...?"

"Soleil. I'm not sure she ever told me her last name."

"Where does she live?"

Rupert gained a modest dollop of composure. "Why are we talking about her? What about us?" He tried a half-hearted seductive leer, but it had no effect. She barreled ahead.

"She's wanted for murder, Rupert. Perhaps you know something about that." She eyed him. "Perhaps you know a great deal, even helped, with that crime."

The blood ran out of Rupert's face, and his stomach churned. He sat bolt upright in the bed. Fear took center stage. Who, what, was this woman?

Fiona lay next to him, her head propped up on one arm. The sheet had slipped down, exposing her breasts. "That's it, luv, isn't it? Mayhaps you were the wheelman for the job, or one of the trigger pullers himself?" Her leer was feral. Rupert started to shake.

"Now, Rupert, luv. Tell me everything that you possibly remember about Soleil. I have all night. Who knows, I might even throw you another mercy screw. Got a cigarette?"

Soleil stood at her office window and looked down into the Bahnhofstrasse. Morning traffic seemed thick, but she had no yardstick for this observation—maybe it was heavy like this every morning. Clouds lay over the city.

She turned and sat at her small desk. Before her lay one of the ledger books from Tom's hidden desk compartment. It contained what appeared to be an address book of clients or contacts. Scotch-taped on the inside cover was a business card:

Ballas Trading Advisors
300 S Wacker Drive, Chicago, IL 60606
(312)555–6730
Kurt Ballas, Pres.

Soleil had heard the name before. Tom had mentioned Kurt Ballas—he had once helped Tom stay in the commodity business by lending him money. She dialed another Chicago number that was penciled in on the bottom of the card next to the word "private." As the phone rang on the other end, she realized that Chicago was six hours behind Zurich—it was around 4:00 a.m. in the Windy City.

She was about to hang up when a sleepy voice came on the line: "Yuhhh?"

"Oh, sorry, I forgot it was so early. I'll call later."

"Wait, don't hang up." The voice was thick but awake. "I was getting up anyway to check the markets." A few muffled grunts and then, "Who's this?"

"Is this Mr. Ballas?"

"You got him. And who're you in the middle of the night?"

"I'll call back later. I'm really sorry."

"No, no, I like your voice. Keep me company while I shave. What's your name, where are you, what's on your mind?"

Four thousand, five hundred miles to the east, Soleil rolled her chair to the window and said, "Soleil Tangiere. I'm a friend of Tom Patel."

The sound of running water. Ballas looked into the mirror, and his thirty-eight-year-old face looked back. His tawny hair fell over his brow, and his 6'3" frame felt stiff from a bad sleep. I'm a wreck, he thought. "Tom Patel—long time. How is Tom?" he said into the cordless phone, which he had balanced on his shoulder. Soleil listened very carefully and concluded the question was sincere—he didn't know about Tom's demise.

A moment, then: "I have some bad news, Mr. Ballas—"

"Kurt."

"Kurt. Tom had an accident. He died a few weeks ago."

The water turned off.

"What happened?"

She weighed the possible responses but opted for the truth. "He fell from an office window."

"Jesus." Silence.

"Sorry, it was pretty bad."

"Did you work with him?"

"In a way. In fact, I was his silent partner, and now I'm going to be running his business. And that's why I called you. I need some help, and I'm willing to pay for it."

A minute, and then Kurt said: "I knew Tom at the Merc, the Chicago Mercantile Exchange. He was a good guy, but he fell in with a bad crowd." Soleil suddenly felt a poignant sadness. "I saved his butt one time and he made good, but honestly, if it's a loan you're looking for, the Ballas Bank is closed."

Soleil liked his candor. "No, it's nothing like that. I just took over the reins of the business and I see that there were a lot of contacts, but I have limited experience in the markets, and commodities for that matter. You've got your own trading company. Can I pick your brain? At your convenience, of course."

Kurt let out a puff of air. He already liked this woman—she had nerve and was direct. A "no" would be an easy way out for me, but let's see how this plays out. "What did Tom tell you about me?"

"Not much, and not recently. Only that you were a stand-up guy." Soleil was surprised that she used that expression—she avoided trendy expressions if she could. But she was talking to a Chicago guy, so...

"OK, Soleil. Are you in town? In Chicago?"

"No. I'm in Zurich."

"Oh, Lake Zurich, Illinois? That's around an hour away, and—"

Soleil smiled. "No, Zurich, Switzerland."

Kurt stared at his reflection in the mirror. Oh, man.

"All right," he said slowly. "What would you suggest?" Is this chick for real?

Soleil thought for a moment. Then: "Let me come to your office and hang around for one week. I'll be generally out of your way, and I promise not to hijack your time with too many questions. And of course I'll pay you."

"You'll come from Switzerland?"

"Yes."

"And you just want to hang around. And pay me for the privilege? And then go into competition against me?"

"Yep."

Well, this is something that doesn't happen every day. And she probably doesn't know it, but the odds against this woman making a mark in the "boys club" business of commodities are huge. Well, why not?

"When did you want to do this?"

"Not for at least two or three weeks. After that, just let me know me when I can come to Chicago, and I'll be there."

"I must be nuts. OK. What's your number?"

Soleil gave him her phone number, and they said their good-byes. She heard Kurt hang up.

She started to hang up her phone, but thought better of it and put the receiver up to her ear. She heard a faint scratch and then a click.

Then the dial tone.

Camille Tangiere Weston was exhausted from flying as she walked along the Jetway with the other tired passengers. She had only been on a plane once before, and now this: Minneapolis to JFK to Heathrow to Zurich. She felt as if she had been traveling forever. At least Soleil had sprung for a first-class ticket. In that way Camille felt special.

She had traveled with only a carry-on as per her youngest sister's suggestion and was now grateful for that—she didn't feel like waiting another minute, certainly not for some luggage.

She walked out of the terminal and to the left as Soleil had instructed.

Near the taxi queue stood Soleil.

They hadn't laid eyes on each other for four years. Camille was eleven years Soleil's senior, and they shared the same birthday, August 20. She was darker than Soleil, having inherited their father's Gallic looks, and striking in her own right: thick auburn hair, olive skin, piercing dark hazel eyes. Together the two sisters covered all the bases of beautiful.

They hugged for almost a minute, the taxi drivers in the queue being afforded a chance to let their imaginations run wild. "Let's splurge for a cab, Cami," Soleil said. "I came here on the train, but I'll give you a quick tour by car. It will give us a chance to talk."

She gave the cab driver instructions in rapid German, and they headed toward the city. "I'm impressed. Where did the German come from?" asked Camille.

Soleil told her how she had started picking it up in New York and then easily built on it once she got to Zurich. "This town is mostly German speaking, but you can get by in four or five different languages. How's your French, Cami?"

"*Bon, salope!*"

They both laughed. And after a minute or two, there, in the back of the cab, Soleil did something that she hadn't done since her brother Kent died—she cried.

At the apartment Soleil set up the couch with some bedding while Camille looked for a place to unpack her small carry-on. "I followed your instructions and came poor," she said as she dumped the contents of the bag on the kitchen table.

"Good. Tomorrow you shop. Use this." Soleil took a wad of money out of a dresser drawer. Camille's eyes went wide.

"What bank did you rob? How much is this?"

"Three thousand Swiss francs and two thousand US dollars. Don't feel guilty or anything; it comes out of my business account." She thought about Tom for a bitter second or two.

"And do me a favor: wait at least a half an hour before you start wrecking my apartment." Camille's casual attitude toward the orderliness of her immediate environment was as legendary in the family as Soleil's neatness. Soleil eyed the mess on the kitchen table and frowned.

Camille rooted through her things and then tossed a manila envelope through the air at Soleil.

"Is this it?" asked Soleil after holding it for a moment. Camille nodded.

Soleil slit it open and studied the single page with its Federal Bureau of Investigation heading.

Camille sat in a chair as Soleil read.

After looking at the floor for a full minute, Soleil said, "I don't know how to thank you."

"Don't thank me, Soleil, thank my ex."

"Jake?" Soleil was incredulous.

"Yep. Here's what happened: Old Smiley himself got into another mess and started on a fourteen-month gig in federal lockup in Milwaukee. Don't ask why or how it started. As his ex-wife, I was able to access his rap sheet with the locals and the FBI. Then I wound up sort of dating this FBI agent—Raymond—who got me all the information the bureau had on you. It's in your hand."

"'Sort of?'" Soleil eyed her.

The document contained more than she could hope for. Soleil discovered that there was nothing on her with either the FBI or local law enforcement in Montana or any other state. She had a clean sheet.

"Raymond asked around, and as far as he can tell, no other agency is looking at you. And of course you never can be completely certain. But this doesn't cover Canada."

It was enough for Soleil. She could travel to the United States without looking over her shoulder. Finally: confirmation after four years. Her relief was palpable.

"Let's get dinner. It's on me!"

"Well, it sure as hell ain't on me, Miss Moneybags." Camille chuckled as she grabbed her coat.

"It's Ms. Dyche, Mr. Clooney."

John Clooney held down the speaker button on his office phone and said into the instrument, "No calls until I tell you." He checked the black bug detection device attached to the phone. When he was satisfied that the call was protected, at least on his end, he picked up the receiver.

He deepened his voice by habit. "Hello, luv."

"Hi, Johnny. Reporting in." Fiona's voice had an ironic lilting quality.

Clooney stared out the window at the familiar shape of Big Ben in the fog. "How's the land of Swiss cheese?"

"You mean the land of Swiss *watches*. I found a beautiful Vacheron Constantin in Zurich today. It's platinum with diamonds, Johnny..."

He was exasperated. Fiona was a girl of high maintenance and higher prices. But she *did* have a bloody ruthlessness that transcended money—a rare trait, especially in a young woman, and it was the feature of her personality that Clooney found himself most coveting as of late.

Ignoring her implied request, Clooney went on: "The latest on the Tangiere girl?"

"Well, I will say she's striking, John. I'm glad we're on the other side of the equation—wouldn't want your mind, or your nob, wandering." Fiona giggled inside—it would be far more likely that Fiona herself would think of making a pass at Soleil if it came to that—John was all sizzle, no steak.

Getting back to business, Fiona outlined the lay of the land in Zurich, which included Soleil's new apartment and her new office. She left out her methods of obtaining this information, and Clooney was smart enough not to ask. After all, he still held a vaunted post in a high-profile platinum company. This whole thing was very risky, he thought. If it hadn't become personal now, I'd have likely dropped this whole Soleil Tangiere business, he thought. But it *was* very personal.

Fiona told Clooney about the existence of the accounts at ZSB, Soleil's intention to carry on with Tangiere International, and the phone-tapped fact that she would be seeking the help of a Chicago trading firm to establish herself. Clooney had never heard of this Kurt Ballas and dismissed the idea of Soleil going into a competing business as rubbish—she wouldn't last six months.

And the existence of Tom Patel's slush fund was no news to Clooney. Carrington Metals' money was languishing in that fund right now, he thought. And payoffs from even shadier operations such as those run by such ruthless luminaries as Josh Fowler or the Poong brothers were certain to be keeping that money company. And now Fiona had confirmed that the slush fund was there and under the Tangiere woman's control. Good girl, Fiona.

But Fiona had one more piece of information. Before her mind had shut down, Yvonne had told Fiona about the key that had lain next to the checkbook in Tom Patel's hidden desktop compartment and now was in Soleil's possession.

"Johnny, there's one more thing. There's a key."

Clooney's next breath caught. What?

A key? *The* key?

After a long silence, "Johnny, are you still there?"

"Fiona." His voice was very low.

Suddenly she was on high alert. "Yes. There was a strangely shaped key that the Tangiere girl took along with the checkbook." Silence on the other end of the line. "What's this about, John?"

"You're positive? You're sure there's a key?"

"Yes." She had listened very carefully to Yvonne's desperate words.

"Fiona," he said carefully, "can you see if you can get that key?"

"What does it unlock?"

"The Tangiere woman probably knows. Make her tell you, Fiona. Make her."

Fiona could taste the avarice dripping from each of Clooney's words. She liked it. *At the very least, Johnny boy will pay me for that key one way or the other. Whether we find the lock or not.*

"OK, I'll get the key. Is that all, Johnny? Is there anything else?" She already knew the answer.

"This can't lead back to me, to us. So far, everything that's happened in Geneva was risky, and the Geneva police are taking it seriously. Take your time. Go skiing or something. Then do what you do best. This has to be sanitary work, Fiona. Clean.

"And if you can get me that key...if you could get me that key...I would be very grateful." He could hardly control the intensity in his voice.

"The world, Fiona, my world, would be yours."

"Mademoiselle Tangiere?" the familiar voice came through the receiver.

"Ah, M. Deshautels, how have you been?" Soleil kept her tone even and courteous. For all she knew, Henri Deshautels had left his wife. Or even worse: he *hadn't* left her and was even more discomfited.

"I'm very well, thank you, but I need to speak with you about something." The tone of his voice raised the light hairs on the back of Soleil's neck.

"It concerns a Miss Yvonne Goulet." At Yvonne's name, Soleil's heart skipped a beat. She had been trying to contact Yvonne for weeks.

"She has been incarcerated at a rehabilitation center in Chenes-Bougeries."

"What happened?"

After a brief moment, Deshautels said, "Ms. Tangiere, to believe that what happened is *not* an effect of your presence would be naïve. It seems that wherever you go, trouble follows closely." A brief silence, then: "Ms. Goulet was admitted to hospital with a severe neurological problem accompanied by burn marks on parts of her body. Unfortunately, her mind has undergone a serious trauma. She no longer can communicate in any effective way."

Soleil didn't know where to begin thinking about this.

He continued, "Do you have any knowledge about exactly what happened or who is responsible?"

"*Non*, monsieur, not at all." Deshautels was listening carefully and could detect no artifice or evasion in her voice. At least over the phone. "When we parted, Yvonne said she would come to Zurich to help me out with trying to get my company off the ground. When I hadn't heard from her, I tried contacting her many times by phone. In fact, I was thinking of calling you about it if any more time went by."

Silence for a good fifteen seconds. "What do I need to know, Soleil, I mean Mademoiselle Tangiere? What is the missing piece to this grand puzzle? You do not strike me as a criminal or deceiver, yet we are speaking once again about a violent, heinous incident. Can you help me? What is left to know?" Deshautels sounded as tired and whipped as any policeman who has come to a dead end on a high-profile case about which his superiors are demanding a solution. Or at least a scapegoat. With dead bodies littering the International City of Peace, all of whom met their de-mise in the vicinity of this Tangiere girl, Deshautels was up against it.

But not as much as Soleil was. A point will come, she reasoned, at which they might just haul her in and throw away the key until she either confesses to something or dies of old age. And this Deshautels, well, he's been more than patient with me, for whatever obvious or ulterior reasons. I can't expect that to go on forever.

She forced her voice into a lower register. "Henri, I do not know," she said in velvety, perfect French. "I am at your service. I will come to Geneva anytime you wish. You have inadvertently served me a new dish of guilt topped with the possibility that my acquaintance with Yvonne has left her injured or worse. Now I need to know how it happened. I will do anything to help you, but you must promise to help me find who did this as well."

Deshautels's pulse annoyingly quickened at her re-sponse. She had the tact and silken bravado of a woman twice her age and experience. For the umpteenth time, he felt that he wanted to be near her. "You want to know who did this. Do you seek revenge?"

"I seek the peace that only justice can provide, Henri."

"I will be in touch, Soleil. *Au revoir.*"

"*Au revoir*, Henri."

Soleil gazed out the window of her small apartment. Who did this to Yvonne? The top of the list screamed Smythe's people or even his son. Yet it could be someone else, an enemy of Tom Patel who was owed money. Yvonne knew a lot of things about Tom's business dealings and associates. Soleil had anticipated leveraging that knowledge when Yvonne came to Zurich.

But she never made it, and deep down Soleil knew one thing: what was done to Yvonne was a message to her. *I have to end this, end all of it. And soon.*

She picked up the phone on her office desk.

"Tangiere International." *I'm owner, secretary, telephone receptionist, and window washer here,* Soleil thought as she answered the phone. *You have to start somewhere, I guess.*

A man's voice with a slight accent. "Is Mr. Patel available?" Soleil had had the phone number transferred over from Geneva, and a few calls had dribbled in, mostly sales solicitations.

"I am sorry, Mr. Patel is no longer associated with this company. May I help you?"

"Oh. Well, probably not." After a pause he said, "Or perhaps maybe. This is Edward Sierra from Rio Plata. I need to speak to someone about buying Col Tan in quantity."

"Pardon?" Soleil's heart sank. She was way out of her depth.

"Columbite-Tantalite. We have open orders across Europe and are touching base with your firm, among others." He sounded a bit pompous and impatient. "A Mr. Stepanov recommended you."

Soleil thought fast. "Certainly. Let me put you in touch with the right party." She hit the hold button and dialed Kurt Ballas's private number in Chicago.

"Yes?" came a drawl.

"Kurt, quick, it's Soleil Tangiere. I have someone from a place called Rio Plata on the other line. They need to buy something called Col Tan, and I haven't the faintest notion about what it is. Can I transfer them to you?"

Kurt Ballas was impressed. Normally he would have opted out on this random call, but Rio Plata Mining was a huge commodities company with offices around the world. How did this girl...? Pretty slick.

"OK, can you transfer him over?"

"Yes. His name is Edward. Good luck."

Her phone rang an hour later.

"Thanks, Soleil. I owe you."

She smiled. Good. Kurt got this order, and I gained face—a perfect situation.

"Oh, that's OK Kurt. No charge."

"On the contrary, Soleil, there's a very big charge. Rio Plata Mining is a major player, and they don't do business unless it's big business. I found what they wanted, and we made a deal. And I set it up with us being a kind of introducing firm with the deal coming through your company, Tangiere International. Your commission comes to—"

"No, Kurt, I don't want to make anything on this."

"Sorry, Soleil, this is a business where commissions are factored into every level of every deal. Your cut comes to one hundred seventy-five thousand dollars—same as mine, if that's OK with you. My office will handle it all. Send me your banking info, and Rio will wire you the money when it accepts delivery."

She looked straight ahead. What? This is the commodities business? A few phone calls and you're that much
richer?

Oh.

OK.

She broke her own silence. "How nice. Thank you, kind
sir." Kurt could hear the smile in her voice.

"Soleil?"

"Yes?"

"When did you say you're coming to Chicago?"

"Soon. Why?"

"I was thinking. The ball is a week from Saturday in
New York. Why don't you meet me there?"

"The ball?"

They sat across from each other at the Brasserie Schiller
on the Goethestrasse and worked on their delicious onion
soups. It was a little late for the lunch crowd, but the staff
was happy to have them—were these obviously American
women famous in any way? They looked as if they could be.

"I don't get it," said Camille in her direct way. "Tom
wanted you to come to Switzerland and help you with his
company, which he kept secret? Why didn't he just tell you
what was going on? You were going to marry him anyway."

"We were engaged, and just barely. I had started to think
about marriage earlier on but kind of put it on hold in my
mind." A pause. "He was a really great guy at first. He wasn't
loud or gross or a braggart, and he treated me well. Since he
had money, though, he thought that it would cover all sins.
I don't think he ever figured out that money wasn't my god

or my yardstick." After a moment: "Thinking back, I never really loved him."

Camille put down her spoon. "Face it: on the surface, you did better than I did in some regards. But even though Jake and I had our moments, he never betrayed me like this."

"He smacked you around, Cami. Come on."

"Well, truth be known, I smacked him a little as well. Remember it was me who taught you how to neutralize a man in heat." They both laughed. Then Camille got serious. "In spite of everything, even though we're divorced, there's something about him that I'll always like. You know, the bad-boy syndrome. I'll guess we'll always be connected. He had a violent side, but I know he'd never Bullwinkle me."

"He'd never what?"

"Bullwinkle. You know, knock off, kill. It's kind of a mobster expression that popped up in the Midwest. You remember that murder of the cop in Montana." It was a statement more than a question. "Well, for some reason a little folklore grew up around that incident, and the term 'he was Bullwinkled' became a synonym for 'murdered.' Don't ask me why." She looked at Soleil.

"I won't. As I was saying, Tom used me, and badly, and nearly got us both killed."

"Not to mention wrecking a perfectly good BMW." Camille's loyalty was the kind that took no prisoners.

"All right. Enough of that."

"Why didn't you just come home, come back to the US or Canada? Why are you staying here? On top of that, why on earth did you take over that business? Are you a glutton for punishment?"

Their salads arrived, and they waited for the flurry of beaming busboys and waiters to abate.

"I don't like being pushed around. Dad spent his life being pushed around by bosses who couldn't shine his shoes. He wouldn't want me to run away anytime there was trouble or it got uncomfortable. Tom Patel used me badly—worse than anyone. He lied and lied, and I'm not dead just because I'm quick and I'm lucky. Oh no," she said, as if Tom were sitting at the table with them, "you wanted me in the business, Tom. Well, don't wish too hard. See, you just might get what you want."

Camille smiled inside. Though they were never that close, Camille was always a tad envious of the way that Soleil was always the wild card, always the unknown quantity. Always Soleil.

"I can't go anywhere because the heat's still on about Tom's death and the Wild West scene that went down at the Geneva airport. And Tom's secretary has been seriously injured by someone involved in this mess. I know I'm still being hunted, certainly by the people who killed Dad and those other miners. So I'm going to use the money and the contacts that Tom left in the business to help me settle the scores." She smiled in a secret way and brought a forkful of arugula to her mouth.

"I nearly forgot how scary you could be."

Soleil bared her teeth in a mock snarl. "Yeah, scary."

They chatted on through the rest of the meal about family. Soleil had been out of touch with everyone except Camille. She found out that her sister Nanette and her husband had settled into a new life in Texas. Soleil vowed to get in touch with them soon. Her brother Rolf was living with an exotic dancer in Crotch Lake, Ontario. Previously divorced, he had been unemployed for the better part of a year after coming out of a three-month lockup in Quebec for check fraud. Soleil had just about lost hope that he would one day make something of himself in honor of his deceased brother, Kent. She sighed.

"What's happening with Lana?" she asked Camille about her other sister.

Camille fidgeted for a moment and then said, "No one knows. She's divorced again, I think, and as far as I can tell, she's wanted on both sides of the border for a boatload of petty scams. You know Lana."

Soleil did. "It's embarrassing to be a Tangiere sometimes," Soleil said quietly.

Camille looked at her little sister. You have nothing to be embarrassed about, Soleil. Everyone makes their own light in the world and they're the ones who have to take the responsibility. Blood may be thicker than water, but so what—it doesn't give people the right to do any damn thing they want in the name of "family." "One thing I know for sure, Soleil, is that even though people have been dropping like flies all around you, they brought it on themselves. You wouldn't hurt anyone—who didn't have it coming, that is." A bright smile.

"Watch your step."

"Speaking of step, what's our next?"

"'Our?' Oh, Cami, I love you, but I don't think you should hang around Europe much longer, especially around me. The heat is really on."

"Shut up. I'll do what I want," Camille said archly.

Soleil saw that her sister had really made a comeback from what Soleil feared was a terminally depressive life. Renewal is a wonderful thing, and I'm not going to derail it. It's Camille's life.

After a moment she said, "OK, but I'm moving you into a hotel, you slob. I need neat. And besides, knowing you, the boys will start rotating in and out of my apartment any day now."

"Whatever do you mean, Soleil? Here, I'll pick up the tab." She waved her left hand in the air without taking her eyes off her sister.

The pack of waiters swung into action.

In the world of mining and metals, the most highly anticipated event of the year was far and away the Metal Moguls Ball, the signature feature of the International Metals and Commodities Forum.

The CEOs and owners of some of the most powerful commodity companies on Earth flocked to the five-day-long forum event each year to wheel, deal, network, connive, and hobnob with their friends and competitors. It was also a chance to celebrate their lofty status as heads of the companies that supply the metals and minerals the world needs to run on. And the opulent and exciting gala night, known to one and all as the Metals Moguls Ball, was an opportunity to dance, dine, show off wives and girlfriends, and let monstrous egos loose in some of the most exciting cities in the world.

This year the ball was being hosted at the Clarendon Hotel at Broadway and Forty-Fifth Street on Times Square in New York City. At the time one of the largest and tallest hotels in the world, it featured the city's largest rooftop restaurant, which, since its opening in 1985, had hosted a smorgasbord of glittering international events.

Attendance was by invitation only. Tickets were sent out by the major metals and commodities industry organizations around the world to its movers and shakers. And this year, with the rumored dissolution of the Soviet Union still the main focus of the commodity world, the crowd was expected to be larger and more interesting than ever. The USSR was said to have the Earth's lion's share of many critical commodities such as oil and the precious metals. And the accelerating changes that were opening up that huge country to world trade were on everybody's minds.

In fact, this year's Metal Moguls Ball had its own slogan: "The Russians are coming."

8

THE RUSSIAN

Maxim Stepanov was coming. His invitation was in his suit jacket pocket.

He stood speaking with his friend Vlad in front of the Russian embassy in Brunnadernrain, a residential street in the city of Berne. Thirty years old, around five foot eleven, Stepanov was stocky and powerful—not in a phony workout way, but in the way of a farmer-laborer. His hands and fingers were thick and strong. He had thick black hair, a strong nose, a wide chin, and piercing black eyes—eyes that always moved and were always watching. Now they were smiling.

A taxi was waiting to take Max to the train station. The Swiss sky was heavy with clouds, but Max was in a fine mood.

"Maybe, Vlad," Max was saying in Russian, "for the first time Russia has a bright future. One day we may not need this embassy anymore—the Soviet Union is changing. People like us have an opportunity of a lifetime."

Vlad looked at him critically. He was about the same age as Max, and it was rumored that he was Gorbachev's nephew, but Max knew that was laughable. What wasn't laughable was the fact that Vlad was almost certainly KGB. Max had known him since university and corresponded with him when Vlad was working in Dresden, in East Germany. Max believed that his referrals had helped Vlad climb the party ladder, but in recent years, it may have been the other way around. Russia, Max mused.

Vlad said, "Maybe I would use this opportunity to start over in a new place, Max. Like America or even here in Switzerland."

Max laughed. Vlad would never leave Russia—he was loyal to everything Russian. He was either playing with him, testing him, or most likely both. "You go, Vlad." said Max. "Find a new life. For me, I have a plan, and even the changing of the guard in the motherland is just a bump in the road—a very fortuitous bump." He watched his friend. Vlad was a good man, and Max always thought that his bland demeanor was a put-on—Vlad was smart and crafty. And he was mostly old Russia, Max thought: strength and toughness wins the day and all that. He sighed inside. One day I will leave Russia, but it will be on my own terms, on my own schedule.

"I will write to you, my friend. I'll send you a post card from Zurich. The Alps." They laughed and hugged in the Russian way, and Max got in the cab. He rolled down the window, gave Vlad a short wave, and told the driver, "Go."

Born in Riga in the Soviet Republic of Latvia, the son of a midlevel apparatchik, Stepanov had bullied his way up in the Communist Party partially by using his father's connections with the local party bosses, but more so by sheer guts and brains and his ability to stay sober while all those around him were perpetually hammered. He hated the Party, but he was practical—it was the only way to advance.

After university, where he cleverly decided to study geology, he was sent to work in Siberia at the Soviet palladium and diamond mines near Irkutsk as he had hoped. While despising the abominable weather at what was commonly termed "the frozen asshole of the world," he set his sights on a different target and looked on his frigid ordeal as a necessary trial by fire. Finally returning to Moscow and pulling every string possible, he wrangled a post as an assistant minister with the Soviet metals and gem monopoly Almazjuvelriexport, or Almaz for short. *Finally, a place where I can learn how business really works, how capitalism really works. Almaz deals with the world, unlike so many other Soviet enterprises, which are mostly dead ends.*

But in the USSR, the structure of the Russian economy was slowly vaporizing. As with so many other institutions, the higher-ups at Almaz were looking forward into the future and consolidating their power and their assets, and people of Max's age and employment level were given the ax. So after just two years, Max was let go.

Not to be deterred by what he knew was an inevitability rolling toward him, Max was able to make a move to Cenkhran, the secretive Russian state precious metals and gemstone repository, where gold, precious metals, and diamonds were being securely maintained off the books of the Russian balance sheet. His experiences in Siberia and business contacts at Almaz were invaluable, and his prodigious capacity for work, coupled with his knack for evaluating people and leveraging friendships, helped him immensely. Vlad also gave him a sterling recommendation.

And the fact that Max had been strategically sleeping with the daughter of the head of Cenkhran's administrative department on the side didn't hurt either.

Until it did. But there was more to his rapid exit from Cenkhran than just that slight error of youthful miscalculation. It was just another factor that made his move to Nevsky easier.

Nevsky Nickel was a state-owned-and-operated company, but its chief officers were quietly preparing it to be denationalized—and then, who knows? A public corporation? It was the largest nickel, palladium, and platinum mining company on Earth, and it already owned some very capitalistic assets such as a modern world headquarters and a small fleet of corporate jets.

Nevsky, like other Russian mining companies, was not allowed to sell its refined nickel, platinum, and other metals without a waiver from Cenkhran. So Max, his roster of inside contacts under his arm, was warmly welcomed at Nevsky.

And now he was in Switzerland ostensibly to scout out a location for a satellite office for Nevsky Nickel and then to travel to New York to represent the company at the conference and ball. Switzerland was critical to Nevsky: it was the land of sheltering assets and of the tax break, and the Russians weren't fools: there were serious reasons why the largest commodity companies on the planet had their main offices in obscure towns like Baar and Zug, where taxes were shockingly low.

He loved Switzerland. Hell, I love anywhere that's not Russia. Back home I live in a small one-bedroom flat in a drab, smelly apartment block that I waited ten years to get. I work at what should be a job with some prestige, but most of the time I live like a beggar, like the rest of the proletariat.

And like the rest, I have some secrets. One of them is waiting for me in Zurich.

To say my life is stalled out is the understatement of the year. When I get back from this trip, I will have to deliver the bad news to Katia. She's a good girlfriend, and we've been on and off for four years, but she, too, is a dead end. Likely she will go into the entertainment field sometime in the future. I hope for her sake she gets out of Russia— she's a natural beauty and deserves better things. But we're doomed—we've grown too far apart.

After all, where am I going in Russia? What am I looking forward to? I've been sucking up to the party for so long it's become a way of life. I need to be able to operate outside of the state. I know I could burn up the world, accomplish great things, given the chance. And now finally I will have a chance.

Vlad can stay in Russia. Nevsky Nickel is my bridge. I'll keep working my way up in the company and learn all I can and then leave. I will go to the West and create my own destiny. I even have an engraved invitation.

I just have to keep up the façade of a displaced party loyalist until it's safe not to anymore. Patience. Hah, the word should be emblazoned on the Russian flag.

On the train to Zurich, he patted the invitation in his jacket pocket that his superiors at Nevsky Nickel had handed him. "Stepanov will have to go to New York; his English is by far the best," said his bushy-eyebrowed bosses. He could hardly keep the jubilation off his face. New York! *Chorosho!*

The panorama of the Swiss countryside unfolded outside the window as Max sat on the train from Berne to Zurich, his mind idly circling back to the day when his position in Cenkhran came undone. He had been ordered to sit in on a meeting with two Englishman, a Mr. Smythe and a Mr. Clooney, who represented a company Max had never heard of and had not conducted business with. Max had stood in the back of the room with three or four managers and said nothing—just observed.

Being nobody's fool, Max understood that this obscure Patel + Co, run by one Mr. Tom Patel, was just a front for a large Western metals company that was prohibited from dealing with the Soviet Union under its sovereign laws—Carrington Metals. *That* company he knew about. Bad business. Max thought the whole idea was ill conceived and of low cunning, and his impression of the two men after observing them for just a few minutes was that of a pair of jackals.

Odds were that this Tom Patel was just a dupe for this nasty *sobaka*, Smythe, and in the process was probably being ground up in the scheme. The other man was a mirror image of Smythe, but younger and a little shorter. He could have been his son. On the way out of the meeting, Clooney completely ignored Max and his small group. Displaying arrogance is not a good idea when you are the guest of Cenkhran, thought Max.

But Max had underestimated the influence of these Englishmen and was under no illusions when he was suspiciously fired within a few days of the meeting. He wrote it off to the backroom dealing, the cutting out of possible leaks, and the overarching paranoia of his bosses—not uncommon states of affairs in the Soviet Union, to say the least.

Max made his move over to Nevsky Nickel as the USSR was trundling down the path to disintegration, and he didn't think of the incident at Cenkhran for almost a year until he was contacted by Edward Sierra at Rio Plata, a huge mining and commodities company. Sierra needed Columbite-Tantalite, a critical element in the production of electronic components, and Max had no access to it.

Looking back, Max had felt slightly embarrassed that he had recommended that Sierra contact Patel—the virtually unknown company probably didn't even exist, and if it did, it probably would be unable to supply Col Tan legally. He gave Sierra the phone number that Smythe had supplied to him at Cenkhran because the two Englishmen had boasted about their direct pipeline to the Ivory Coast, where the majority of the world's Col Tan was mined. After hanging up with Sierra, he had immediately put it out of his mind.

But surprisingly, Sierra called Max to thank him for the contact, which was now called Tangiere International. Curious. When I get to Zurich I might just look these people up. If they have easy, and legal, access to rare metals and minerals, then we can surely make some deals. Edward Sierra and Rio Plata do the proper due diligence: if there were anything illegal, they would have spotted it and would have had nothing to do with it.

I'll touch base with this Tangiere when I get to Zurich. But first I have a date with an egg.

This wasn't Fiona's cup of tea.

Waiting around while Whipple mucked up her days in Zurich was tedious and nerve-wracking.

John Clooney sent Winston Whipple to Switzerland to "surveil" the Tangiere situation and "help" his fiancé. The man was an abomination: he was running to fat, badly attired, and dull. The only attribute to this man was his nervous reaction to Fiona herself—she scared him. Good. I feed off fear, she liked to say to herself. Stay out of my way, Winston.

After what must have been a contentious and extremely weird conversation with his grandmother, John had called Fiona to let her know that it would be unwise for her to be seen in Zurich. Let Whipple try to find the key first. Then Fiona could get Soleil out of Switzerland, where she could operate far more efficiently and without the specter of the police around every corner. That was when she would force Soleil to tell her everything. That kind of thing was Fiona's specialty, not Whipple's.

Well, she *had* been seen in Zurich, but not by Soleil, or at least she didn't think by her. And now this oaf shows up. The tweedy lout spent his time bugging phones, going through garbage, following the sister around—a total cock-up and waste of time. Of course, he had little to report. The Tangiere woman must know the key is of great value and is guarding it zealously. Well, enjoy yourself now, Soleil—*our* eventual meeting is in the cards. And that's when I intend to have my fun.

With time to kill, Fiona followed Soleil at a distance. She had easily started to hate Soleil, and now she hated her sister, who seemed to have shown up out of the blue. Viciously competitive, Fiona couldn't abide Soleil's confident poise and fresh beauty. And now the older sister shows up—another bloody pageant queen! Fiona's drinking and drug use edged up a notch. Oooh, revenge will be very, very sweet.

Whipple knocked hesitantly on the door of Fiona's hotel suite. She let him in. Without any pleasantries, she barked, "Well? What's the latest?" You dumbass.

"Can I sit down?" He started to lower himself onto a chair, but Fiona's eyes shot daggers. He thought the better of it and remained standing.

"All right. A man was in her office this morning."

Fiona stood in front of him, her hands on her hips. "Go on."

"I didn't get his name or what he's doing there. The bug went down."

Fiona blinked. "What do you mean?"

Whipple looked like a deer caught in the headlights. "I, I don't know. She let him into her office and, well, here, listen." He pulled his little mini-recorder from his pants pocket and switched it on. Voices in German.

"Come in." A woman's voice.

"Good morning, Ms. Tangiere." A moment or two of quiet.

"OK."

Then the tape ended.

It hit Fiona.

After the "good morning" the visitor must have found the bug and gestured to Soleil to be quiet. Hence the "OK." Then he disabled it.

"What did he look like, lummox?" Fiona was furious.

"I don't know. A lot of men were walking in and out of the building at that time. They kind of all looked the same. You know—suits, ties..." his voice trailed off.

Fiona rolled her eyes. "Where did they go when they left?"

"I didn't see him. I followed *her* to the train station."

Fiona waited. "And then...?"

Whipple stared at everything but Fiona.

"I lost her."

After Fiona had thrown the idiot out, she called Clooney.

"Why did you send me Inspector Clouseau? He's a moron! Tangiere is hobnobbing with everyone in sight, going hither and yon with hardly a care in the world, and we don't know a thing about the key. All my efforts have brought up zilch. And your joke of a spy is making things worse. C'mon, John!"

Clooney held the phone six inches from his face. She was scary all right. "Don't discount Winston. He's a good fellow if a little too literal, and you must admit he's inconspicuous. Sort of blends in with the scenery."

"Oh, give me a break. Look, Soleil's going to New York next week to that ball. I'm going, and—"

"Of course you're going. We're both going. I'm always invited to the Metal Moguls Ball. Last year it was in Cannes. Boy, was that a fun ti—"

"Bully for you, John," she interrupted harshly. "Listen, if I can get her by herself in New York, it will all be over. She'll be away from her precious Swiss police protector, Deshautels—who, by the way, is cheating on his wife, but not with Soleil—and I'll be able to sew this whole thing up. Screw Whipple and screw Switzerland, and I'm going to New York to get this show in motion. Get me a first-class ticket." The phone went dead in Clooney's hand.

He and Fiona at the Metal Moguls Ball? With Soleil Tangiere?

His stomach churned.

Max Stepanov was ushered into a small room in the basement of the bank. He closed the door behind him and checked the room for any possibility that there was a hidden camera. Can't be too careful. Hence the hat, the tinted glasses, and the ridiculous pencil moustache that he had donned for this one chore. The bank certainly had cameras everywhere else, and Swiss or no Swiss, what he had to do was his business only.

He produced a key from his pocket and opened the safe deposit box that he had put on the table in front of him. He flipped the hinged lid open and carefully extracted the contents: $100,000 in neatly banded bundles of hundred-dollar bills. A Swiss passport. An American passport. A Smith and Wesson .38-caliber police special. A green cardboard box.

He counted out $20,000 and put the rest of the money, the passports, and the gun back in the safe deposit box. That should tide me over in case of an emergency. He was about to put the green cardboard box back with the rest but then hesitated. All right, one look—he felt like indulging himself, and besides—he hadn't seen her in a long time.

The green box measured around six inches on a side. He opened it. Inside was tightly packed cotton. In the cotton was an egg.

It was a golden egg, around five inches long. Its surface was decorated in gleaming red and gold guilloche enamel, and tiny diamonds and rubies were interspersed in an elaborate design all around it. He pulled gently, and the hinged top of the egg opened. Gingerly he pulled out a tiny model of a ballerina made of gold standing on her toes on a tiny purple amethyst stage. The detail work was astounding: she seemed to float and twirl on her miniscule toes, a clear quartz crystal tutu circled her waist, and Max held his breath at the thought of what this was.

The little masterpiece was the work of Peter Karl Faberge, court jeweler to the czars of Russia. This particular egg was part of the collection secretly owned by Almaz, and how it came into Max's possession was something he didn't want to think about at this time. It was a piece of Russian art, a symbol of its cultural history, and it was priceless.

But all Max knew at the moment was that he loved this artifact of another time, a time before the era of Lenin and Marx, and it was, if he ever needed it to be, his insurance policy.

He carefully fitted the tiny ballerina back in the egg, closed it, and repacked it. When it was back in the safe deposit box and he had finally left the bank, he breathed a contented sigh and ripped off the ridiculous moustache, which he tossed in a trashcan.

It was a nice day, so he decided to walk to the building where the woman, Soleil Tangiere, was expecting him.

"Come in," in German.

Soleil had gotten the call yesterday, and a man with a slight accent had asked if he could stop by for a few minutes. He said he was a representative of a Russian commodities firm. Right. Sounds like a spy for you-know-who. Might as well let him come by, though. I meant it when I said I've got to end this.

Max stepped through the door, and Soleil tilted her head slightly. Well. Here's an interesting-looking man.

"Good morning, Ms. Tangiere." But the man was already in action. He put a finger to his lips to indicate she should be quiet and carefully made his way around her office. In his other hand was what appeared to be a small Geiger counter.

"OK." Soleil looked on, intrigued.

After a minute or two, Max stopped in front of Soleil's desk and passed his electronic device back and forth. After a moment, he grabbed the desk lamp and picked it up. A light on his little machine was flashing. Under the base of the lamp they both saw the bug—a small metal pickup with a thin wire disappearing into the lamp. Max ripped it out, replaced the lamp, and plopped the tiny metal device into the vase that held Soleil's morning flowers. It made a quick crackling noise when it hit the water and then was silent.

"Good. Now we can talk, yes?" He sat down in front of her desk, an open smile on his face, dark eyes glowing. He passed a Nevsky business card across her desk. It was in Russian, but his name was spelled out in English. Now Soleil was a little more than intrigued.

"Mr...." She looked at the card. "Stepanov. How do you do?" She reached across the desk. The touch of his rough hand was reassuring, and his eyes held no lies. So far.

"No, no. Max, please," he said.

"Soleil," she said back.

"Soleil." He lifted the Geiger counter. "Sorry for the theatrics." He clicked it off. The little light on it went out.

"Pardon?"

It suddenly hit Max. "Would you prefer we speak in English? I love English, and I hate German."

Soleil was relieved. "Oh yes, absolutely. So what can we, I, do for you?" She was stumbling over her words. What's wrong with me?

"It doesn't surprise you when a strange Russian shows up at your office and rips listening devices from your lamp? You must lead a very interesting life."

That smile again. Do all Russians have such white teeth? Maybe it's from all that vodka. OK, Get a grip—this is serious!

"No, I'm not surprised. I'm learning fast that in this business, anything can happen."

"Huh, don't I know it."

Soleil forced herself to remember that this Max had been in 'this business' far longer than she had. If he was on the level.

She sat up straight and said, "Why are you here?"

"A mutual friend, Edward Sierra, told me he was very pleased with the way you handled a complicated deal for his company, Rio Plata Mining. Your company came on my recommendation. I gained face, and I came to thank you."

Soleil suddenly remembered. Yes, that Mr. Sierra had mentioned that he was referred by a Mr. Stepanov. And here he was. And he had known Tom. Suddenly her heart sank. Forget the hope of him being on the level, at least for now. Her tone turned cold.

"You did business with Tom, er, Mr. Patel." It was more an accusation than a question.

Max looked at her carefully. Why was she suddenly a closed book?

"No, I never laid eyes on him. His name was mentioned in a business deal that never came to fruition, and from a source that was, well, not a good one." He spent the next few minutes telling Soleil how it all came about, about seeing Smythe and Clooney in the Cenkhran offices. When she sensed the contempt that Max had for the two Englishmen, her skepticism started to wane. Also, Max apparently had no idea of what had transpired at the Geneva Airport.

"I can't imagine that you were part of this," he ended up, looking directly into her eyes.

Soleil explained that she had started from square one in this business only a couple of months ago and Tom had taken her on as a sort of junior business partner. Better keep our lovely little affair close to the vest until I can get a better fix on this man.

"You know that Tom is dead, don't you?" she finally asked.

Max stared at her. He didn't. Now it was his turn to turn a jaundiced eye.

"What happened?"

Decision time, Soleil said to herself. Should I tell him what happened? He was obviously on the other side of the deal that they were supposed to have made in Moscow if the aborted abduction of her and Tom had been successful. But like her, if he was to be believed, he was also in the dark. Was he telling the truth? She looked at him closely. I need a friend to take on CM and their people. This man may know a way for me to get to them before they get to me. Besides, could it get any worse?

She made up her mind.

He was genuinely stunned as she told him the details of Smythe's and Tom's deaths. Finally she said, "I'm in serious danger. It seems useless to hide that from you. It looks as if you know the score." A moment, then: "For all I know, you're here to kill me."

He shot her a serious look.

"No, I'm just a Russian businessman. But I know that in this world of giant metals deals where millions are at stake, things like this happen. You were just in partnership with the wrong man." This girl was unlucky but resourceful. And to take over a company when her partner has just died, single-handedly and with just about zero experience—even a tough Russian would have run away. She was really something. He looked at her with undisguised admiration. After a quiet moment, he said, "Tom Patel had it all. He blew it."

"He blew it," she repeated before she realized that Max might have been testing the waters.

"Who was on the other end of the bug?" he asked.

"Probably CM. Smythe's son is more or less running the company now, and he's obviously using his power to find and silence me. And now that you're in the mix, my life may be getting even harder. But don't worry, Max. You couldn't have seen this coming."

His face fell. Why am I so concerned about this woman? Why don't you admit it, Stepanov—she is, as the Americans say, a hot fox, and a smart hot fox at that. Control yourself. Katia is still in the picture, waiting for you back in Russia, and she's—no, face it—Katia may be a shimmering star, but this woman is like the sun blazing. Eeeeh!

He slowly shook his head and said, "You are wrong, Soleil. Now that I'm in the mix, maybe things will be changing for the better. Maybe I can help you end this mess once and for all. I know how this business works." He paused. "At least from the Russian point of view." He looked at her.

She sighed inside and considered why he would want to help her, but then thought maybe, just maybe there's something more there. OK, Max.

A full minute passed in silence. Then: "Tell me about yourself," Soleil said with genuine interest. "Tell me about Russia."

She leaned on her elbows on the desk and looked straight at him. Her sapphire eyes had a life of their own. He suddenly felt his own heart beating.

Klass! Max thought. What a woman! How old is this beauty? Twenty-three? Twenty-five? What's wrong with me? *Nyet! Da!* I think I have to have this woman in my life. At all costs.

Then he told her about himself. And about Russia.

They left the office together, Soleil having been treated to a fascinating and sometimes humorous glimpse of Russia and surprising herself with how easy it was to accept Max's dinner invitation for the following night. Max seemed solid and old fashioned, and she liked him instantly. Must be the Russian upbringing, she pondered.

Once they were out on the sidewalk in front of the building, Max told her to go on ahead of him. This would confuse the silly amateur who was following her, whom Max had spotted on the way into the building. A heavyset man with sunglasses, hiding behind a newspaper while standing in the lobby? You've got to be kidding.

He advised Soleil, "Go to the train station and step on and off a train once or twice. That should do it. If a man like this was working for the KGB, he would have been sent to a gulag by now." He chuckled.

He kissed her on both cheeks in the Russian fashion and watched her walk away. When she got to the station, she lost Winston Whipple on the first try.

The phone in Whipple's cheap hotel room rang, and it woke him up. He lunged across the bed, knocking the phone to the floor. Then he bent down and picked up the receiver.

"Hallo."

"Whipple, It's Mr. Clooney. What are you doing?"

He shook his head to clear the cobwebs. "Sleeping, sir."

"Ms. Dyche called me earlier." Whipple knew what was coming.

"Don't screw up anymore, Whipple, do you hear me?" Clooney yelled into the receiver. "How could you lose that girl? What's wrong, she was too fast for you? Or did your nob take over and you became cross-eyed with lust, you loser?"

"I, I..."

"Don't aye-aye me, Winston. You're an oaf! Now get on the stick, and I mean it!" The phone went dead.

Whipple sat on the side of the bed. You called me for that, Mr. Clooney? Damn.

The car dropped them off at the Baur au Lac Hotel. The Pavillon, the hotel's restaurant, was one of the finest in Zurich, in all Switzerland. The tuxedoed maître d' snapped his fingers, and in a moment they were sitting at a small table in a private alcove.

She was dressed in a simple skirt, a fawn-colored silk blouse, and a well-cut, high-collared jacket. He was in a navy suit, which did its best to compliment his stocky, muscular physique.

He was relaxed, and they ordered some drinks and some food and talked.

"What are you doing here?" she asked.

"Here, where? This restaurant, Zurich, the West?" He loved this. Certainly not all Western women were like this. But then he saw the change in her face.

"None of the above. What are you doing here with me? What don't I know, Max?" The eyes were suddenly serious.

She went on: "I'm out of trust, you see. If this wining and dining is going to turn into lying and betraying, then please, Max, please don't start. I'm burned out—there's nothing left." She turned two palms up.

He looked down at her hands. The fingers were long and tapered. I wish I could read the future in those palm lines.

"If I were lying, I would simply hold those hands, look in your eyes, and say 'of course I'm not lying to you.' So...of course I'm not lying to you." He took her hands in his. She didn't pull them away.

Her eyes narrowed. "Yeah, you're lying," she said, a smile starting at the corners of her mouth. He had better not be. I'm going to have to come down on one side of this or the other.

"So go ahead, Max, tell me about the wife and kids you have back in the USSR."

"Lots of kids," he said. "Seven of them. Two wives." He took a sip of wine. "In Russia, that's called 'available.'"

She smiled at his wit.

"And you..." he made a "come on" gesture with one hand.

She thought for a minute and decided to watch his face carefully when she said, "I lived with Tom Patel for two years."

"Truly?" His face told her the story: he didn't know that. Good. If he had, he would have been lying all along—his visit would have been based on prior knowledge of her personally, and that would have been that. He would have been left with an empty chair and a half-eaten salad as company for the rest of the night. She breathed a mental sigh of relief.

"Truly. We met in New York, and I made a major mistake—I trusted him and believed him. Then I got sucked into this mess, and now it doesn't look so good." There was no self-pity in her voice—just a recitation of facts.

Max realized that this woman's lover had recently fallen to his death, and she seemed to be taking it pretty well. Wow, she's tough. Patel had used Soleil and used her badly, he calculated. How could anyone do that to this woman?

"Soleil, in Russia the truth can sometimes be as rare as hen's teeth. People lie all the time. Sometimes a lie is more comfortable than the truth."

She looked at him. "Seven kids, huh?"

"Well, that's not very comfortable, is it? OK, I lied. No wives, either."

"Plenty of girlfriends, though."

"Aaaaay!" he drawled, making a fist and hooking the thumb in his armpit.

"What was that?"

"Russian imitation of the Fonz?" He winced as he said it.

She shook her head, said, "*Nyet*," and took another bite of salad.

Oh God, that face, he thought: that radiant, beautiful face. His heart sang.

He handed her an envelope. She peeked inside and smiled at Max's bravado as she pondered its contents for a moment.

Finally she looked up and said, "Thanks for the plane ticket, Max, but I insist on paying for it."

He smiled and said, "Don't thank me—tickets, cars, hotel rooms—all are fleas on the back of the elephant expense account of Nevsky Nickel. When I pay, you'll know. It will be with your money!"

They laughed and flirted lightly, and their main dishes were served with a professional flourish. The wait staff had them pegged as some kind of power couple—likely a movie or entertainment duo, as they looked the part.

They ate slowly, and through the small talk, Soleil kept gauging and weighing and thinking, and then finally she made a decision.

When they had finished their dessert, a chocolate soufflé that they had fought over with two spoons, she said, "Max, I need to show you something."

She reached one hand into her bra and put the other one in front of it as a shield. Max's eyes widened, and he held his breath. She looked in his eyes, extended her hand toward him, and opened her fingers. A key fell on the tablecloth.

She looked at Max. "Max. This key—do you know what it is?"

He scowled slightly and looked at the key. No, I don't kn—Oh God, what's going on here? Could it be? He picked up the key and looked closely at it. Soleil was watching his face.

For the first time since leaving Russia, Max felt suddenly tired, suddenly empty. *Da*, I know what this key was. I know, and I wish I didn't. And most of all, I wish this woman were not involved in this. Damn.

After some moments of silence, he said, "Where did you get this, Soleil?"

She tensed a little—his face showed a deep sadness: not a reaction that she expected. It was impossible to miss.

"Tom Patel had it hidden in his office the day he died. I found it. Should I lose it now?"

"*Nyet*. No, you can't lose it now."

"Tell me, Max. Tell me about the key."

Her face was entreating. He should have said no, but that face—he had to tell her.

Max took a long sip of his wine.

"All right. I've worked in three giant companies in the Soviet Union over the last seven or eight years. One of them, Cenkhran, is now considered the state repository for metals and gemstones. It is, of course, a monopoly. The people weren't supposed to really own anything in the Soviet Union—only the state, which meant only the people in power."

He paused for a second and seemed far away.

"When the country began to implode recently, those in power knew they might be in peril, and Cenkhran, their Fort Knox, was in danger. In fear of an assault, even a military one, on their stronghold, they decided among themselves to spread the wealth, the entire inventory of the vaults, so as to make it impossible for a single faction or even an army to steal it.

"Over a period of two or three months, gigantic quantities of diamonds, gold, objets d'art, and precious metals were spread around the world in numbered bank boxes, secret vaults, even buried in strategic locations. No names. No individuals. Everything was account numbers and map coordinates. No one person knew everything, but there had to be some kind of control, some kind of inventory of locations and codes. So they made a list." Another sip of wine.

"List?"

"Yes. A list of all the boxes and burying sites and locations. Those in power believe the list is in a safe deposit box in Leningrad or Moscow."

"Max, it's just a list. Surely the people who made it have more copies."

The Russian looked at the key on the table between them.

"No. It was a bad time—and it may get even worse. There's a whole new crop of big shots jockeying for survival and power as we speak. There were many murders, and there will doubtless be more. And the key was handed off from one criminal to another. It kept floating. I think that our old friend Smythe may have been in possession of it and then handed it off to Tom Patel to hold for a period of time. Then both Smythe and Patel had the bad luck to die, and you had the worst luck of all: you now have the key.

"And no, no one living has a copy of the list. But whoever can obtain it will have the ability to access wealth, great wealth. And with that wealth comes the ability to buy power, to buy an army if necessary. It boggles the mind." He thought he saw a question on her lips. "How much is there?" he asked rhetorically. "I would think two, maybe three billion dollars."

"Billion? With a *b*?" she asked.

He nodded.

Soleil was impressed, but not with the dollars or the treasure or the power—that wasn't what her life was about. No. She was impressed with the depth of danger that she was in.

Thanks, Tom, she thought bitterly. I've become a target for a flotilla of very bad people who will go to any length to get this key. *Any* length, I'm sure. They might kill me because I have it, and they might kill me if they think I do and I don't. Now I get it. Now I understand the sadness in Max's eyes.

"Couldn't someone just break into the box?"

Max shook his head. "There are microscopic encoded instructions on the key explaining where the box is, and besides, there are certainly people watching and waiting there. Whoever comes to open it is a dead man unless he brings an army with him." Or a dead *woman*, he finished the thought in his mind.

She was thinking, What do I do now? Give it to someone? Who? And how do I explain that I came by it? Throw myself on someone's mercy and promise to keep quiet?

This is bad.

Max looked at her carefully. Only a *svinya* would leave it at this and walk away from her. As the situation stands, she is doomed unless I help find a way out for her. She needs a solution—a Russian solution.

Well, certainly there is such a thing as fate. The people trying to corner her know, or at least think they know, what the key is for. They won't stop until they get it, and even if they leave her alive, that condition won't last long. Somehow Soleil and I collided, and I know about her key.

Fate.

They lingered over coffee, and little more was said. Max paid the bill, and the two wandered out into the hotel lobby. Soleil walked close to Max, but her thoughts were far away.

Finally, she said, "C'mon Max, walk me home. It's about a mile from here, and I need to burn up those calories." She patted his flat stomach. "So do you."

The touch of her hand on his belly instantly vaporized any hesitation that might have been lurking in Max's heart. They walked out of the hotel and zigzagged through the Zurich night. Finally they came to Soleil's apartment building.

She had already decided what she would do before they got there. Even though her nerve endings were screaming to take Max upstairs, her head was saying no. Wait. Not yet.

But Max made it easy.

"When will I see you again?" was all he said as they stood on the sidewalk.

After a minute she said, "Whenever you like. Just not tonight."

"All right." He took her face in his strong hands kissed her.

He didn't remember walking back to his hotel.

"Come on, Soleil. Give it up. What happened after dinner?" Camille was sitting across from her in her office, squinting her eyes and slowly moving the tip of her tongue over her lips.

Soleil would have none of it. She seemed a little distant.

"He's going to meet me in New York," she said vaguely.

"What! What are you talking about?"

"That industry convention is taking place a week from Saturday in New York. I'm *in* the industry now, in case you forgot. So is Max. He has an invitation, and I'm going as his guest." Camille started rolling her eyes. "This other commodities trader named Kurt Ballas says he has an invitation waiting for me in New York as well. Lots of invitations out there, Cami..."

Camille was suddenly worried. Soleil was acting strange—she could sense it more than see it.

"Soleil, what's wrong? What's eating you?" Her hazel eyes flashed.

Soleil shook her head as if to clear it. "Max has a plan. He thinks he can get these CM people off my back for good."

Camille was skeptical. "Why would he do that?"

"I think he may have other motives, but he's not telling me. Or maybe he sees the seriousness of the situation and is just a good guy. I do think he wants to help me."

He wants to help me, but he's handed me the biggest weight of all to wear around my neck: the facts about that key. Thank God I never mentioned the key to Camille. If what he says about it is true, it's complicated matters tremendously. It feels as if I were back in Montana, back on the run.

"Come to New York with me. I need your help." She looked at her oldest sister. Soleil had always felt that Camille was far better looking and smarter than she was. It bothered her when she was younger. Now, not as much, but still a little.

Camille looked at Soleil and knew there was something that she wasn't telling her. I used to resent you, Soleil, she thought for a second, for being Dad's favorite and also for being so beautiful and clever. But lately I like myself a lot more, and it's kind of nice to be needed. You're in trouble, of that there's no doubt. And the Russian and I are all you've got, I guess.

"All right," Camille said. "Let's go to New York."

9

LIVING LARGE

There was a commotion at the front of the jewelry exchange.

Now what? I'm getting too old for this, Izzy said to himself for the thousandth time. Brenda sat at the little jeweler's bench inside the booth going over some invoices. Izzy leaned over the counter to get a better view. There were a number of voices, and then he heard it: "Soleil, Soleil, hi Soleil!"

She came down the same aisle that she had walked down four years ago wearing a blood-stained parka and near death. Izzy's heart leaped.

"So, young lady. What can I do you out of today?" He could hardly get the words out of his mouth. Soleil stood in front of him, beautiful and happy, the small diamond cross at her throat winking at him. His Solie. His old eyes misted over. It had been only a few months since they had seen her, but it seemed like forever.

Soleil lifted the wooden flap that let her walk into the booth, and the three hugged for a full minute. Tango, who had been sleeping behind the counter, couldn't believe she was there and was barking and jumping like a dervish. Then Brenda took over.

"Oy," she said, taking a step back and giving Soleil the once-over. "They ran out of food in Switzerland? You're so thin, Soleil. We have to load you up on some good brisket and *knaidlach*!"

Soleil laughed. They talked for almost half an hour. Izzy stood outside the booth leaning against the counter while Brenda and Soleil chattered away. Soleil showed off some of her German. The Gutthelfs tried a little French, and everyone laughed. When the topic turned to Tom, Izzy went serious.

"We were fooled too, Solie. Somewhere in the world there is a good man who will be worthy. Don't let any man call the shots for you again. You are very strong. *You* decide your life." Brenda stood nodding solemnly. Izzy smiled.

"Hey! Ice Queen!" Soleil felt the finger poking her in the small of her back and heard the familiar voice. Aimee stood there in her new hairstyle and the latest in Brooklyn chic. And of course she was balancing on nosebleed high heels.

"Hey, Flashy and Trashy," said Soleil, and they hugged fiercely. Aimee was genuinely happy. Soleil's absence had left Aimee to assume the role of queen of the jewelry exchange. She wasn't Soleil, the jewelers quipped, but she made for a pretty good sequel! "Thanks for getting me this job, Soleil," she said.

Brenda overheard and scowled. "Aimee, she didn't 'get you the job.' She merely made a suggestion." Everyone smiled. The world seemed so right.

"Moving back?" Aimee asked around her Juicy Fruit.

"Sorry, I'm only here for a little while, but I'll see you before I go."

They chatted for a few more minutes, and then Soleil glanced at her watch. "I'd better be off," she said.

As Soleil was making her good-byes and promising she would visit one more time before returning to Europe, Izzy gently took her arm and said, "Solie. Someone was here just yesterday asking about you."

Soleil's heart sank. "Who was it, Izzy?"

"I don't know. A woman, maybe thirty or so. Short black hair, angry eyes. Crude manners. English accent. She never told me her name. She wanted to know if we knew where you were living in New York."

Brenda interjected. "Don't worry, honey, we told her nothing. Izzy and I know the bad guys when we see them. And the bad girls. She asked a lot of the jewelers here, but they knew less about where you were than we did. We didn't even know you were coming back." Soleil thanked her stars that she didn't give the Gutthelfs any advanced warning of her visit.

"She asked *me* what I knew about you, and I told her to douche with it," Aimee said in her usual colorful style. "Looked and sounded like skank to me," she added.

"That more or less sums it up, I guess."

Who was the woman? Soleil fretted.

A chill raced up her spine. The vision of a black-haired woman in a dark Mercedes following her in the streets of Zurich came suddenly to the front of her mind. There it is.

"Brenda, Izzy. I don't think this woman will be here again. Don't worry about it." Worry wouldn't help anyway. Not with these people. "Just stay safe," she added.

"OK, Solie. Go. Enjoy the Big Apple. Have fun at your ball on Saturday."

She left the exchange and stood on the sidewalk in the middle of Forty-Seventh Street looking left and right. She liked it here, but it was no longer her home. She walked to Sixth Avenue, turned left, and headed south toward the Clarendon.

At that moment, Fiona Dyche was taking a long, hot, boring bath in her suite at the Sheraton at Fifty-Third Street and Seventh Avenue. *When my loving fiancée shows up, I'm going to skewer him. This whole drawn-out plan has wasted weeks of my life, and now I'm here in New York.* She fiddled with a bar of soap. *I hate waiting around. I hate New York. I'm starting to hate John Clooney.*

But money I like, and up to now, he is far and away the best meal ticket to wealth and independence out there. At least for me. I came from the gutter, and he has faith in me. Not exactly Pygmalion, but close enough. He does appreciate my talents, my obsessions. And now Soleil Tangiere is number one on my obsession list.

What gives that Canuck frog tramp the right to be happy and gorgeous? Why is she allowed to have wealth and respect? She's a damn tart, for God's sake, and she's still a baby—how old is she, twenty-three? You've got to be kidding! The word "hate" doesn't even come close.

She looked down. Without realizing it, she had squeezed the bar of soap into the shape of an hourglass. Damn her!

Downstairs, Kurt Ballas paid for his cab and entered the lobby of the New York Hilton. The Hilton, directly across Fifty-Third Street from the Sheraton, was closer to Sixth Avenue, and both hotels were a short walk from Times Square.

He was tired from his trip from Chicago. I should have taken a train, he reflected wearily. But instead he had flown: Cab ride to O'Hare. Plane ride to LaGuardia. Cab ride into New York City. It was a drag.

Ballas went to a pay phone in the lobby and left a message for Soleil, who was staying at the Clarendon. The newer Clarendon, where the Metal Moguls Ball was going to take place, was directly on Times Square at Forty-Fifth Street, and its rooms had been sold out far in advance. Nevsky Nickel was among the group of global commodities firms that had booked suites months ago.

After leaving a message for Soleil to call him at the Hilton, he checked in at the desk and made his way to the bank of elevators. Then he heard a familiar voice: "Kurt!"

He took a deep breath and turned to face a red-haired woman dressed in an expensive outfit and fur coat. Jewelry dripped.

"What are you doing here, Amanda?" The last person on Earth that Kurt wanted to see was his ex-wife. Well, not my ex-wife, not yet. This separation is killing me, and she's gaming the lawyers like a pro. And of course the kids are paying the price. Sometimes I hate the world, hate everyone.

"For the same reason you're here, Kurt. The ball."

"Well, you're not going with me. Not this time."

She made a face. "Why would I want to? I don't need you to take me to a party. I've been invited to go with Josh Fowler."

Ballas knotted his brow. "Josh Fowler? The head of J. Fowler Metals? He's a snake, a pirate, and an all-around bad guy. It's amazing he's not in jail or worse. Everyone knows that. You know that."

"Sounds like sour grapes, Kurt." She looked past her expertly shaped nose at him and grinned. "I always liked going to the Metal Moguls Ball, Kurt. At least at this one, I'm going to have someone smart and fun to be with." An elevator hissed open, and she stepped in and turned to Kurt.

"C'mon, Kurt, get in. What floor are you on?"

"I'll wait for the next one," he said and a split second later regretted it: he sounded babyish and trite, like her. Yechh.

When her elevator doors had closed, he went back in the lobby and sat on a long couch looking out onto Fifty-Third Street. The large windows faced the side entrance of the Sheraton across the street.

I should never have gotten into it with Amanda. Besides, it's the pot calling the kettle black when it comes to infidelity and pettiness. I'm not exactly a saint, sorry. And look at me now, waiting like a little kid to meet this Soleil. What, to teach her about commodities? Sure. No, I guess we are pretty much the pair after all, Amanda.

He watched a man in a hat and long gray coat get out of a cab in front of the side entrance to the Sheraton. He watched him walk around the cab as a bellhop pulled his luggage from the trunk. He watched the cabbie getting paid and driving away, and John Clooney and his luggage disappear into the hotel.

Another poor sap, thought Kurt, at another convention.

I should go to the airport now and get the hell out of here.

John Clooney arrived at the Sheraton from the side door, as was his habit, and immediately went up to the suite. The conversation he had had with his grandmother before leaving London had resonated in his head for the entire plane trip. Fiona isn't going to like what I'm going to tell her. I'm too tired to care, though. Fiona is turning into bad karma.

She let him into the room, and he instantly realized that it was worse than he had feared. He had never seen his fiancée like this: she was out of her tree ranting and raving about knocking off this one and "offing" that one, and "Bullwinkling" someone else, whatever that was. I should Bullwinkle her, he thought tiredly. Finally she settled down.

"You're not killing anyone, Fiona," he said, sitting on the side of the bed, his jacket still on. "Grandma and I had a talk before I left London." His foot was idly kicking something on the floor near the bed. What the hell! Is this a hand grenade?

Damn it, Fiona thought bitterly. That crazy old lady again? Oh, John of the tiny twig, you have to think for yourself. A little longer and we'll be able to return home, older and wiser and richer. Much richer. Besides, you don't want *your* name to land on *my* list, do you?

"Oh, Grandma? Really?" she said, suddenly calm and sweet. "What was the talk about?"

But he was on to something else: "A *hand grenade?* You gotta be joking!" He was purple with rage, and he held it at arm's length.

"Cool your jets, sweetie. It's not real, it's my lighter." She snatched it from his hand and flicked a small flame by squeezing its handle. "What kind of girl do you think I am?"

He scowled. "Grandma insists that the Tangiere woman give us all she knows about where the key is and especially who else knows about it. We have to get the key at all costs, but Soleil Tangiere stays alive." He watched her face.

"Okey dokey, Johnny." Her grin was oddly frightening. Stays alive. Sure. "Where are we going to dinner?"

"I'm going to take a shower. Where would you like to eat?"

"Le Cirque."

John Clooney groaned. He had to make some phone calls.

Later, while he was in the shower, he came to a decision. So did she.

"She's not here. Who's this?"

Camille had answered the phone in their suite. Holding the instrument in her hand, she gazed at the breathtaking view from their fortieth-floor suite's window. The Empire State Building and a large swath of Manhattan spread out before her. Some difference from where I came from—I could get used to this.

"This is Kurt Ballas. Will she be coming back soon?"

"Oh, yes, Kurt. She's been trying to get ahold of you for a few days, but we've—she's been traveling. She wanted to let you know that she wouldn't need that invitation to the ball; she already has one." Camille could feel the man's disappointment over the phone.

Hastily she added, "but she's looking forward to meeting you there. She told me you're a nice guy."

Kurt looked into the phone receiver. Another downer. Oh, stop acting like an ass, he told himself. "Who are you?" he asked.

"Camille. I'm her sister. Older sister." She liked his rough Chicago accent.

Then, "Kurt?"

"Yes."

"Kurt, Soleil told me you were leaving a ticket at the ball for her. Is that right?"

"Yes."

"You never actually asked her to be your date for this event, did you?"

Kurt cursed himself. In a dejected voice he said, "No."

"Kurt, what do you expect? You must have sounded like a Ticketmaster agent, not someone asking for a date. Pardon my bluntness. Soleil attracts dates like sugar attracts flies. You snooze, you lose, Kurt."

"You're going to the ball, too, Camille?"

"No-o," she said slowly. "No, I don't have an invitation."

It took him less than a second to decide. "I have that famous Ticketmaster ticket. Can I use it to take you to the ball?"

"Now there's a line from Cinderella. OK, Kurt. Sure."

Then he said, "Are you married?"

"Nope. Divorced." Then she had an intuition: "Are you?"

"Separated. But I'm warning you, my ex might show up there. Is that a problem?"

Oh Soleil, you can be such a jerk sometimes, Camille thought. I guess I *am* helping you here—this is the kind of drama you don't need. I'll take this Kurt Ballas business off your hands and take it on myself. Besides, this could be kind of fun. This guy sounds pretty OK.

"Not for me, Kurt. I never even heard your voice until three minutes ago. You can bring a whole damn Little League team with you, for all I care. But a word to the wise: Soleil didn't know much about you, and she knows nothing about this ex-wife stuff." Kurt started to interrupt, but she continued. "You sound like a nice guy, Kurt. Take it from me: it's good that it's working out this way. Soleil is going through a rough patch, and I'm trying to tone down the drama in her life if I can. My little sister is very cautious and straightlaced about a lot of things, though she won't admit it."

"But you're not?"

Camille laughed. Time to puff this guy up. "Kurt, you're quite a man—you figured out a way to pick me up in five minutes, and on the phone, no less. And thanks for dinner, by the way."

"Dinner? What dinner?"

"The one you're thinking of inviting me to tonight so you can check me out first and determine whether your date for the big ball is going to turn out to be a butterfly or a basset hound."

They both laughed. "Very clever, Camille. Can I call you Cami?"

"Pick me up in the lobby at 8:00." She hung up.

"How will I know you?" he asked into the buzzing phone. Then he realized it was a very amateurish question.

"You did what?"

"I picked up your commodities boyfriend, Kurt." Camille munched on an apple from the complimentary bowl of fruit on the sideboard.

"What are you doing, Cami? You can't do that!" Soleil all but stomped her feet.

Camille smiled. "Sometimes you can be a real dope, Soleil. This Ballas guy thought he was taking you to this shindig and I knew he was in for a letdown, so I picked up the ball, so to speak."

"What letdown?"

Camille got serious. "This is where I have a problem with you. You're irresistible to men, even over the phone, but sometimes you just don't get it. Sometimes you wind up playing with their heads, and you don't even know you're doing it. This guy was ready to have you as his date, which wasn't going to happen since you're going with Max, and I just stepped in to soften the blow. So there." She took another loud bite of apple.

Soleil smiled inside. Camille was right. Soleil knew that most men had generally one-track minds, and sometimes those tracks were really narrow. Cami's solution was actually pretty clever. Soleil would meet Kurt Ballas on a neutral level. Then, in the future, she would hopefully be able to learn some of the commodities business from him without any other distractions. Kurt would have his date, and that should cool him off. *And I can be close to Max—everyone wins.*

"By the way, Einstein, his wife will be there," Camille said.

"What, whose?"

"Kurt's. Don't ask me—sounds like he used to take her to these things, and now she found another commodities guy to take her since their separation. It would have been a bad scene for you, Soleil."

"What about for you?"

Camille threw her a crooked smile. "Me?"

Soleil knew enough to end it there.

"Oh, and Kurt's taking me to dinner tonight."

"Pretty quick work, Cami."

"Ha! Spoken like an amateur."

Soleil smiled. "OK, have a nice time at dinner."

"Not until I get something to wear."

Camille grabbed her purse, and a minute later she was gone.

Le Cirque was located on East Sixty-Fifth Street, and it was always crowded, especially on a Friday night. It had taken a lot of heavily pulled strings from CM in London for Clooney to get a table on such short notice and a literal wad of cash when the maître d' announced that his reservation had been suddenly "lost" at the last minute. When they were finally seated at a small corner table, John was already in a black mood.

But Fiona wasn't. She was hyped up and wired and dressed to the nines and was already winking and flirting shamelessly with the celebrities who sprinkled the tables at this, New York's most interesting and trendy restaurant of the era. Is that Mel Gibson? Oh God, it is. "I'll be right back," and she was off. Clooney tried to hide behind a menu.

After a nail-bitingly, profoundly embarrassing, and hideously expensive meal, Fiona was impressively drunk. John decided that he was fighting a losing battle here and ordered after-dinner drinks. "More drinks? Fine with me, Johnny boy," she said, smiling at someone else in the room.

"Listen, Fiona. Tomorrow everyone arrives early for meetings and speeches during the day. I have to be there for all that. You can be with me or not; I don't care. That part's over around 5:00. Then the Metal Moguls Ball starts at 7:00 with a cocktail hour, and then dinner at 8:00. After dinner is when it really heats up. Now, Fiona, there are some guidelines: I want to tell you exactly what I expect as far as Soleil Tangiere is concerned."

Fiona took a swig from her balloon glass of Courvoisier, put one arm over the back of her chair, and belched. "Sure. Shoot." Belch.

Nice, thought John. Real nice.

The Clarendon's lobby is disorienting at first sight. The James Porter-designed hotel was completed in 1985, and its most astonishing feature is its four-hundred-foot-tall internal atrium lobby, with its pod-shaped elevators scaling the inside of the enormous space on their metallic tracks while shuttling passengers quickly up and down the forty-five floors and to the restaurant on the roof.

Kurt Ballas stood in one of the open areas of the lobby and slowly turned in a circle. He had on a Brooks Brothers suit with one of his best ties and felt much better. The idea of his sudden blind date was energizing him.

All right, now am I looking for a butterfly or a basset hound? I guess she'll find me, but how will she know?

"Kurt?"

He turned around. "Cami?"

She stood ten feet away, a hand on one hip, one leg slightly bent. Her thick auburn hair cascaded past her shoulders, its color closely matching her beautifully fitting, knee-length, low-cut Gucci dress. Kurt was stunned. Her deep-hazel, laughing eyes were frankly appraising him.

"You *are* Kurt, aren't you? Kurt Ballas?"

"Cami? I mean yes. Hi!" He smiled broadly and reached out to lightly shake her hand. Her skin was cool. "Wow!" He couldn't help it—she was gorgeous.

He looks pretty good, she thought—nice build, nice smile. Helping you out could turn out to be lots of fun, Soleil. "C'mon, Kurt. What, you've never seen a girl before?"

He laughed. He held his arm out, bent at the elbow. "I'm hungry, Cami. Let's go eat."

She slipped her arm in his. "You're playing my song, Kurt."
They walked out of the lobby onto Broadway.

"Hi."

"Hi."

"Where are you?"

"Kennedy Airport." Max stood at a pay phone with his luggage at his side.

"How was the flight?"

"Long." But not that long, he thought: I had you to think about. "Is everything all right so far?"

"Not bad, but it feels like the bad guys are all around. I'm sure of it."

"Your hotel is full of commodities moguls. As they say in America, 'nuff said.'"

"What's your plan?"

"I'm getting a cab right now. See you in an hour or so."

"OK."

"Soleil?"

"Yes?"

"You know the city. I've only been to New York once, and that was with a bunch of cheap Russians. Pick the nicest place you know for dinner. I'm famished."

She held the receiver in her hand for few seconds and then smiled before carefully replacing it.

So was she.

"What I expect is this." Clooney, his drink on the table in front of him, was a little tipsy himself. "I expect you to be at my side, and we'll watch and wait for Soleil to leave the ball, then you'll follow her from there. Wherever she goes and whatever she does, she'll have to return to the hotel as her last stop. You have her room key, which I was able to obtain from my contacts. That wasn't an easy feat, you know."

Fiona wasn't impressed. She was drunk, but she wasn't stupid. "So I take all the risks, huh?"

"Whipple will be with you as back up. He'll neutralize anyone else she's with."

"Whipple? Send him back to England."

She looked as if she could topple over in the next breeze. Then she said, "How do you know she has the key?"

"She has to have it. This ball is the one place where she can find out what it is if she doesn't know already, and she'd have to show it to someone: the power people will all be there. The key will be on her, or if she brings someone with her, it will be on the person she'll be with. Grandma figured it out, and whatever you may think of the old bag, she's never wrong."

Fiona groaned inside—Grandma again. A waiter came to the table to try to sell another brandy.

"What if I need'ja tomorrow? How can I get a hold'a you?" She was slurring her words.

"I'll be at the meetings all day. You're a big girl—wing it. We'll be leaving for the ball at 7:00. Wear something attractive."

"Huh! You lizard—I always dress right."

He narrowed his eyes. "What I meant was, don't look like a murderous bitch if you can help it."

She hiccupped. "I'll put myself out."

Frank Sinatra was looking over Camille's shoulder. So were Mickey Mantle and Zero Mostel.

Kurt and Camille were at a table by the wall at Sardi's on West Forty-Fourth Street. The restaurant was a landmark, and even though it was a bit of a tourist trap, it was always a fun place to eat. Rows and rows of signed pictures and caricatures of famous Broadway, movie, and sports figures jammed the walls, and the place had a lively New York feel.

This was all new to Camille, but she more than rose to the occasion. She couldn't remember when she had been happy like this. She liked New York, she liked this place, and she was starting to really like this man. They sat across from each other laughing over their food.

Kurt was in high spirits as well, holding forth about his adventures as a commodities broker and how he had gotten to this point from a poor beginning on Chicago's South Side. His ex-wife and her proximity to them was not part of the conversation.

Camille was telling stories about life in Canada and the Midwest. Kurt loved the way Camille had a devil-may-care way of speaking her mind, and her discourse was decorated with a gritty palette of epithets when she felt they were needed—which was often.

When she came to a pause, Kurt said, "This all started with your sister. She seems pretty direct, like you."

"Soleil thinks 'aw shucks' is a curse word. It makes me itch."

Camille sighed inside and continued: "We're all direct, we Tangieres, Kurt. Soleil was always a kind of underdog, a loner, in our family, but she really is the best, the strongest one. You shouldn't be surprised that she called you in the middle of the night to butt into your life. That's her."

"I'm glad that you came to New York with her. This is great." She saw his sincerity and was flattered.

"I hope you can dance, Kurt. What's a ball without dancing?"

"Like a man on fire." He grinned at her and gestured for the waiter.

He asked the waiter if there was good dance club nearby. A moment later Kurt had the names of three.

"Let's go. I need to brush up for tomorrow night."

He left an impressive tip.

Lion's Rock Restaurant was on Seventy-Seventh Street east of Second Avenue, squeezed between two townhouses.

It was beautifully detailed with a small bar and a dining area with lion motifs scattered around. Its main draw was an outdoor courtyard in the back of the restaurant that faced a surprising, two-story-tall rock that somehow was preserved by the building's owners. Lion's Rock was what the geological formation was called in the NYC historical records, hence the name of the restaurant. Some tables were scattered at the base of the rock in a tranquil garden, and a few tables for two were up on some of the rock's low ledges. Soleil and Max sat at one of those.

The night was cool, and the subtle lighting played over the garden and the rock. The sounds of soft conversation and the tinkling of ice floated around them. Sitting in this oasis, it was hard to imagine that one was in the middle of New York City.

They laughed at how the waiters had to carefully negotiate small stone steps in the rough rock while balancing their trays of drinks and food, and Soleil was feeling a little better. Max was attentive but not obsequious, and he realized that he was falling harder and harder for Soleil Tangiere.

And being Russian, he embraced the tragedy of her plight but thought he had a way out. If the stars lined up perfectly, he mused. And if I don't lose Soleil forever.

They spoke about how Russia was changing rapidly, how it was going through the growing pains of a regime change, a people's revolution, and the imminent explosion of a new kind of economy, a new kind of culture.

They spoke about what it was like growing up in Canada and the Rockies.

But finally they got around to the inevitable.

Soleil put down her fork and looked directly into his eyes. "What's your plan?"

Max's mouth tightened.

"Look, Soleil. This is very bad, but there may, just may be, a way out. A lot hinges on what happens tomorrow night. If we can be absolutely sure who the people are who want to get the key, all of them, then we have a chance. You have to trust me."

Soleil had learned not to like that phrase, but she was cornered by circumstance. Her eyes were unreadable.

He continued, "We have to survive this ball and find out who all our enemies really are. That won't solve everything, but it will give us the leverage to get out of this once and for all."

Soleil gave her shoulders a slight shrug.

"And then we need to neutralize the key."

He looks very troubled, she thought. That's probably a good sign: he cares.

"I ask only one favor," he continued. "Where is the key now?" After a thoughtful moment, she reached into her bra with one hand while holding the other hand up as a shield, the same as she had done that night in Zurich. "Here."

"It has to come to the ball with us," he said, glancing at the key in her hand. "If something very bad happens, we may have to give it up, even though that's not part of the plan. We need it there as an insurance policy, just in case."

Her face showed the frustration she felt, but she knew he was right.

"Fine. I'll keep it safe." She slipped it back in her bra and smiled at him. Max was falling faster by the minute. *Does she know what this little bra stunt is doing to me? How could I live with myself if something happened to her?*

"I'll be right by your side all the time," he told her.

She was thoughtful for a moment and looked closely at him. *You're a good man, my kind of a man, but sorry, Max, I have my own plan. If you can't share everything with me, it means that your version of trust is supposed to work only one way. No good. I still have to take care of myself, even if your plan makes the assumption that I can't.*

And I do have my own plan. And I can't tell you anything about it either, because I don't want you hurt. So we are really star-crossed, aren't we?

"No, Max. I don't want you around me every minute." The hand lifting his drink stopped moving for a second. "If someone's coming after me, as long as I know you're near and aware, I think I should try to circulate alone. Let the sharks feel secure in their power. They'll be more likely to make a mistake. I can take care of myself." She threw him a harsh look. "And if you can't tell me all of your plan, then I can keep a few things under my own hat as well." She lifted her chin a fraction, and her eyes glowed in the low light.

"You're sure you're not Russian?" he said.

"Not a chance, *Comrade Stepanov.*"

His heart did a backflip.

"Dessert?" It was the waiter. "Cappuccino?"

They ordered some coffee and spoke no more of the ball. Tomorrow would take care of itself.

10

THE METAL MOGULS BALL

Soleil sat on the edge of the bed and stared out the window. It was 6:30 a.m., and she watched the red edge of the sun peek over the borough of Queens. She thought about the Gutthelfs. Izzy's probably going to *shul* in a little while, she thought idly. I have to visit them before I leave New York. *If* I leave New York.

A shudder ran through her. A simple thought like that seemed oddly dangerous and unconnected to reality. She needed to clear her head. I have to shop for a dress for tonight. That chore should take my mind off things for a while.

She threw on a pair of jeans and a thick, cable-knit sweater and left the suite. She made sure the door was locked and then walked to the railing across the hall with its tremendous view down into the cavernous atrium. From this height, the metal and glass lobby fountain in the shape of a huge, twenty-foot-high ball looked like a toy. The elevator was also disconcerting—it felt as if she were a mile above the lobby floor when she stepped into the glass-walled pod.

She was able to buy a cup of coffee in the lobby, and she wandered out onto Times Square. At this early hour, only a few stray hookers and grifters were still up and about. The raunchy storefronts and general messiness of Times Square was depressing. She ducked back into the Clarendon.

On a whim, she walked to a house phone and dialed Max's room.

"Uhnn."

"Hi. It's me."

"Uhn, oh, good morning, *devochka*." Max liked the idea of waking up to her voice.

Soleil let the endearment pass. "Are you busy?"

"If you call snoring work, very."

"Oh, sorry, you can go back to sleep."

"No. Please, come on up."

"Coffee? Milk and sugar? I'll bring some up."

"I'm Russian, remember? No milk, lots of sugar. No coffee. Make it tea, please."

"Try to be awake when I get there." She hung up.

He let her into the room. He had made a mad dash for the bathroom after he had hung up the phone and was now in the process of tucking his shirt in.

A wry smile. "You didn't have to dress, Max. I had no designs on you."

"We hardly know each other," he replied. "Is that good or bad?"

They sat on the couch with their cups and looked out over the city.

"When this is over, are you going back to Russia?" It was an innocent little fishing question, but it brought on a strange reaction. Max's face seemed to get a little flushed, and he said, "Eventually, yes, but for just a short time." *Should I tell her that if somehow we both get out of this unscathed, I will return as soon as possible? That nothing would hold me back from returning to her?*

There was a minute or two of silence. Finally Soleil said, "Well, I'll be getting ready for the ball later in the day. I need to get something to wear unless you *really* want me to wow the crowd. I hope you brought your tux."

"I did. Don't laugh when you see me in it. The last time I wore it, they tried to ship me to the Moscow Zoo to live with the apes."

In spite of his humor, Soleil sensed a small undercurrent of tension. She told him she had much to do and had to get to doing it. Then she levered herself off the couch, and he jumped up to join her. She closed the final two feet between them and threw her arms around his neck. Her face was an inch from his.

"Be careful, Max. I need you around." The kiss was deep, and they both melted into it. *Can I trust him? Oh God, let me trust him and let him trust me. And help us both through the night.*

Finally they separated. Max's dark eyes glittered, and he started to say something but then changed his mind. Then he said, "Until tonight," and they both walked to the door.

"Until tonight," she said.

The door closed behind her.

The International Metals and Commodities Forum kicked off at 10:00 a.m. The highlight of the five-day convention was the gala, known far and wide as the Metal Moguls Ball, and the cocktail party would start at 7:00 p.m. that night in the huge restaurant on the roof of the hotel, which had been reserved in its entirety for the event.

At 1:00 p.m. there was a welcoming address by a famous New York City builder-contractor well known for his bravado, self-promotion, and strange, windswept haircut.

"This is great," he blasted from the mike in front of hundreds of guests in the largest meeting hall in the Clarendon. "All the people here are great, terrific people. We love this event. My wife Avona says the ball is her favorite in the world. And she's great. Terrific."

Fiona Dyche sat near the front of the audience and wondered if she could finagle a little time with this man later on. Now here's someone with *real* money, and that Lithuanian wife or whatever she is: no problem.

It never occurred to Fiona that her grip on reality was slipping off the edge.

John Clooney was outside the meeting hall in conversation with a tall, handsome man in an expensive dark-blue suit and red tie.

Manny Rauch was a notorious commodities trader who had been dealing with shadowy governments for years, many times in contravention of US laws. He also had large, secret deals with the Soviets and now was thrilled that the regime had begun to implode so he could expand his commodities empire. John Clooney worshipped him. The two were just putting the final touches on a verbal proposal for CM to buy and sell platinum through Rauch in Afghanistan.

"Have your lawyers contact mine next week. Good-bye." Rauch turned to leave.

"One more thing, Mr. Rauch—or may I call you Manny?"

"No."

"One more thing. There is a small company called Tangiere International that has gotten tangled up with Rio Plata in a thoroughly illegal Col Tan deal in the Ivory Coast. The owner, a young woman named Soleil Tangiere, is here now at this event but will soon certainly be arrested on criminal charges. Her company will be up for grabs. When she is neutralized, I can arrange for M. Rauch + Company to waltz in for next to nothing and take it over. As an added bonus, Tangiere is located in Zurich, too," John said, referring to the location of Rauch's Swiss shell corporation.

Rauch looked down at this weasel and thought, why not? At some point, you little nothing, I'll own your company as well. Here, I'll throw you a bone for the sport of it:

"Fine. Contact me after the convention." He turned and walked away.

"Will I see you tonight?" Clooney called childishly after him.

"No. I'm only here on business," Rauch said over his shoulder. "Good-bye."

John Clooney talking to Manny Rauch—he felt stimulated. A little too stimulated.

It never occurred to him that, in concert with his fiancée, his sanity was beginning to seriously erode.

Max Stepanov was in his suite on the thirty-eighth floor. The man with him was uneasy and said so.

"You are crazy," he finally said to Max.

"You owe me. You said so yourself. You are a man of your word, aren't you?"

The man looked at the floor for a moment.

"Let me get this straight. On your signal we move in and have the girl arrested. Why wait for your signal? Why not just go to her room now, knock on the door, and do it? It would save everyone a lot of trouble."

Max scowled at the man. "I need to know everything and everyone involved in this mess. Think carefully—I'm not really asking that much."

"Yes, you are. You are asking more than much." He paused. He moved to the window, sighed, and then turned to face Max. He said, "How does the song go: What's love doing with it?"

"It's 'What's Love Got To Do With It.'"

The man smiled inside. How interesting. How serendipitous this little affair has become. They spoke about details for the next few minutes.

The man sighed. He liked Max, and Max would be in debt to him for the rest of his life if he did this for him. It was a no-brainer.

"We'll be there." He walked out of the suite.

Damn it, thought Max. Damn everything.

I'm sorry, Soleil. God, am I sorry.

It's not exactly a hangover, but it's a pretty good impression of one, she thought. Camille stood before the bathroom mirror in a hotel robe and peered at herself through eyes that were slits. Oh, man. The wages of sin, I guess. Nah, the wages of fun—last night was the most fun I've had in I don't know how long. Kurt is something else.

She had snuck into the hotel suite at 3:30 in the morning, treading carefully as to not wake Soleil in her room. If Kurt Ballas had his way, she would have woken up in his hotel room at the Hilton today, but for all her bravado, Camille wasn't that way. She knew how to handle men. And she really liked Kurt. A little waiting could only help.

Now it was around noon, and the phone rang. Camille walked into a bedroom and picked it up.

"Hello."

"Up so early? I heard you coming in at 3:30. You're losing your touch." Soleil's voice couldn't conceal an undercurrent of anxiety.

"Where are you?"

"I just found a dress for tonight. Want to have a late lunch?"

"I'm meeting Kurt. Do you want to tag along, want to meet him?"

"No, have fun. I'm good."

Her sister sounded exhausted. "Can I do anything for you, Soleil?"

"No thanks. I'll see you later."

Camille hung up. I better keep an eye on Soleil tonight. I wonder where she found a dress?

As usual, Winston Whipple had followed orders to a *T*. He had tailed the girl from the hotel and cleverly concealed himself as she went into a few clothing stores. He was disappointed when she kept leaving the stores empty handed.

Having recognized Whipple from the Zurich train station and after studying his bumbling attempt at surveillance through one of the store windows, Soleil figured she could kill two birds with one stone.

She window-shopped a little more and then went into Neiman Marcus at Broadway and Forty-First Street. To his chagrin, Whipple discovered there was more than one entrance to the haute couture fashion bazaar that was Neiman's. *Drat, I have to go inside and try to remain inconspicuous.* He suddenly felt extremely nervous. He checked his sunglasses and adjusted his hat. *This is man's work,* he kept reminding himself. Then he went into the store.

Arlene Margolies was frustrated. With both kids in college now, she had ample time to finally shop for herself, and her husband had made sure that her credit cards were good all over the city, for any amount.

It wasn't that Neiman's didn't have one of the most extensive and au courant selections in the country. It was the fact that nothing was made for her size. *These damn European designers didn't know what they were doing. What, is everyone in France and Italy anorectic?*

She stood in a small stall in the fitting room with a dozen outfits spread around her, on a chair, on the floor, and tried in vain to lever yet another YSL creation onto her zaftig frame. That was when she heard a light knock on the thin dividing wall.

"Excuse me," came a small voice. Arlene carefully opened the saloon-style louvered door and peeked out. A very attractive young woman in jeans and a sweater stood with a shiny evening dress over one arm. "Sorry to bother you."

After abandoning his post in the cosmetic department, Whipple worked his way around to a better view of the fitting room. When is the girl going to come out? How the hell long does it take to try on a stupid dress? I'm vastly unappreciated by the bastard Mr. Clooney. Immediately upon my return, a raise it will have to be for me, or I'm seeking other employment. Ahh, to hell with Mr. Clooney. He has absolutely no class. Now this Soleil Tangiere girl—she seems to have a lot of class. And she's so beautiful.

But something was wrong. Women were coming and going out of that fitting room, but the Tangiere woman was nowhere to be seen. Could she have made me? Nah, impossible. Or is it? Is there another way out of there? Oh, crap, Mr. Clooney will be apoplectic. OK, Winston, old stick, you'd better check this out, he said to himself.

The large man waited until it seemed no one was around, and then he literally tiptoed into the fitting room. He saw the row of stalls, all with open doors except the one second from the end. A pair of bare feet and assorted clothing were visible below the door.

He crouched down on the floor on all fours and tried to get a better view.

Suddenly the door swung open and smashed Winston in the head, and a heavyset woman with a fierce look on her face came charging out.

"Pervert!" she screamed. "Help! A molesting pervert! Someone call security!"

Whipple scrambled to get off the floor, but at that moment two women rushed into the fitting room. They began screaming and kicking at him with their very pointy Ferragamos. Arlene joined in. He awkwardly gained his footing and sprinted out into the store, only to collide full force with a young woman handing out sample bottles of perfume. Man, woman, and a hundred bottles of L'Air du Temps skidded along the aisle in a whirlwind of breaking glass and a cloud of heavy scent, the intensity of which was increasing by the second. That was when a beefy security guard showed up.

Back in Arlene Margolies's fitting room stall, Soleil stepped carefully down from the chair she was standing on, thanked the woman sincerely, and walked calmly out into the store, being careful to steer clear of the chaos taking place down the center aisle.

She paid for the dress, which had fit her perfectly right off the rack, and walked out onto Forty-First Street.

Kurt Ballas had just gotten off an elevator and was heading across the Clarendon lobby when a thin man in a gray pinstripe suit approached and buttonholed him.

"Excuse me, Mr. Ballas? Mr. Kurt Ballas?"

"That's me."

"We have spoken on the phone. Edward Sierra from Rio Plata Mining."

"Edward, how are—"

Sierra had a cold look in his eyes. "We need to discuss something."

Kurt was caught up short.

"The deal that my company did through Tangiere International," Sierra said.

"What about it? It was a good deal, wasn't it?"

"I'm not so sure. I just came from a conversation with John Clooney of Carrington Metals. He tells me that CM has been in contact with government officials in the Ivory Coast, and they never authorized the deal." His face was dark.

"What are you talking about? I handled the due diligence on that deal myself for Tangiere. It was a clean deal." He looked at Sierra carefully. "And I think you know that."

Sierra hesitated for a second. "Look, Ballas, this is just what I heard. And not only from Clooney—it seems like this rumor is spreading all over this convention. Rio Plata will not stand for this kind of negative publicity, especially where it concerns Third World countries and regimes." He sniffed. "Someone could easily get themselves arrested for this kind of behavior."

Kurt stepped toward him and spoke forcefully.

"First of all, I'll bet the farm that it was Clooney who *started* this dangerous gossip. Second, any deal with my company or with Tangiere International is strictly confidential, and the odds of anyone other than CM taking the risk of involving themselves in something like this is remote. And finally, this is just the kind of scandalous rumor that unfortunately is part and parcel of the business. It gives us all an undeserved bad name, and you know that as well as I. Hell, not less than a half hour ago, I saw John Clooney upstairs whispering to Manny Rauch. Probably about this latest lie. I suggest Rio Plata check the facts for itself, and I suggest you do the same."

Sierra cooled down rapidly. "All right, I apologize. We have done business with Clooney and Smythe in the past, and it's never, ever been 100 percent straight. I'm sure Ballas Trading is on the level, as is Tangiere." He paused to gauge Kurt's demeanor. "For some reason, I feel this Clooney will not change his ways. He makes us all look like thieves."

"You have nothing to worry about, Edward," said Kurt reasonably. "There's no way I'm going to bend over while someone drags my company name through the mud. And that applies to Tangiere International as well." Sierra looked at him strangely. "One day Clooney will get his."

I'll make sure of it, he thought as he headed for the lobby door.

Kurt met Camille at the Carnegie Deli at Fifty-Fifth Street and Seventh Avenue. Sitting at a small table in the middle of the yelling, laughing, cursing activity that characterized the famous establishment, they had to raise their voices to hear each other.

"Where's your sister?" Kurt yelled over his pastrami sandwich. "I thought I would have had a chance to meet her by now."

Camille was midchew on her turkey club. Finally she managed, "Oh, you'll meet her tonight at the ball. Don't worry about that." Changing the conversation, she said, "That was fun last night, Kurt."

Kurt smiled. They had danced at two different clubs and had closed the second one down. He had felt as if he were twenty again. *Camille is something else. I won't let her go.*

"Where to after tonight? How long will you be in New York?" he asked.

She thought for a moment. "I'm probably going to go back home tomorrow, or maybe Monday." Anticipating his next question, she said, "Saint Cloud. Minnesota."

"What do you do there?"

"Oh, I've done it all, and don't take that in the wrong way! At the moment I'm on a kind of sabbatical." She didn't want to tell him that she was on the way to whipping her old, bad habits. *I can hardly believe how well it's been going in that regard. I'm becoming a new me.*

Kurt was saying, "You should be a dance instructor. Do you want to come to Chicago?"

"Do you want to come to Saint Cloud?"

"Damn right I do."

Camille looked at him. *This is the kind of man I should have hooked up with to begin with. Not that crappy crowd from Bear Hair, Quebec, and Phony Falls, Minnesota, who seem to spend their time marching in and out of correctional institutions. But this has to happen the right way, not the convenient way. After all: after just one date? I'm becoming as bad as Soleil. It must be genetic or something.*

"Kurt, I think we had better wait for that divorce of yours to come through."

He suddenly felt cornered, and she knew he did.

"I told you: we Tangieres are direct, and I'm being direct with you. I think you are the best man I've met in a long time. But I don't think we should rush anything as long as you're still legally married. It's not good for anyone."

Kurt hated the old-fashioned and seemingly unassailable logic. After a minute, "You're something else, Camille. And you're right. Let's have a good time tonight. We'll have all the time in the world to sort things out after that."

They looked at each other and took big, aggressive bites of their sandwiches.

"I'll pick you up at 7:30."

"No, I'm going to pass on the dinner."

"If that's what you want."

"That's what I want," said Soleil Tangiere.

"All right, I'll have dinner with the crowd and then come down to get you."

"No, Max. I'll just be there at 9:00." There's stress in her voice, Max thought.

She started to hang up the phone.

"Soleil?"

"Yes?"

Max wanted to tell her then and there but knew he couldn't. He wanted to tell her that somehow, in some way, the stars had placed them together, and now the only way to make it work forever was to take it down a road that most likely held pain and what could be looked at as a kind of betrayal. He wanted to tell her that there was a light at the end of the tunnel. But the way to that light could be too difficult and might shred her trust in him forever. Or worse.

So he just said: "See you at the ball."

At 6:45 the band started warming up. They were one of the hottest groups in New York, a lot of brass and a lot of sass—rock, salsa, jive, disco—whatever you want, man, we're it. They set up against one of the walls of the restaurant, the city glittering behind them through huge floor-to-ceiling windows.

The long, extravagantly stocked bar was across the restaurant from the band, and large round tables, which seated ten or twelve, had been jockeyed and placed so a dance floor could dominate the center of the room. Waiters, busboys, and managers were going about their business. Guests started dribbling in. Out in the hall, the people from TV, the journalists, and a few paparazzi were gearing up for the ball. They crowded the hallway and gawked over the railing that faced the atrium. Someone dropped a camera lens cap over the railing by accident. It took a long time for it to land down in the lobby.

In his hotel suite a few blocks uptown, John Clooney was straightening his bow tie. His tuxedo was expensive, but it didn't fit very well, and looking in the mirror on the wall of the suite, he made a mental note to complain to his bespoke and, to him, violently overpaid tailor in Bond Street. That his body had gone to seed of late and his posture had deteriorated never occurred to him to be part of the problem. At least his shoes looked good.

And where was Whipple? He was supposed to have called in hours ago. Now I don't know where the Tangiere girl has been, who she's been with, nothing. That big lummox. He's fired when we get back to London. No, he's fired now.

In the bathroom, Fiona was taking her time in front of the full-length mirror. Her gown was a black Versace creation with a neckline that plunged almost to her waist. There were some wings and folds that made no sense on the otherwise daring garment, but Fiona found them to be useful. After all, this was a working event. Must come prepared and all that. She popped a few uppers and washed them down with a glass of water.

"Might as well make yourself comfortable, Johnny," she yelled through the closed bathroom door. Clooney paced for another minute and then sat down to wait. He didn't know what to expect. That was why beneath his left pant leg, strapped under his sock, was his small-caliber Sig Sauer automatic.

"Let's go, Fiona," he said to no one.

Kurt got in the elevator on his floor at the Hilton and then realized he had made the one mistake he had been trying to avoid all this time. Before he could react, the door closed, and he saw that his fellow passenger was Amanda, dressed to kill and arm-in-arm with a man.

"Oh, hey, Kurt! This is great. We can walk to the ball with you!" She smiled broadly.

Kurt cringed inside and turned to Amanda's date.

Josh Fowler was the CEO of J. Fowler Metals, a mid-size mining consortium famous for dirty deals, illegal kickbacks, and rapacious business practices that exploited the people in the poor countries in which most of those deals took place.

He was a head shorter than Kurt, with slicked-back, thinning black hair, an outrageous hawk nose, and a small chin. His eyes held every kind of sinister duplicity there was, and there was an air of violence around him. His reputation, or more accurately his notoriety as a nasty piece of work, was not only legendary—as bad as it was, those who knew him agreed that the reality was even worse. Good pick, Amanda, thought Kurt.

"Good to meet you, Ballas." The voice was surprisingly high pitched. "Amanda said you would be here. Didn't we meet before?"

"Yeah, at this same event in Paris last year." He glanced at Amanda. "Remember, Amanda?"

She ignored the remark. Fowler went on: "I heard you and Rio Plata got into a mess in the Ivory Coast. You should have called me first. I know how to set up real deals with the right people." He winked. Kurt cringed. The only mess that I'm aware of is my wife's choice of friends, he said to himself. The elevator doors opened.

"See you at the ball, Kurt," Amanda said over her shoulder as she left the elevator on Fowler's arm.

Kurt hung back until they were out of the lobby. He wanted to be as distant from that pair as possible. Forever, if I'm lucky.

"Well, Fowler, how's business?"

The pod-shaped elevator in the Clarendon was packed with people, and Clooney was pushed up against Josh Fowler for the quick ride up to the forty-fifth floor. Fiona and Amanda were mashed together, and neither was very happy. No introductions were made, and the awkwardness and discomfort was heavy.

"Great, Clooney," Fowler said to John's chin. "In fact, so good of late, I was thinking of buying your company." The ears of a few men in the elevator suddenly perked up.

"What a coincidence, Josh. I was eyeing yours, but it's too small to really make a dent." The sophomoric banter went on for a few more seconds, and then the doors opened.

The people poured out and had to produce their invitations at the restaurant door. TV and other media people were milling about. Fiona went into overdrive, striking poses and flashing looks that made no sense—no one knew who she was, and no one seemed to care.

Whipple slid up to Clooney and Fiona as they were approaching the restaurant. He had a bad suit on, and Clooney gestured for him to follow and quickly. In a nearby alcove down the hall, Clooney let it fly.

"Where were you? Where was the Tangiere woman today?" A look of fury on his face.

"Neiman Marcus. Well, in the morning at least." Whipple looked everywhere but at Clooney.

"What about the afternoon?" Clooney watched as Whipple fidgeted. "You lost her, didn't you? Idiot." He let his face pour his anger all over Whipple. Sniff, sniff: What's the dope wearing, perfume? Echhh. Then: "Find a way to get back to England, or wherever the hell you want to go. You're not working for me anymore!" He turned his back on Whipple and went to find Fiona. When he finally did, he took her by the arm and pulled her into the restaurant.

Whipple stood there for a full minute. Then he turned and walked down the hall until he found a sofa. He sat down to figure all this out.

"Who is it?" she said to the knock.

"Kurt Ballas."

Soleil opened the door. "Hi, Kurt."

"Soleil?"

It was the first time he had ever seen her. She was in her jeans and sweater and bare feet. He towered over her by a good six inches. She shook his outstretched hand and then stood on tiptoe to give him a quick hug. "Sorry about the mess with the invitation and meeting you and all. I apologize."

"No, it's fine, Soleil; it all worked out. I never really formally invited you to the ball, and I wound up getting to meet your sister. Now I almost feel as if I'm becoming a member of the family." He smiled.

Soleil laughed. "One thing you *don't* want is to be a member of this family, Kurt."

From one of the bedrooms: "Shut up, Soleil. And keep your grubby mitts off Kurt. He's got a little class, in case you didn't catch it."

Kurt and Soleil smiled.

"My offer still stands, Soleil. I'd like to teach you about the commodities business." He saw a look on her face.

"I appreciate it, Kurt, and I'd like to take you up on it. But it may be a long time until I'm able to get to Chicago. Events have intervened. After this party I'll be heading back to Europe." I think.

Camille came out of the bedroom wearing a daring, black, low-cut gown that complemented her figure. A faux-emerald cuff bracelet flashed on her wrist and almost matched her hazel eyes. Her stiletto-heeled shoes gleamed. Kurt forgot to breathe for a second. Wow.

He's seems nice, thought Soleil, and I'm glad this is happening. It wouldn't have worked, he and I—I can see that right away. And now, thank God, there's Max. But there are problems there too, she suddenly thought bitterly. And maybe big ones.

"You look terrific, Cami." Kurt meant it as Camille came to him for a kiss on the cheek. Then, "Ready?"

"See you later, Soleil," Camille said on the way out with a surreptitious wink. "Better get dressed."

Soleil closed the door behind them, walked to where she had placed her purse, and took out a small sewing kit.

The bar was filling up fast with the movers and shakers of the metals and commodities industries and their wives and girlfriends. It was a completely male-dominated business in which only one or two women in the world had positions of power. Direct power, that is.

Amanda and Fowler were standing having drinks in a clot of people by one of the windows when there was an obvious flurry in the crowd. Suddenly the actor Brock Whalers was standing in the center of the group in a maroon tuxedo jacket. Whalers was basking in the afterglow of his latest successful blockbuster, *Hit Hard*, a story about a cop who rescues a building full of people from a ruthless terrorist. Now he was in New York scouting around for a location for the sequel, *Hit Harder*. "This building is awesome. It has amazing possibilities," he said.

And *he* has amazing possibilities, thought Fiona, who had rushed over. Whalers was married to another Hollywood star, but she was nowhere in sight, and...

Suddenly she felt Clooney's hand pulling her away. She looked at him, and his face scared her just a bit.

"Enough, damn it, Fiona! Get me the key, and then I don't give a damn what you do! Just get this done!" For once Fiona demurred. John was stone cold furious, and well, it kind of turns me on, she said wonderingly to herself.

Max came into the restaurant and decided to just walk around for a little while. He was in a black mood and couldn't wait to see Soleil. He had a Russian conversation with himself for the hundredth time: Am I doing the right thing? Is there any other way? He couldn't find answers in himself.

His tuxedo was perfect—it slimmed down his muscular physique, and his thick black hair was freshly barbered. Women stole glances as he walked by. One stopped to speak with him.

"And what famous consortium are you the leader of?" Max noticed the woman's pupils were hugely dilated in her mahogany eyes.

"I'm in the processed zinc business," he said, and the bland, boring answer accomplished its purpose.

Fiona mouthed a silent "Oh" and walked away.

From a few yards away, Clooney watched the interchange. The man Fiona was just talking to looked familiar. He walked up to Max.

"John Clooney. Do we know each other?"

Max remembered with crystal clarity the day Clooney and Smythe were in the Cenkhran offices. They had hustled past Max and the other managers with barely a glance. He didn't like Clooney then, and he hated him now. Might as well play the game.

"If you've ever been to Latvia, we may have met. Max Smirnoff, Chermasov Metals," he lied.

Clooney shook his hand and thought: they're inviting anyone to these events nowadays. But the face haunted him. They spoke for a moment about nothing, and then Clooney excused himself. Max looked at him as he walked away. So far he doesn't remember me.

But he's thinking about it.

Kurt ordered Camille a glass of champagne at the bar and a bourbon neat for himself. He waved to a few people he knew from the business and was pleased with the many admiring looks that shot toward him and his beautiful companion.

Camille was enjoying every second and wondering if the people here took all this for granted. Is this what the rich and powerful are up to all the time? How hard would it be to get used to this? Now that's a dumb question, she admonished herself.

"Well, well, hello again. I haven't seen you since our hotel." The voice came from behind Kurt, but he was ready for it. He knew that Amanda would do what she could to embarrass him, and he had given Camille a little warning.

"I can't stop her from coming to the ball," he had told Camille in the elevator on the way up. "And I can't predict how she will act. If you don't want to come to the ball with me, you can back out now."

Camille had already put a few brakes on the relationship at lunch. A snotty, soon-to-be-ex-wife? Are you kidding, Kurt? I eat those kinds of sardines for breakfast.

"Oh, Kurt," she said sweetly. "Don't worry. Everything will be fine. We probably won't even see her." The elevator doors opened, Kurt presented their invitations at the door, and they walked in.

"No, not since this afternoon at our hotel," Amanda repeated, emphasizing "our" to underscore a possible trysting place for her and Kurt that didn't exist in the real world. She frankly stared at Camille.

Normally, after knowing a man for such a short period of time, Camille wouldn't care or even bother to respond, but she saw there might very well be a future with Kurt, and now she was able to get a look at a part of his past. And Camille also had to let everyone know who she was without leaving any doubts—it was her nature.

Men were so stupid when it came to women, she said to herself. They made the biggest mistakes. Men believed everything women said, took it as gospel, and then let their lives be run by girls who normally couldn't run their own. Of course, women were just as dumb about men.

Amanda Ballas was tall and slim, but her face was hard and the China-blue eyes beneath the red hair had a cast of only moderate intelligence. In a moment Camille figured out the whole tired story: After the novelty of being married to a good catch with financial wherewithal wore off, Amanda had turned bored and started grasping. When Kurt began wondering why he was still with her, she closed his exit door by giving him two children, one after the other—the oldest trick in the book. Living in a marriage based on guilt and the fear of a child-damaging separation was a major mistake. Now Camille hoped he had the grit to go through with the divorce.

If he doesn't, we're finished before we're out of the gate.

Since Kurt stood there without offering a response, Amanda had to break the silence again. To Camille she said, "I'm Amanda Ballas, Kurt's *wife*," and held out a gloved hand.

Camille shook it. "I'm Camille Weston, Kurt's *date*," and then immediately she turned to Fowler and asked with interest, "Is this your date?" She smiled lightly at Fowler, holding her outstretched hand out, palm down.

As sleazy as Fowler was, he appreciated her gesture that demanded he touch her palm and kiss the back of her hand. "Josh Fowler," he said as he did just that without taking his eyes off Camille's.

Nonplussed, Amanda looked from Camille to Kurt and pressed on: "Did you and Kurt just meet?"

Camille turned to her: "Yes, I picked him up on Forty-Second Street an hour ago, while my pimp was out getting coffee. Kurt said he wanted to relive the way he met you just one last time." Sweet smile. "For old time's sake."

Fowler nearly gagged on a suppressed laugh, and Kurt looked for a place to hide. Amanda didn't have the wit to respond in kind, so she smiled a dagger or two and led the coughing Fowler away.

"Cute." Kurt said to Camille, watching their backs.

"What?" She looked at him with a raised eyebrow. "Isn't that how they solve problems in Chicago?"

By 8:00 p.m. the room was almost filled. The excitement of being at the event, mixed with a torrent of alcohol, was infectious. The band was playing soft background riffs. When dinner was over around nine o'clock, the serious partying would begin. But for now the avalanche of conversations just about drowned out the music. Some movie celebrities made brief appearances to the delight of many guests and the photographers. The sky outside the windows was dark, and the galaxy of lights that was New York glittered.

At the table with John Clooney and Fiona sat five more couples, all the men being business honchos from the commodities world. None of them knew John personally, so conversation was relatively polite and centered on business and politics. Fiona fidgeted and drank. She kept looking around the room. Where's the Tangiere bitch? Let's get started here.

I don't want to pass out from boredom. She jabbed an elbow into John's side. When he looked at her quizzically, she said, "Just because," and went back to her seviche.

Camille liked the seviche—she had never eaten it before. Hell, I never even heard of it before. She glanced at Kurt and was delighted that he was having a grand old time. After the little dustup with his wife, he had led Camille over to a table near the band, and they immediately took it over: Kurt became the table's natural storyteller and joker—the perfect complement to Camille's spicy banter, and soon the other five couples at the table were laughing and yelling, and everyone felt that this was table to be at. Even Brock Whaler and his wife stopped by for a minute to see if they were missing anything.

Amanda and Josh Fowler sat at a table close to the door. One of the couples at the table was Edward Sierra and his wife. The chair next to Edward was empty, and on the other side of it was a handsome man with dark hair and a faint Russian accent who introduced himself as Max. Max listened carefully as a conversation got started between Edward and Josh Fowler. They were discussing doing platinum and palladium business in sub-Saharan countries, and to pass away the long minutes, Max was taking mental notes.

But most of the time he had his eyes on the door.

By 9:15 dinner was just about done, and couples were up and moving on the dance floor. The band was terrific, and whether it was a slow dance or rock or retro disco, everyone wanted to move, to celebrate their success, to show off and impress their sexy companions, or just have fun in the greatest city in the world.

Max sat at the table and watched the dancers.

Then, for what seemed like the hundredth time, he glanced toward the door, and he felt his heart skip a beat.

Soleil Tangiere stood there in a pool of light.

Her silvery platinum gown fell perfectly on her trim, modest figure. It was composed of a myriad of tiny seed pearls and sequins—the light softly exploded off her gown and her matching stiletto heels in diamond flashes.

The front of the dress was modestly cut, but the back was a large open *V* from the shoulders on down. Just under the shoulder blades, a thin line of the gown's glittering material traversed her naked back. Hanging at the center of that line, a slim cascade of flashing crystal rondelles tumbled almost to the base of her spine. Long, pointed sleeves hugged her arms and ended in flares below her wrists.

Max was transfixed—he could hardly move. A hundred heads turned to see the woman in the spotlight at the door. Her straight blond hair fell past her shoulders on either side of her perfectly symmetrical face. A few errant chin-length strands hung in front of her calm sapphire-blue eyes.

Mid-dance Camille saw Kurt's head turn suddenly toward the door, and she knew what had happened without looking. She sighed. Soleil must have finally shown up, she thought.

And Fiona Dyche, in John Clooney's arms, came to a sudden stop on the dance floor, nearly causing them both to slam into another couple. Clooney's eyes followed her gaze. He instantly saw the slim woman in the shimmering gown standing in the doorway. Well, hello Soleil—we meet again, he thought. Oh man, is she gorgeous.

Fiona didn't have to read his mind: he had unconsciously whispered that last little bit out loud, and her jealousy turned to hatred. She pulled Clooney violently to her until her mouth was almost in his ear.

"I'm doing this for us, John, and I expect my life will vastly improve starting tonight. You better not be jerking my chain!"

Clooney pushed her from him. Another couple dancing near them moved away.

"Get me the key." He grinned sadistically as he stared across the room at Soleil. He remembered the last time he had seen her. It was quite a different circumstance. The grin got wider.

"The key, Fiona. She has it here with her in New York. It may even be in this room. Just do that one thing and then let her go, and all your dreams will come true."

I'll let her go all right—straight to hell, Fiona thought wildly, but her face remained inscrutable, if not a bit overly made up. I won't allow Soleil Tangiere to live on the same planet with me, and that's my *own* law of nature. When are all these stupid people going to stop staring at *her?*

Max was suddenly by Soleil's side. She looked at him, and he gave her a quick, light kiss on the lips. "I'm glad to see you. You're beautiful," he said softly.

Her face was impassive, clear. She leaned into him and whispered in his ear, "Whatever happens tonight, let's remember to forgive each other."

What? What did she mean by that? The soft words shook him visibly, but he held her arm and began to guide her to the table.

Suddenly, across the room, she saw someone, stopped short, and everything—Max, the ball, everything—went away...

She could barely see three feet in front of her. All had gone quiet, a silent lull in the midst of the hurricane caused by the mine cave-in. Then men were yelling, and there was the rumbling sound of muffled explosions. Smoke laden with a heavy brown dust swirled around Soleil's head, around her eyes.

Out of the clouds a figure suddenly loomed—a man in tan overalls. The letters MMSO were stitched in thick black letters on one of the pockets.

"What's happening?" Soleil yelled.

The figure stopped to look at her. Her heart skipped a beat when she saw a weird grimace on his face—wild and unreadable. It almost looked like a grin—a devil's grin. He came within a foot or two of her, and then he was lost in the cloud of dust and soot...

And there, forty-five stories above Times Square, in the midst of the Metal Moguls Ball, she saw that face for the second time in her life. The overalls melted away, and the man was wearing a tuxedo now, and he was dancing with the woman from behind the wheel of the dark Mercedes. Soleil's spine stiffened.

"Max," she said finally while still looking across the room. "Who's that man dancing with the woman with the straight black hair?" Her heart already knew the answer.

Max had been looking at her, knew this moment was unavoidable, and then he followed her gaze. In a moment he said, "That's John Clooney. I think the woman is his girl-friend or fiancée." He saw Soleil's face turn to stone.

That man is the reason I'm here. *He's* the reason I came to New York, because otherwise he had himself set up to be safe and protected behind his guarded doors at his precious company in London where I would never be able to get at him. That grimace, that grin—I know where I saw it now—it was *him* at the mine; it was also the grin on Smythe's face, his father's face, a minute before he was fricasseed in the Audi at the airport. This man is the "son" he said would come after me. And now that I've seen his face, now that I know beyond a shadow of a doubt it was he who set those explosives, that it was he who killed my father along with six other innocent people, now Max my love, I have to do what no one else will do.

She looked at Max. "Buy me a drink," and they changed course toward the bar.

"I hate you," said Camille, looking at Soleil's gown appraisingly.

"Cut it out. You look better than I do, and you're smarter than me to boot."

Camille was still laughing inside at the reaction Soleil had gotten when she entered the room. She had seen this before when Soleil was younger. It comes with being a Tangiere girl, she said reasonably to herself.

She and Kurt were standing near the bar, and Soleil had a hand up against Max's arm. He was carefully watching the crowd. At first Soleil thought he was just keeping track of Clooney, but there was something else. It troubled her, but she pushed it to the back of her mind.

She pulled Camille aside to speak privately. "I love you. I got you here, I even got you Kurt Ballas and everything that goes along with that. Now I need you to do something."

Camille looked at her and closed one eye slightly.

"I'm not leaving," she said to Soleil, anticipating the request.

"I want you to go home tonight. Or go with Kurt to Chicago. You have to get out of New York."

"No."

"Darn it, Cami! I told you that things were eventually bound to heat up, and tonight they will. For my sake, please, go." She threw Camille a hard look.

"'Darn it?' Tsk, tsk, your language is going all to hell, little sister." She grinned. Then she leaned into her until their foreheads almost touched.

"I'm not leaving. And Soleil," she whispered, "I've been holding something back."

"What?" Soleil suddenly felt a chill.

"I know you killed Dorsey."

Soleil stared at the hazel eyes a few inches in front of her. Her face turned to stone.

After a moment Camille went on: "Jake overheard us the first time you called after Dad was killed. He heard me say Dorsey's name and then ask what you had to do with it. You never said you did and never said anything about it after that. But you know Jake—he collects odd bits of information." She paused.

"Around a year after that call, while doing a short stretch in work camp, Jake met a second-story man who was in for burglary, and he told Jake he knew that Henderson didn't kill Dorsey. This guy said he was casing the cop's neighborhood that day from across the street at the edge of the woods, and he saw a young blond girl going around the side of Dorsey's house with a compound bow and arrows strapped to the back of her navy parka. Curious about it, he hung around and then heard gunshots and saw her leave in a pickup. That must have been Dad's pickup, right? It wasn't long before Jake put the whole thing together. Soleil."

Soleil appraised Camille's face. "Great. Now something new to worry about."

Camille touched Soleil's arm. "No. Jake won't talk. You became his hero—a cop killer in the family." Soleil winced. "And besides, whoever was there cleaned up and fingered Henderson in a very professional manner. Case closed." She looked deeply into Soleil's eyes. Then she said with kindness, "I know you did this to avenge Dad. No one else in the family bothered to lift a finger." She paused for a second. "So I'm staying."

Soleil's eyes were sad. She didn't feel like telling Cami that Dorsey brought his demise down upon his own head, that she wasn't Bonnie Parker in disguise. Then: "OK. But if anything goes wrong, be careful. Really careful."

Camille didn't know what she meant but knew she should leave it at that. And take it seriously.

Max and Kurt walked up to them. Would they like to dance?

The band started in on a hit left over from the disco years. It was still a popular dance number, and everyone was up and on the floor. One of the band members even did a little imitative singing. He wasn't bad.

Max was a surprisingly good dancer: his moves were natural and efficient, and he let Soleil take the spotlight. And Soleil thanked her stars that she had gone to those dance lessons with Pradeep. She loved this kind of dancing, and as she embellished and built on Max's lead, other couples started giving the two some extra room for what was obviously becoming a professional show.

Now the two were center stage, the ceiling spotlights flashing a million diamonds off Soleil's spinning gown. Max was the swaying partner and anchor, Soleil the unwitting but confident star. Two hundred pairs of eyes watched— some in admiration, some in jealousy—one in rage. Finally the song ended with a fade out:

"Dance, baby, dance...."

The room erupted in applause. Max pulled Soleil to him and kissed her. It was a magic moment for all.

And then what Soleil knew would likely happen, was bound to happen, what *had* to happen, did: There at the edge of the dance floor, dressed in her expensive black gown, her shock of blue-black hair falling down over one eye, stood Fiona Dyche. She held a semiautomatic Glock .45-caliber pistol steady in a two-fisted grip and zeroed in on Soleil.

Everything, everyone was frozen for the smallest fraction of a second. It seemed like an artist's tableau, with people painted into the scene. But then the moment passed.

"She's got a gun!" someone screamed.

A riotous yelling and scrambling erupted, and the crowd quickly parted while a rush for the door began. Shouts were everywhere: "Watch out! Stay back!"

Max's instinct was to step in front of Soleil, but to his utter astonishment she literally shoved him aside.

Kurt and Camille rushed at Fiona, but Soleil's surprisingly commanding order stopped them: "Wait!"

"What do you want?" Soleil said over the din in an amazingly calm, almost otherworldly voice to Fiona and started walking toward her.

"Well? C'mon, what exactly do you want?"

Fiona's mind was gone. What did the bitch say, what? That key, that bloody key. That's what I want, of course.

Give me that key so I can get this done. "Give me the key, Tangiere!"

Soleil slowly reached into her dress under her left arm and tore the key from the tab that she had sewn in there. She brought it out and waggled it in her fingers. She was ten feet from Fiona's gun.

"This key?" she said in an odd tone. Then she looked at Clooney, who had quietly walked up and now stood next to Fiona. He was aghast, his mouth open in silent wonder mixed with uncertainty. His fiancée had lost her mind. Totally. He remembered Grandma's admonition not to harm the Tangiere girl. He said loudly to Fiona out of the side of his mouth, "Fiona. Don't shoot her. She's going to come over and give us the key, and then we're leaving so we can start our new life. Fiona?"

A thin line of spittle was dripping from the corner of Fiona's mouth. She gripped the gun tighter and sighted down it to the center of Soleil's chest. Give *us* the key? No. No no *no*. "Give *me* the key!" she growled between clenched teeth. "*I* need that key, not him! Me! Now give me that..."

But Soleil suddenly felt as if she weren't really there at that moment: she had gone to another place, a place six feet above Fiona and Clooney and everyone—even herself. From that place she was listening and watching calmly and then understood everything, and this is what happens some-times, like that time with the bear, and then I knew, I *knew* that it would be all right, and sorry Clooney, because now, without a doubt, we know it's going to be OK. Right, Dad?

Then she was back and knew just what to do.

"John Clooney's got the key," Soleil said to Fiona in a firm voice.

"NO! Give...me...that...KEY!"

Soleil looked into Fiona's mad eyes. Then she looked at the key. Then she looked straight and frankly at Clooney and winked seductively. And finally back at Fiona again.

"Nope." Now she spoke in a light, small, offhanded voice. "This is a copy." She made a little head toss toward Clooney. "I already gave him the key."

She winked at him? Fiona asked herself wildly. She's in this with *him*? He's in this with *her*?

Fiona's whole body made a quick quarter turn toward Clooney. The gun swung around to point at her fiancé, and the sound of the shot blasted through the room. Everyone froze.

Fiona Dyche, her blue-black hair suddenly exhibiting a deep new scarlet part, toppled to the dance floor.

Clooney was onto Fiona's Glock before it hit the ground. Now with his still-smoking Sig Sauer automatic—the one he had removed from his sock—in one hand and the Glock in the other, he turned full circle, waving both guns wildly. The crowd pushed away from him. Then he lunged at the nearest woman.

He almost knocked Amanda Ballas off her feet as he crashed into her and wrapped one arm around her neck, his Sig Sauer sweeping the crowd, while with his other hand he pushed the muzzle of the Glock under her chin.

She was immobilized with fear. Clooney shoved her, and the two pirouetted until Clooney was facing Soleil. He pushed the Glock into Amanda's chin painfully and said to Soleil, "You! Out the door. You know what I'm capable of." His Sig Sauer pointed at Soleil's heart.

Soleil stood there for a moment, her eyes holding Clooney's, and then the three shuffled awkwardly out the door, the crowd held at bay by any number of voices and shouts of "Stay away from them!" and "Careful, don't rile him!"

Josh Fowler, his monstrous facility of self-preservation coming to the fore, had melted back into the crowd. Amanda never saw him again.

Max, Camille, and Kurt were cautiously following them at a distance of four or five yards. Out of the corner of her eye, Soleil saw that Max was about to hurl himself at Clooney and damn the consequences. She said just loud enough to hear, "No, Max. Don't. I've got this."

He held himself back.

Clooney's eyes were filled with avarice and unstoppable insanity.

"Kurt!" It was Amanda's sob-filled voice. The barrel of the Glock was making an angry red circle in the soft skin under her chin. "Kurt, help me."

"Stay away, Kurt!" Clooney growled at the man who must be Kurt as they moved farther out into the hallway. He yelled to anyone within earshot: "Back in the restaurant. Now!" He quickly fired the small automatic into the ceiling with a loud bang. The several dozen people outside the restaurant hurried around them and did as he asked. Then the gun's barrel pointed at Soleil again.

"Listen carefully, Kurt," Clooney said slowly with craziness in his voice. "Take your friends back into the restaurant. Do as I say, and I'll send this woman back in to you unharmed. Then shut the door behind you. Do anything else, and she and Soleil die on the spot."

Camille's mind was short-circuiting. She wouldn't move from where she was standing, trying to figure a way out of this standoff. Clooney had Amanda in his hideous headlock, and Soleil was standing at the end of his outstretched gun. *Soleil. God, Soleil, what are you made of? You're standing there as if you haven't a care in the world. Are you human?*

Max was like a leopard in a cage. I have to do something. But Clooney seemed to read his mind. Suddenly Clooney said, "Oh, Mr. Russian. Take your friends back in that restaurant, and she might live to see tomorrow." Then, in a strange tone of voice, without taking his eyes off Soleil: "I remember you now, Russian. My father and I were in your office at Cenkhran making that deal..."

Soleil looked over at Max and tried to read his face.

"And you thought you could hide under your desk and avoid any involvement. Stupid. Just like you're doing now, because you and I both know that if she were able to walk free now with the key, she would be looking over her shoulder for the rest of her very, very short life."

Soleil looked at Max. Her eyes were unfathomable. Then looking back at Clooney, she said loudly, "Take them inside, Max."

Clooney's eyes were everywhere. The group of onlookers was back in the restaurant's doorway. Clooney slowly pulled the Glock away from Amanda's chin and pushed it harshly into the center of Soleil's chest. Amanda ducked under his arm and sprinted into the restaurant. She nearly knocked Kurt over.

"Kurt, oh Kurt, oh God." She was crying hysterically.

Kurt looked at Amanda. Damn it.

Camille was focused on her sister. How do I save Soleil? She looked at Max, and he put a restraining hand on her shoulder, holding her back from doing anything rash, anything at all.

Clooney had both guns on Soleil. Without taking his eyes off her, he yelled savagely, "Close the door!"

Max closed the door halfway. He was ready to barrel back out into the hall at any second. His powerlessness was killing him. And I'm afraid I've lost Soleil forever.

There was no one in the hall with Soleil and Clooney. It wasn't really a hall in the classic sense of the word because one side of it was open to the atrium. The waist-high railing afforded an incredible view down the inside of the hotel all the way to the lobby forty-five stories below.

They stood almost up against the railing, and Clooney said, "Give me the key. Nothing's stopping me now, so just hand it over."

Soleil looked in his crazy eyes.

"No."

"I'll finish what Fiona started."

"You need me alive, and you know it. Otherwise you would have let your psycho girlfriend kill me long ago in Zurich."

Then Soleil added, "You killed my father."

"You killed mine." His lunatic eyes glazed over for a second.

"Your father killed himself," she said. "Just like you're about to do."

"Give me the key."

"Never."

She stood coldly staring into his eyes as he carefully pressed both guns into her chest.

He said, "Your choice. The easy way or the hard way."

When he saw no reaction, he said, "OK. The hard way. Good-bye."

He tensed the two guns and snugged his fingers on the triggers.

Winston Whipple had been sitting quietly on the backless sofa down the hall from the restaurant considering his life. His clothing was wrinkled, and he realized that he didn't smell very good. Like stale perfume, he thought sadly.

The large man had been going over the events of the day in his mind, and then the events of the last few weeks. He reasoned that even though he wasn't the smartest man in the world, he always tried hard, sometimes embarrassing himself in an effort to do his job, and since Mr. Clooney had been "promoted" due to the demise of Mr. Smythe, he had been treated like, well, like shit.

And look at all these people going and coming at this party: glittering women, tuxedoed men, all successful, all laughing and celebrating themselves. Damn it, what's wrong with me? I'll tell you what's wrong—nothing. I'm just as good as they are, just as worthy as...

And as the night wore on, Winston Whipple quietly went a little bonkers and made some bad resolutions and came to a decision: When Mr. John Clooney comes out of that restaurant, he is going to have a problem. And that problem will be me, because I'm going to get real angry, and he might get hurt, and so what? I'm a person and a good person, and...

And then suddenly people exploded screaming from the restaurant, and there was a gunshot, and then more screaming and milling around and trying to get on the elevator, and then *there he was*, Mr. Clooney, you bastard, and this time you have *two* beautiful women with you, and another gunshot and more milling and running and now just you Mr. Clooney.

Just you and Soleil...

"Give me the key."

"Never."

She stared levelly into his eyes as he carefully aimed both guns at her heart.

"OK, the hard way. Good-bye..."

Then he fired both guns simultaneously. The double roar was gigantic. But Whipple had silently come up behind his ex-boss and had rammed Clooney's arms down to his side in a bear hug. The two bullets flew into the floor on either side of Soleil.

"We need to talk, Mr. Clooney," Whipple said in an obviously crazy voice as Clooney struggled like a snake trying to break out of the hold. He furiously tried to raise his arms. The Sig Sauer fell from his left hand and thumped on the carpet.

"Winston! What are you doing?" Clooney growled between clenched teeth as the restaurant door crashed open.

Soleil lunged at Clooney's right wrist and gave a two-handed twist with all her strength, and the Glock dropped from his hand. She bent and picked up both guns, then backed up a step and aimed the Glock at his head and the other gun at his chest.

"Wait," she said in a loud voice to Max and Camille and Kurt as they piled into the hall. "Wait!"

They came to an astonished halt.

An elevator door opened a short distance behind Soleil, and three men in dark suits came running out. After a second to evaluate the situation, they drew their guns.

"Soleil Tangiere?" one of them said with a Russian accent. He stood five or six yards down the hall.

She didn't move or turn around or drop the guns. She kept staring at Clooney struggling in Whipple's bear hug.

"Soleil Tangiere, put down those guns. You are under arrest." After a few more seconds, the voice added, "Interpol."

Her mind was racing furiously. There was something very wrong with this picture. She looked quickly toward Max. Her eyes met his, and their sapphire flashes said: Tell me it's not true.

Then she turned back and slowly, deliberately cocked her head and looked deeply and lovingly over John Clooney's shoulder and into Winston Whipple's eyes. This won't be fair, she thought, but life hasn't been fair about any of this, has it?

She looked at Whipple's face, and her eyes changed. Her eyes did all the asking, all the coaxing. Soleil willed her face to tell him the story of the paradise to come for the two of them, of the soft heaven that awaited them together. "Winston," she whispered, "now I'm yours. I love you." Winston's eyes opened wide as saucers as she gently bit a corner of her lower lip.

Then she backed away a step, slowly opened her fingers, and the two guns dropped from her hands to the floor with two loud thumps. Without taking her eyes off Whipple, she ran the tip of her tongue over her lips, and then she slowly put her hands behind her back and heard, more than felt, the click of the handcuffs. She turned her head as if she were trying to see behind her back and then turned once again to look lovingly at Whipple.

"Please, Winston," said her eyes.

John Clooney's blood surged in triumph. Now it's just a matter of time, Soleil! I won't make this mistake again. I swear I'll get to you and that key, and soon. And you'll have to answer for Fiona as well. He wrenched his head to the left and right.

"Let me go, Winston," he said in a loud voice, now wriggling like a fish. "We'll talk this out," he yelled over his shoulder. "This woman is finally going to face the music, Whip—Ow! You're hurting my..."

And John Clooney's very expensive bespoke patent-leather evening shoes slowly left the floor, and he felt himself being lifted, higher and then higher still, and then he was being levered over the railing, and he heard himself yelling Winston, man, what are you doing? Stop! Put me down, Whipple, stop! We'll talk, Whipple...Whipple!

Hans Petzenfelder loved New York.

He had flown in this morning from Geneva and congratulated himself on his meticulous planning. *Ja*, it was very clever of me to make this reservation at the Clarendon six months in advance—the hotel, as I understand it, has been booked solid for months. I love sitting here on this bench in the center of this magnificent atrium, in this magnificent lobby.

Wow. What a fountain, what a beautiful display—it's like a water-filled globe of the Earth made of metal and glass. *Ja*, It's beautiful, and it's perfect. I love perfect.

Clooney had just about reached terminal velocity when he crashed into the twenty-foot-tall spherical fountain, causing a booming, shattering explosion of glass, metal, and water across the entire lobby.

Hans instinctively curled into a ball as jagged, whizzing pieces of the fountain, torrents of water, and what was left of John Clooney blasted over everything.

When the cacophony of falling glass finally stopped, Hans straightened up. His new suit was drenched.

Perfection, he said to himself, even in New York, is rare indeed.

11

FOLLOWED

Sirens filled Times Square as the NYPD showed up in droves. From forty-five stories up, the cops looked like ants rushing into the ruined lobby. The first group headed to the elevators.

At the restaurant the crowds were desperately trying to get as far away as possible, running down halls and stairs, looking for more elevators. A crowd had gathered around the body of the black-haired woman, but no one tried to help her—she was obviously dead. The whup-whup sound of a helicopter outside the restaurant windows filled the air.

One of the remaining guests calmly helped himself to a drink at the bar and sat down to think...

Moments after Clooney had disappeared over the railing's edge, the three Interpol agents, guns drawn, herded Soleil, Max, Camille, and Kurt through a side door in the hallway and down a back staircase. One of the men quickly took the handcuffs off Soleil's wrists. She turned to him with venom in her eyes as they made their way down to the fortieth floor, where they pushed through the fire door. When they got to Soleil's suite, they all went in except for one of the agents, who posted himself in the hall.

Up on the forty-fifth floor, Whipple was left leaning over the railing looking down at the lobby. The first New York cop to get off one of the elevators tackled him and slapped the handcuffs on immediately. As they led him away, he was meek as a kitten and kept repeating something about a woman.

Standing in the middle of the suite, Soleil faced the agent who was obviously in charge. She was at the end of her rope. "Who are you?" she said quietly. I don't even want to talk anymore.

The sandy-haired man collected his thoughts for a second. "My name is Vlad. Vlad Spiridonovich." He glanced at Max.

"You're Max's friend, I guess," she said with ice in her voice. And then at Max: "Whoever Max really is."

"He is who he says he is," said Vlad. "But we are not Interpol. We are from Russian Internal Affairs, and we are here at Max's request."

Camille and Kurt looked on, speechless. What?

Without taking her eyes off Vlad, she said, "This must be his big plan, his big brilliant plan."

Max began to say something, but Soleil swung around toward him and said harshly, "Don't you *dare!* Don't talk to me, don't tell me anything, don't explain anything. Just *don't!*" Her eyes gleamed.

She looked down at her feet for a moment. Her left foot was unconsciously tapping, and she stopped it. "OK, Vlad, what's the next part of the Master Plan? Where are we going—Siberia?"

"Please, Ms. Tangiere." Vlad was almost whispering. "Can we please go in the other room?" He motioned toward one of the suite's bedrooms. She glared another withering look at Max and then walked into the room that Vlad indicated. Vlad followed, closing the door behind them.

Max, Camille, and Kurt stood looking at one another. Finally Kurt spoke up: "Can anyone tell me what just happened?"

Camille said, "Oh Kurt, I warned you about us. Don't try to figure this out. I'm only up to speed on half of it. But Max, here, I suspect he knows the whole story." She made a vague gesture toward Max, sat down on the sofa, and crossed her legs. And her arms. And stared daggers at Max.

Max looked at Camille. He couldn't say anything. His face was stern, and though his soul was shattered, his heart was singing a song that Soleil was still alive. Hate him forever she might, but she was still alive. Now to just keep her alive—there's just a short way to go.

A few minutes later, Vlad walked out of the bedroom and closed the door behind him. He looked at his watch: twelve midnight.

"There can be no change in time and place," he said to Max in Russian. "I've arranged for Viktor and Pyotr to be stationed here at the hotel, but please keep a close eye on the girl tomorrow and Monday. Tuesday we will send transportation to take you to the airport. Your company jet will take you and Ms. Tangiere from there."

"And her sister, if she wants her to come," Max said. It wasn't a question.

"Does she?" Vlad glanced at Camille.

"I'm not certain," said Max. "If it would make Soleil more comfortable, what is the downside?"

"Fine. And her sister, if she wants." Vlad continued: "After that, all debts are canceled. I don't like New York anyway." He hugged Max, nodded to Camille and Kurt, motioned to the other agent to get the door, and then they were gone.

Camille got up and turned to Kurt. "You'd better go." He stood, and she kissed him and then added, "Call me when you've resolved the issues in your marriage. This was a little much for anyone," thinking about the near-fatal incident with Amanda Ballas.

He looked at her and smiled thinly. He kissed her cheek. "I'll see you soon. That's a promise." On an impulse Camille took his hand in hers. Then she let slowly go without taking her eyes off his. Kurt turned to Max and nodded. "Say goodbye to Soleil from me." A moment later, he was gone.

Max was still standing.

Camille said, "Well?"

Max turned to the window. Without turning back to her he asked her, "Did she tell you about the key?"

"Not all of it. Now I know it's worth dying for, I guess."

"No, it's not," he said to the glittering lights of New York.

"Max, I'm pretty sure you broke Soleil's heart, and she won't let that happen twice. She's young, and her record with men is pretty dismal. This could be bad for you as well as Soleil."

Max cringed inside and turned away from the window.

"Camille," he said. She liked the way he said her name, with that light sexy Russian accent. He *is* kind of attractive, she thought, but then quickly refocused. He was saying, "Soleil could have given that man Clooney the key, or anyone else, but it wouldn't have mattered."

"Why?"

"It unlocks bad secrets, and the person who owns it, even for short while, would always be thought to know those secrets and thereafter be open to danger from some very, very bad people. They wouldn't care if she had given the key away. If they found her, she would be doomed no matter what." Camille started to look sick.

"So. I think I found a way to protect her, but I didn't want to tell her until the very end."

Another voice said, "How's that?" Soleil stood in the bedroom's open doorway. Max and Camille looked over. Neither had heard it open.

"How's that?" she repeated. "Max?"

Max told her. When he was done, she said, "Go. Just go." I'm just too weary.

She watched him cross the room. A moment before his hand touched the doorknob, she said to his back, "If you want..."

He stopped abruptly, turned, and looked at her. Looking at me like a naughty puppy being given one more chance, she thought.

Then, for the first time, she realized that Clooney was no more. The last murderer is gone from this earth. And then a tight band that had been circling her heart for these years was suddenly removed, and she could breathe.

"If you want," she said to Max, "you can bring me things I need." She stood there with a stern expression on her face. "Since I'll be a prisoner, I expect that Russia would want to cater to my comfort and necessities..."

Max nodded, his heart on fire. He noticed Camille's conspiratorial look and left.

The New York City Police Department had their work cut out for them.

They had a dead woman named Fiona Dyche. They had a dead man named John Clooney. The British company Clooney had worked for confirmed that the two were engaged but were surprisingly reticent about providing any kind of motive for what had transpired in the ballroom from the time Ms. Dyche pulled her gun in the middle of a crowd until the moment when Mr. Clooney obliterated a four-ton glass fountain with his hurtling body. That reticence would have to be addressed.

Witnesses tended to agree that both victims appeared insane or close to it. The Dyche woman profoundly so.

Then there was the Brit who was still breathing named Winston Whipple, the admitted murderer of John Clooney. In police custody he made a strange, flowery confession featuring paranoia, delusions, and a detachment from reality, which, the police discovered, had evidenced itself earlier that day via a strange incident he was involved in at Neiman Marcus.

Whipple professed love for his mother, one Sally Preston Whipple, who had been beaten to death by his father twenty years ago. He kept chanting something that sounded like, "Sally, Sally." Police inferred that he was obviously calling out to his mother. He was transferred to an observation ward at a secure location prior to formal booking.

As to the woman who had been threatened by both the deceased Brits, she had been observed by dozens, if not a hundred guests at the event, but her name was never mentioned or overheard, and it was assumed that she was either the girlfriend of one the guests or a professional dancer or call girl who was at the wrong place at the wrong time. The fact that she fled the scene probably indicated the latter.

In any event, the police were grateful that she had avoided injury or death in the affair.

When Max called her on Sunday she told him, "I need to be alone, Max," and hung up. Camille watched as she stood leaning against one of the suite's big windows.

"Chinese water torture, huh?"

"C'mon, Camille, I don't know if I'm ever going to forgive him completely. And I need space."

"He's really..."

"No, Cami, not now. Let's talk about you. What are you going to do after I leave?" The future still seemed shaky and uncertain, and talking about it made Soleil uneasy.

"I have to go home for a little while. I have to close up my life in Minnesota." She turned and looked out the window at the New York skyline. "As hard as all this has been, it's opened my eyes about how sick I was before and how happy I want to be now. New York, Zurich, Kurt Ballas, what next? I want it, Soleil. I want an interesting life."

"Huh! Interesting? If looking down the barrel of a gun is interesting, you can have it." Then: "You saved my life, Cami. Thanks."

Soleil suddenly had a new thought and continued, "Cami. Don't go back home just yet. Come with me. It will only be a week or less, and you need to give your passport a little more of a workout or it will dry up and blow away. Please, I have a hunch about it."

"I'll let you know later." She looked around for her purse. "Shopping sharpens my decision making. Besides, I have a nice shadow escort courtesy of Vlad. Can I bring you something when I come back?"

"An end to all of this."

After a moment Camille said, "You're not going to like it, but we have to trust Max."

Soleil's face was unreadable.

"I know. When Vlad brought me into the bedroom, he explained everything."

The phone rang late Monday morning.

"How are you?" he said in a quiet, tentative voice into the phone.

Boy, for a big strong Russian, you really know how to walk on eggshells, don't you? she thought, smiling inside.

"Fine." Then, "Better."

Max said, "How about I bring you some borscht?"

Soleil stifled a laugh.

Then, "Cheeseburger," she commanded.

Fifteen minutes later there was a knock on her door.

"You decided to gamble with my life, with our lives, and you didn't tell me. Why should I believe you now?" she asked the French fry before biting it in half. She looked to the left, to the right—anywhere but at Max. The other half of the French fry disappeared. "The ends don't justify the means," she said to no one.

Max thanked God for the hundredth time that she was alive.

"We leave tomorrow. Are you OK with it?" he asked.

She said, "Do I have a choice?" Then, "I want Camille to come with us. Just a feeling that she should get out of the US for a little while longer."

"Absolutely. No problem." Max wasn't going to disagree with anything. Besides, he had already discussed the possibility with Vlad.

She looked at him.

"Max. I got myself into this mess partly with my own bad decisions, but a lot of it was caused by other people. I realize I can't get out of it alone, that I need some help. But my trust factor is zero."

Who can I trust? she thought. Can I trust the police who were knee-deep in a murderous conspiracy in Montana, which resulted in the death of my father and many others? Can I trust a man I lived with for two years who quietly used me for his own financial gain, putting me in mortal danger? Can I trust powerful but essentially stupid business people who have tortured and killed others over money and who have been using me for years? Can I trust the next man who comes into my life with smiles and promises?

She looked into his eyes. "The only thing no one expected was that I would fight back." The sound her glass of Perrier made when she put it down on the table sounded abnormally loud.

He sat looking at her without saying a word.

Well, Max, she thought, at least you're smart enough to know that right at this second silence is golden. Nothing you say now would work, not denials, not promises, not apologies. At least you're starting to see who I am. That's a good first step.

There was the sound of a key in the lock, and Max stood up. Camille came into the room.

"Max." She walked over to him and accepted a kiss on the cheek. "I don't know about Soleil, but I want to get this show on the road."

"Tomorrow morning," he said. "Tomorrow morning."

The Nevsky corporate jet was parked out on the tarmac near Terminal Eight at Kennedy International Airport. It had been sitting in that spot since Max had arrived in it last week.

The car that had picked them up at the Clarendon pulled up a hundred yards from the plane. A slight wind brought the promise of rain as Max, Camille, and Soleil got out of the car.

When Soleil got to the top of the boarding steps, she stopped to look around her one last time. She had a quick warm thought about Izzy, Brenda, Aimee, and Tango. The she boarded the plane.

The inside of the plane was luxurious, and obviously no cost had been spared in its appointments. Max thought: this is the future for the quick and the smart in Russia now. The times are changing, and fast.

There was a leggy flight attendant, impeccably dressed, and a pilot and copilot in starched uniforms. Max went up to the cockpit to speak with them while Soleil and Camille chose plush facing chairs.

They chatted for a few minutes, and Soleil glanced out the window. She saw the usual baggage handlers and jet-fuel personnel moving about. Below one of the mirrored terminal windows, a man in a long gray coat wearing sun-glasses was watching the plane.

When Max came out of the cockpit, she said, "Max?" and gestured out the window at the man. Max looked out the Plexiglas at him for a thoughtful moment. Then he ducked out the exit door, down the retractable stairs, and strode up to the man. Watching out the window, Soleil saw him talking to the man with the sunglasses for a minute, and then he returned to the plane.

"False alarm?" Soleil asked when he was inside.

He looked at her and said, "Maybe not."

Ten minutes later they were in the air. Soleil looked out the window as the plane banked, and she watched the island of Manhattan slip slowly beneath them. Then they were out over the Atlantic, heading east.

"Dance, baby, dance..."

And then the room went crazy.

The man was stunned, just as his date and everyone else in the crowd was.

"What do you want?" The beautiful young woman had said in a strange, almost otherworldly voice across the dance floor as guests scattered in panic.

Then she brought the small object out of a fold in her gown and dangled it in front of the woman in the black dress, seemingly oblivious to the large gun pointed at her.

"This key?" she had said to the woman.

The man looked carefully at Clooney, who was now a part of this deadly drama. What is John Clooney's role, why is he...?

Then it hit him like a freight train. Is this all about that key? Is that the Key?

Of course! It makes perfect sense...

And if it is truly the Key, it confirms the rumors that it was in the possession of Smythe, and now somehow this girl has it. In this confusion I could just run up and grab it, but this brunette looks totally crazy, and I wouldn't argue with that big Glock. Besides, even if I could get away with it, anyone else here who might understand what the key is all about will see me, and then I'll be in the soup.

No, I'll just watch and find out who holds the key at the end of this little drama. Then I'll know what to do...

"You have good instincts," Max said to Soleil, sitting in the aircraft's plush leather seat next to her. "Sunglass man back there got nervous when I approached and was ready with some couch-and-bull story. That only convinced me that he was watching us."

"Cock-and-bull," Soleil corrected. "If you'll pardon the expression."

Camille looked at the two of them from a facing seat. After a minute of frankly studying them she said, "You two make a cute couple."

Soleil's eyes shot her a couple of daggers. "Not now, please."

They would land in London in seven hours. And continue on from there.

"Do you know who I am?" The voice was dry as dust.

"Yes," he said.

"She's killed off my whole line. She. That Tangiere girl."

He listened without saying anything.

"I know what you're trying to do," the arid voice said. "What you are trying to acquire. How would you like to add ten million pounds worth of CM stock to your larder, eh?" Dry as the Sahara.

He knew this woman meant business. Her outrageously dangerous reputation and unstoppable determination were well known in many dark corners of the Western business world.

"Bring me her mortal body. Alive. And come claim the prize."

He thought for a moment. This woman meant what she said.

"Very well." And he hung up.

That Vlad was able to orchestrate his own personal political symphony would impress any Russian.

The Soviet Union was collapsing, and it might be just a matter of months, so this most likely was his last opportunity.

Maybe there is a God, thought Vlad. When Max had made his request, if the political stars hadn't been aligning just so, Vlad would have had to decline. Since timing is everything, he was able to work his plan up to this point in a surprisingly effective way. There was only one way the key could be handled. There could only be one final destination for it as well.

I need to be at the airport early, he thought.

He lay in the bed alone in his hotel room. His wife was still in East Germany with his two daughters. He yawned and rolled over but couldn't fall asleep for hours.

The Lincoln Town Car screeched to a jarring halt in front of the British Airlines terminal at Kennedy International. The man jumped out of the back door and walked quickly into the building.

"The Russian knows that he and the women were followed here," Sunglasses said as soon he laid eyes on him.

"He knows it's me?"

"No, but I think he suspects."

"Have you discovered where the plane is headed?"

"Yes. Geneva via London."

"Switzerland?" He suddenly realized how stupid that sounded.

He went up to the counter and purchased a ticket on the next Concorde for Paris and instructed Sunglasses to quickly arrange a connecting private jet to Geneva when he landed.

If Josh Fowler played his cards right, he could be there to meet and greet Soleil Tangiere and her key. *My* key.

And make John Clooney's Grandma very, very happy.

The Nevsky jet touched down for refueling at Heathrow airport outside of London. Though they had been traveling only around seven hours, because of the time differential, they arrived in the dead of night. They had slept on the plane—the plane's nationality precluded them from setting foot on British soil without the proper entry papers. They would be taking off after refueling and should be arriving in Geneva in the morning.

Soleil and Camille appreciated the fact that the plush seats folded down into beds, and there was plenty of room on the plane for them, Max, the pilots, and the flight attendant to sleep in privacy.

Sometime during the night, Max moved into the seat next to Soleil. He reached over and touched her hand. She didn't pull it back—in fact, her fingers curled around his for a moment and squeezed. Of course, Max never knew whether she was really sleeping or not.

12

CHOPPER

The Embraer jet chartered by J. Fowler Metals had landed in Geneva Airport around 6:00 a.m., hours before the Nevsky Nickel jet would arrive. Josh Fowler stooped in the small lavatory in the back of the plane and shaved with an electric razor. He loved flying and was a natural international wanderer, spreading his own special brand of venom around the globe.

I've got to move fast. She's obviously under the spell of that Russian, and he's surely going to get the key—by subterfuge, lies, force, or all of the above. Jacques and Louis had better be waiting for me with the equipment. We have a lot of work to do and fast. I can't just show up and grab her, though it would save a lot of aggravation and expense.

He finished getting dressed and left the plane. Swiss immigration met them in the terminal and checked their passports. He was striding toward a bank of pay phones at the end of the gate corridor when he glanced out of one of the long terminal windows. Rolling parallel to the terminal, but on the far side of the main runways, was an immense white Tupolev jet with a red hammer and sickle painted on the fuselage behind the cockpit windows. At this distance, the three police cars and the Mercedes limousine that kept pace with it seemed very small.

When the giant plane came to a stop, another car drove up to it, and a man with sandy hair got out on the passenger side. He approached the plane as its engines powered down and a staircase was rolled up to the door. When the door opened, the man climbed up the stairs and disappeared into the plane. Then the door closed.

Fowler stood at the long window carefully watching. It appeared that the plane was the Russian equivalent of Air Force One. What's going on?

A few hours later, the Nevsky jet pulled up at gate 36. As they walked through the Jetway from their plane to the gate area, Soleil shuddered. Heavy doubts filled her heart.

Soleil, Max, and Camille were met in the gate area by two agents of Swiss Immigration. As they were checking their passports, Soleil heard a familiar voice behind her.

"Welcome back to Geneva, Mlle Tangiere."

She froze, stared straight ahead for a few heartbeats, then turned and saw Henri Deshautels standing a few yards away.

He walked up to her and formally shook her hand, and then came the customary kisses on both cheeks. She introduced Camille and then Max. The two men eyed each other with mutual suspicion.

As head of one of Geneva's investigative bureaus, Deshautels had been assigned to meet the official plane from Moscow that had landed earlier this morning. About to leave the terminal, he had spotted the Nevsky jet pulling into a gate and decided to wait and see who was deplaning. When he saw Soleil emerge from the Jetway, a spectrum of emotions went through him.

"You really should not have left Switzerland," he said to Soleil, pulling her aside with a surprisingly harsh grip on her arm. "Now I guess I have to thank you for returning." His eyes narrowed. Soleil saw that he was put out, but his reaction was over the top. She sighed inside. *I wish he would get a girlfriend or something.*

"You don't have to do anything, Inspector Deshautels," she said with a little frost in her voice. "If I have inconvenienced the Swiss people or their government in any way, I formally apologize."

He softened his tone a bit. "Excuse me, Mlle Tangiere. I would respectfully ask you to please keep a low profile from this point onward. The case that you were involved in concerning this very airport is still quite active and is still a thorn in the side of the police. The English company that Mr. Smythe was working for has been raising hell about it."

She looked at him for a moment. Then she said, "Yvonne Goulet's tormentor is dead."

She watched the genuinely shocked expression on his face turn to wonder. Then he said in a surprisingly meek voice, "You?"

She lifted her face. "Of course not me. How could you imply such a thing?"

He made a face and waved his hand as if in dismissal, but before he could say anything else, she said, "You might contact the New York City Police Department. Certainly they will fill you in about her and her identity. I do not know it."

She began to walk away but turned back to him a last time and whispered, almost conspiratorially: "That British company will likely not be following up on the Smythe matter, either. Their head operating officer is likewise dead." Henri Deshautels stared after the three as they were cleared by the customs officials and walked rapidly toward the terminal exit.

Max checked his watch. Vlad had said a car would be picking them up.

From his position at the terminal windows, Josh Fowler stood stock still watching them. He had waited patiently until their plane had arrived and felt smugly confident in the plan he had put into motion in such a short period of time. And now it was time to act.

The conversation on the massive Russian Tupolev was short and to the point. The general secretary and a phalanx of security men and advisors jammed the area of the plane used as its main office. Vlad had everyone's attention.

The Cenkhran Key had been located and was going to be delivered today.

Its importance was such that the courier was going to deliver it directly to the general secretary. She should do it personally, Vlad suggested. The general secretary's televised speech at the United Nations Conference on Trade and Development at the World Court, scheduled for today, would be an ideal venue.

"She?"

Vlad chuckled inside. He knew that would be the response.

"A young woman, a Canadian. She came to possess it by default, a circumstance that occurred without her knowledge of what the key was or any clue as to its meaning. She will be at the World Court today along with my friend and compatriot, Max Stepanov."

"What is the strategy of accepting this 'gift' in public?" asked the general secretary, his eyes narrowed.

OK, now is the moment, thought Vlad.

"There are likely many enemies of the country and the party who know of the significance of the key. More importantly, we are fairly certain the CIA is aware of it as well. By 'repatriating' the key in public, we establish that our country is still well in control of its national treasure and destiny."

He saw the general secretary mulling it over. Yes, thought the secretary, this Vlad apparatchik is clever to a degree, but he can't see six months or a year down the road. We are rapidly losing our empire, and the rule of communism is most likely dead as a doornail. My instincts say that while taking the key in public is a positive step today, it may hurt me personally in the future. My possession of the key will always be suspect: that I cannot afford.

So. I know what to do.

He said to Vlad, "I will accept the key after my scheduled address at the conference. In front of the cameras."

Vlad nodded. "Very well."

The two men whom Fowler regularly hired for what he called "aggressive negotiating" of commodities deals, Jacques and Louis, met him in front of the airport terminal. Louis and Josh Fowler got into a cab while Jacques headed out into the parking area.

But Louis and Fowler's cab didn't take them very far. Their destination was a small private hangar at the other end of the airport. They paid the driver and got out of the cab. The two men walked through a neat row of private planes and headed toward a small helicopter, a sleek blue-and-white Bell 206-B3, which was on lease to J. Fowler Metals' French subsidiary. *Once the Tangier girl is on the helicopter, it will be a series of easy steps to relieve her of the key, get her to London in breathing condition, and collect my ten million,* thought Fowler.

One of Louis's well-paid-for skills was his ability to fly helicopters and fly them well. Fowler also could fly helicopters, but Louis was the champ, and he climbed into the machine while Fowler raised Jacques on his small walkie-talkie. Louis checked the gauges and the fuel—and his gun. Josh Fowler looked at Louis as he was talking on the radio and held his hand out. Through the open pilot's door Louis handed him a gun—a Kohl-Tech .38, a touchy piece that was supposed to go through metal detectors without activating them. Not the most reliable weapon, the gun was considered sexy by wannabe mercenaries.

Fowler shoved the gun in his belt, walked around the machine, climbed in the passenger side, and strapped himself into the seat as the rotors revved faster. The two men donned sunglasses and looked out through the windscreen as the helicopter's skids left the ground.

"*Oui*, I understand completely," Jacques told Fowler over the small walkie-talkie as he walked quickly toward his vehicle outside the airport terminal. He adjusted the driver's cap on his head. He and Louis had been a "problem-solving" team since the seventies, and for the last five years or so had hired themselves out to companies who needed basic thug security.

In point of fact, they didn't mind killing.

Soleil, Max, and Camille walked out of the airline terminal, and before they could reach the curb, an official-looking black car with tinted windows pulled up quickly. The passenger window rolled down, and the driver leaned over and said loudly, "M. Stepanov?"

Max nodded. The women got into the back seat, and Max sat up front with the driver.

Max was irritated that the driver spoke no Russian, but when Soleil started to speak to him in French, he told her in a surly voice that they would be at their destination in ten minutes—it had all been arranged. Soleil shrugged but was uneasy.

The car whipped down the same curves on which Smythe had met his doom, and Soleil noticed that the construction barricades were now gone. At one particular turn, she shuddered slightly. The concrete surface of the road still showed burn marks.

The car started up Route 1, which ran parallel to the airport, but suddenly began to slow. "*Merde*," the driver swore. "Engine."

They slowed rapidly, and somehow the driver managed to get the car off the main road and into the parking area of an office park. There were few cars parked near the place where the cab finally came to a stop. The driver angrily put the gearshift in park and got out to look under the hood. He stood scratching his head under his driver's cap.

The three passengers got out of the car and stood close together.

Something wasn't right. They all sensed it. And they absolutely could not be late.

"Let's go," said Camille suddenly, echoing the rising suspicions of the other two.

As they turned to walk quickly away, they heard the driver say in heavily accented English, "*Non*. Do not move." And then a metallic click.

As one they turned to see the Kohl-Tech .38 in Jacques's hand, and they all froze. Max saw instantly that the man knew how to use it. He was aiming it at each of them in turn in a professional manner. The tableau of the four people was frozen in time for a minute, and it took another thirty seconds or so for any of them to become aware of the sound of an approaching helicopter.

Louis landed the chopper in the parking lot a short distance from the car, the blast from the rotors drowning out any other noise. A fierce storm of dust and bits of street trash flew up in a swirling cloud caused by the rotors' downdraft. The passenger door opened, and out stepped Josh Fowler, shirt open, his suit jacket flapping, the gun held straight out in front of him.

He held his head down as he loped toward the black car. Finally he stopped in front of the group and aimed the weapon randomly. That no one showed much fear didn't encourage Fowler—he had seen this Tangiere girl at the ball—she had real grit.

"Show me the key," he yelled at the three of them.

Jacques came up alongside the group and put the gun to Max's temple. "Show him ze key," he said in his thick French accent. Max angrily hit the gun hand away from him, and Jacques fell back, then charged at Max with the gun and yelled, "You die now, *cochon!*"

Fowler held up his free hand and yelled, "Wait! We need the Russian for now."

"Hey, Fowler!" It was Camille. "You need a helicopter and an army to get a little key from a couple of girls? Who's this," she pointed at Jacques, "your boyfriend?"

It was all Soleil needed. She launched herself at the out-raged Fowler somewhere between "who's this" and "boy-friend." Before Fowler knew what was happening, she had grabbed his gun hand with both of hers and with all her body weight swung it around. She squeezed as hard as she could.

The shot was even louder than the helicopter's racket. The distance to target was ridiculously short, and Jacques's body presented little to no resistance. The bullet crashed through the right side of his rib cage, made an enchilada of his heart and one lung, and exited through his left armpit. A split second later, it whanged into a Volkswagen parked at the far end of the parking lot. The mercenary's body was dead before it hit the pavement.

Max made a quick move for Jacques's Kohl-Tech .38, but as he reached for it, a boot came painfully down on his hand. Louis, who had jumped out of the helicopter and sprinted over to the group, quickly bent and picked up the gun.

Soleil and Camille were struggling with Fowler when they heard the second shot. Louis had fired into the air to make his point. "I will shoot the Russian! Back away!" The two looked over and saw the gun against Max's head again, only this time Louis was holding it. They reluctantly stopped their assault on Fowler.

Fowler's eyes were wild, but unlike John Clooney or Fiona Dyche, he had a firm and dangerous hold on sanity and reality. He yelled, "I say again, before people start dying, give me the key!"

The removal of Jacques from the equation didn't seem to change the dynamic very much. Max stood with Louis aiming his gun at him while Fowler had his gun trained on Soleil and Camille. Fowler walked closer to Soleil and growled between clenched teeth, "Now, the key!" He aimed the gun at the center of Camille's chest.

Soleil stared at him for a few beats and then carefully reached into the slit she had sewn in her bra. Her stare was ice cold, and through the frost, her sapphire eyes blazed. She was out of options. Out came the key, and she tossed it to Fowler. He nabbed it in midair, held it up, stared at it for a few seconds with squinty eyes, and then put it in his inside jacket pocket.

"Louis," he yelled out of the side of his mouth. "Let's go."

He added, "She's coming with me," aiming at Soleil. Then to Louis, "Kill the others."

Louis pushed the gun hard against Max's head. Everyone froze.

Click.

Merde.

The Kohl-Tech .38, with its amazing ability to sneak through scanners, had jammed.

Max flew at Louis, and the two hit the ground in a snarling blur of fists and kicks. Fowler rammed his gun into Soleil's neck. "Back off, bitch!" he screamed at Camille, who had started to make her move at him. She froze when she saw that the slightest mistake would indeed kill her sister.

Fowler roughly grabbed Soleil by her arm and pulled her quickly toward the aircraft. When they reached the chopper's open passenger door, he suddenly swung the gun, and it crashed into Soleil's temple. Her body slumped half in and half out of the machine. He pushed her the rest of the way onto the copter's floor, scrambled over her body into the pilot's seat, and grabbed the controls. Camille ran toward the machine, but before her hands could grab its quickly rising landing skids, the helicopter had lifted off and swept over the parking lot and into the bright Swiss sky.

Max came within a hair's breadth of strangling the *svinya* to death. Louis would be down for the count now, and Max stood bewildered and angry next to Camille—the helicopter had left with Soleil on it while he was wrestling with the filthy pig. *What do I do now?*

Two police cars and an airport security vehicle suddenly screeched into the lot and surrounded the two. Henri Deshautels jumped out of one of the cars. He looked at Camille and Max, the ruined body of Jacques, the moaning body of Louis, and then at the quickly retreating helicopter.

He turned to Max. "Where's Soleil?"

Max scowled at him and then pointed his chin at the rapidly receding machine in the sky.

"Where are they going?" Deshautels asked.

No one had an answer to that question.

A hush in the forest.

He's on his hind legs, his nose quivering.

He smells me more than sees me.

Now he falls back on all fours.

Here he comes. OK, come on, bear. Take a good sniff.

Sniff. His wet nose, his hot breath is all over me.

My arms, my face.

I'm tired. I'll just close my eyes for a minute.

Sniff.

He pushes me with his nose. The arrows rustle in the quiver on my back.

I don't need them.

The ball's in your court, bear.

Now he turns and walks away.

Good decision.

And I won't come here again, bear. This is your place.

We all need to make our own decisions.

The sound of the rotors jarred her awake. Her eyes opened, and she saw the out-of-focus shoe on the control pedal inches away. I need to throw up, and I need to do something about my head. She shook her head gingerly and slowly looked around. Her blurred vision cleared. She carefully turned her head and realized she had a direct view under the seat.

There was a sudden electronic chirping sound, and Fowler snatched the walkie-talkie from his belt. Someone was using Jacques's unit. He switched it on and listened. The voice of Henri Deshautels came from the other end.

"Fowler, this is Swiss police. Air defense has been mobilized and is proceeding to intercept and shoot you down. You have two minutes. Set the helicopter down, and you will survive this."

"You listen to me," Fowler growled into the hand-held radio. "Call off everyone and the Tangiere girl lives. Otherwise her death is on your hands."

"Don't be a fool, Fowler. The Swiss do not negotiate with kidnappers."

"I'm not a kidnapper. I'm a businessman. Now call them off!" He turned the device off and put it back on his belt. He looked down at Soleil but didn't see her because the blast from the fire extinguisher that she had pulled from under the passenger seat hit him full force in the face.

The police car screamed through the city. Deshautels, in the passenger seat, desperately tried to coordinate some way to follow the helicopter as the driver dodged and weaved around traffic while honking his horn incessantly. In the back seat, Camille turned to Max and pleaded, "Max, you have to come up with an idea. Where do you think they're going? What..."

She didn't finish her sentence. The helicopter with Soleil and Fowler aboard suddenly flashed a few hundred feet directly above the car and disappeared between two buildings.

And anyone could have seen it was in trouble.

The cramped interior of the helicopter was no place for a powerful and continuing burst from a fire extinguisher, and Fowler lost all sense of the controls. The helicopter lurched violently.

A few more seconds, and the assault of jet-propelled foam came to a stop. Soleil shook her head to clear it, and then she was up and on him and going for broke. Fast, painful punches smashed into Fowler. He flailed his own arms and fists at Soleil while trying to hold on to the control stick. The helicopter shuddered and twisted violently as it zoomed between the tops of the buildings of downtown Geneva. More than once the machine roared within yards of an office building's wall, and once it clipped off a tall antenna from a rooftop.

Fowler's gun was suddenly in his hand, but the complete chaos in the copter made aiming a useless proposition. Trying to put the gun back in his pocket, he accidently fired. Two quick, obscenely loud shots exploded in the small space. One bullet hit the control panel dead on, and the other disintegrated part of the front windscreen. A blast of

wind hit Fowler and Soleil like a sledgehammer. The helicopter heeled over dangerously before righting itself, but it
was plain that the machine was doomed. The streets and
the buildings zoomed past beneath them, and the wind and
the roar of the engine was everywhere.

He felt Soleil's hand frantically rooting around inside
his suit jacket. After a minute she pulled out the key and
clutched it to her chest. He saw the key for a fraction of a
second, but the reality of the situation suddenly hit him full
force: Screw the key, I'm going to die. And if I die, she dies.
The gun was still in his hand, and the girl was right there.
Kill her, he thought as the machine began to career wildly
and lose altitude at a sickening rate. He tried to fire the gun
one last time.

Out of the corner of her eye, Soleil saw the swirling ka-
leidoscope of the city and its blue lake through the wrecked
windscreen. Her head was throbbing, and Fowler was yelling something about dying while trying to aim the gun at
her again.

OK, she thought. Here you go, Fowler...

The swing of her arm described a perfect arc.

Fowler's hand holding the gun seemed unable to pull
the trigger. His whole body shook violently—what new
hell is this? His mind screamed, and he dropped the gun.
He could scarcely move. Aaaah! Something was sticking
out of his groin just below his beltline: something that was
jammed all the way through him and into the seat and was
making it impossible to move without ripping something off
his body. Pain exploded through Fowler in lightning waves.
He frantically made a futile attempt to pull the object from

between his legs, but his hands weren't working right. Then he looked down, and his vision cleared. It was a knife—a hunting knife. He saw a small oval silver plaque in the knife's bone handle with the letter *S* engraved on it.

"That's mine, thank you," Soleil said to his howling face and tried to pull her knife back out. She had to pull it hard to the left and rotate it viciously to the right and then twist it violently to finally free it.

Then she forced open the passenger door, looked out, and didn't understand what she was seeing. The helicopter was now flashing a mere twenty feet over the blue waters of Lake Geneva and was zooming sideways toward what looked like a column of rainbow light, a pillar of rising ice, a beautiful roaring miracle. She quickly crossed herself and said, "Time to go."

A witness on the lakeshore thought he saw someone dive from the screaming machine into the lake a moment before the helicopter ran sideways at full speed into the Jet d'Eau, one of the highest and most powerful fountains in the world, shooting its single monstrous blast of water 450 feet into the air.

When the helicopter flew into that water blast at such a low level, it was as if it were hit with a mortar shell from a tank. The machine twisted violently, jerked two hundred feet skyward in a single second, and then exploded in a deafening roar—metal, glass, rotor blades, and assorted pieces of Josh Fowler rocketed from a blossoming, billowing chrysanthemum of smoke, steam, and burning fuel.

It was all reflected in the lake, of course.

13

FOREIGN POLICY

It was only a matter of minutes before Max, Camille, and Henri Deshautels showed up at the lakeshore in the police car. They ran out on the concrete jetty that allowed access to the base of the fountain. An uneasy crowd had formed near the fountain's roaring source.

"Let us through." Camille was the first to push herself into the clot of people. She elbowed past a heavyset man. The sight was not encouraging. Debris was everywhere along the jetty, and the air smelled of smoke and fuel. Camille's heart sank. Soleil? Come on, Soleil. Not like this.

Deshautels began questioning people in the crowd. Max walked farther along the jetty. No sign of Soleil. He looked across the lake at the distant shore with its snowcapped mountains ranged against the blue sky. He was done; his life had collapsed around him. He sat on the edge of the jetty.

What have I done?

He looked down into the water and noticed little waves radiating out from under the stone pier. He bent over double and looked under the jetty. Up to her neck in the dark water and holding tight to a piece of iron reinforcement sticking out of the concrete was Soleil.

"Help me, Max." A hand reached out for him.

While the medics were looking after Soleil in the emergency vehicle that was parked on the shore road, Henri Deshautels had once again cut through the red tape for Soleil Tangiere. But this time it was easy. It took five minutes for Soleil to insist to the police that she was an observer on the jetty, really hadn't seen what happened, and that she had lost her footing when she heard the crash and toppled into the lake. She had hit her head on the side of a mooring dock. *Voila!* Besides, how could I have been on that helicopter—I'm alive, aren't I? And who was Henri Deshautels to argue with this innocent girl? He had given his shoulders a Gallic shrug and cursed the day that he decided to become a policeman.

The worst was the head injury, but it was not concussive and Soleil made sure the bandage they insisted on putting on it was small and could be covered by her hair. Nothing else of import—no broken bones or internal injuries. My clothes are ruined, though.

In less than fifteen minutes she was ready to get shakily into the police car with Max, Camille, and Deshautels.

"Max," she said, looking at him as if she were making sure that he was really there. "Max, let's finish this."

They waited in the car while Camille
chase in a clothing store near the lake. S
conservative business suit, blouse, und
always fit her, dammit, I should be so l
naled from the door of the establishment, Soien g
the car and walked in to change in the store's fitting room.

When she returned to the car, Max and Henri couldn't
believe the transformation—she looked fresh as a daisy.

The bump on her head was concealed by her hair, and
when Max pushed the hair aside and peeled back the bandage, he cringed—a hit like this would have knocked me out.
This girl must be made of iron. And how she did fall from
that helicopter and survive?

Soleil seemed to read his mind: "I like diving. I used
to do it back home in the lake near my father's house. He
taught me, and I'm good at it."

Max sighed.

A few minutes later, Deshautels stopped the car at their
destination.

"I need to freshen up," said Camille.

"I have already," said Soleil. Camille gave her a look.

They were standing in the center front hallway of the
Palais de Nations on the Avenue de la Paix. The building
surrounding them was huge, a tremendous and impressive monument to the idea that the world's problems can
be solved by cooperation, committee, debate, social development programs, and political will. That it was original-
ly constructed to house the ill-fated and impotent League

ations was not a topic much discussed in these halls anymore.

The gigantic building with its federal façade now housed the UN European headquarters and all its departments, including UNCTAD, the United Nations Conference on Trade and Development.

In the gargantuan assembly hall, all had been made ready for the important speech by Mikhail Gorbachev, the general secretary of the Communist Party of the Soviet Union. His Mercedes limousine had arrived earlier, and it and its escorting police cars had quickly disappeared into the building's underground garage.

Max looked up to see Vlad approaching with two UN representatives. The expression on Vlad's face was a combination of relief and exasperation. They carefully checked everyone's passports and IDs, which Max had been guarding in his pocket. Laminated cards on lanyards were handed to Soleil and Max. Camille didn't have clearance to attend the speech.

Soleil turned to Camille. "Sorry. Security. Will you wait here for me?"

"Will I wait for you?" Then she said in a whisper with a small grin, "No. I'm going to run out of the building, pick up the nearest Swiss ski bum, go to Saint Moritz with him, get involved in a torrid affair, and wind up with a French-speaking baby. Of course I'll wait for you. Right here."

As Soleil, Max, and Deshautels began to walk down the wide corridor, Vlad leaned over and said to Max, "I'm happy you were able to call us from that police car. When our driver couldn't find you at the airport, I assumed the worst. I was almost right." Max could do little more than shrug.

Then Vlad grabbed his arm and guided him to the side of the wide corridor. Max looked at his friend, perplexed.

"Max, are you going to defect?" Vlad whispered at him blandly. Max was caught off-guard but couldn't read Vlad's face. His defenses flew up.

"No, of course not," he stuttered.

Vlad tightened his grip on the arm. "Listen to me closely; this will be the last time." Max was silent. "When you're ready to follow that girl to the West, let me know before you do. I wouldn't mislead you or hurt you. I can help you with that, you know." He gave the arm a final squeeze and then let go. Max just stared at him.

"*Chorosho!*" said Vlad finally. "Good. Let's go."

"This is as far as I go," Deshautels said to Soleil as they stopped in front of the heavy doors to the assembly hall. "I can't help you from here."

Soleil turned and looked at him. It must be hard being him, she thought. "Sorry for all the aggravation, Henri," she said softly in French. "You won't have any more trouble from me." She looked at him closely with an open face.

He leaned forward slightly and kissed her on both cheeks.

"*Au revoir*, Soleil." Then he nodded at Max and Vlad, turned, and walked away down the corridor. Soleil watched his back and thought: *Bon chance*, Henri Deshautels.

The semicircular Assembly Hall was filled with delegates, politicians, business people from around the globe, and the usual phalanx of reporters and cameramen. The speech was in Russian but was being simultaneously translated to the listeners both in the hall and around the world.

At its close, General Secretary Gorbachev announced a "last-minute piece of important business that impacts Russia and its relations with the international business community and the world in general."

He eyed Vlad sitting on the aisle in the first row. Vlad took Soleil's hand and led her up to stand next to him near the podium. Vlad addressed the assembly in English. The cameras rolled. The journalists scribbled.

"The Russian people are privileged to acknowledge the return of a national property vital to its and the world's security. Without going into detail, this vital property has been returned in its entirety to the country, and its key will now be presented to the general secretary by Ms. Soleil Tangiere, who was instrumental in its recovery."

The cameras flashed and zoomed in on the beautiful young woman, so striking and out of place in this hall of gray men and critical political jousting. Soleil handed the key to Gorbachev. He smiled at her and said, "*Sposibo.* Thank you." As he shook her hand, she felt a sense of relief wash through her. *I guess this worked after all.*

I'll thank Max later.

Gorbachev faced the cameras and said in Russian, "The people of the Soviet Union owe a debt to Ms. Tangiere, and she will remain in the protection and favor of the people of the Soviet Union forever."

And now, as to *you* Vlad, Mikhail Gorbachev thought as he eyed the younger man. Now, whether you like it or not, I'm handing you a new problem that you are going to have to deal with. He looked at Vlad for another moment. He had heard that the sandy-haired party climber and KGB agent had been using his father's name of late, Spiridonovich, instead of his own. That is not acceptable. Time to correct that as well.

He continued in Russian, "The disposition of this property will be personally supervised to every extent by this patriot," he said, indicating Vlad. "The weight of this responsibility is now totally to be borne by Vladimir here. Vladimir Putin."

Vlad showed a thin smile when he heard his real name being spoken by the general secretary and shook Gorbachev's hand while taking the proffered key in his other. Ah, his silent triumph was huge: you fell into my trap, Mr. Secretary. Oh yes, you did.

He smiled, and his mind raced on: soon, Mr. Secretary, you will be finished as you lose your grip on our country, and we will be busy manipulating that drunken boor Yeltsin into power. And then one day he will be gone too, after he has taken the blame for what will surely go wrong over the next few years. And then the true reorganization will begin. *My* reorganization. Russia needs me. The key is in the right hands now.

And everyone, *everyone* knows it.

Gorbachev shook Putin's hand. It was a grand photo op moment.

The confused journalists were busy frantically scribbling theories about nuclear codes, security technologies, and a sexy young Canadian woman.

And across the globe, anyone who had an inclination to bother with Soleil Tangiere instantly gave up on that notion. The key was in the hands of a superpower now, and she was under the personal protection of some of the most powerful men in the world with a nuclear arsenal at their disposal.

Bother with Soleil Tangier now? It wasn't worth it.

It would be suicide.

Shadows began to lengthen over the City of Peace.

Their room at the Grand Hotel Kampinsky overlooked the lake. The city had shut down the Jet d'Eau fountain, and police and rescue boats plied the lake's surface while divers hunted underwater for bodies or pieces of the wreckage. No one had found the person that someone thought he had seen diving from the machine, and now there was no hope of survivors.

Camille watched the activity on the lake from the balcony and considered what to do next. She needed to come to grips with the day's unbelievable happenings and wondered for the tenth time if Soleil was human: a Navy SEAL on steroids wouldn't have made it through Soleil's day.

Soleil and Camille had a two-bedroom suite, and Max had the suite next door. They had heard Max talking on the phone through the wall, mostly in Russian. Some of the conversations sounded angry, and some were too quiet to make out any of the words.

At one point room service delivered a cart stacked with food. Max came in, and they all ate together. No one said very much. It seemed as if words wouldn't work at this time for anyone. Max carefully checked the bump on Soleil's temple, declared it might be looking a little better, and went back to his room.

Fatigue had begun to grip Soleil when she heard a soft knock. Camille walked over and looked though the little round lens in the center of the door. She turned to Soleil and said, "It's a woman, dark hair, never saw her before."

Soleil got up and went to look through the peephole. It couldn't be. She opened the door. The woman stood in the doorway.

"Yvonne! It can't be you!"

"*Oui*, it is," she whispered and burst into tears. Soleil gently hugged her and guided her into the suite. They sat on the couch, and Camille stood by the door and looked on.

"Yvonne, I'm so sorry. But so happy to see you! They said you were very sick, very...damaged."

Yvonne looked as though she had lost weight, but her eyes were bright. Her voice was very soft, and uncertainty lurked at its edges.

"*Non*, Soleil," she said in French. "I betrayed you. I was weak. I told that black-haired witch that you had gone to Zurich, and so I put you in danger. And I also told her about the key. Thank God she didn't kill you as she said she would." A tear rolled down her cheek.

Soleil looked at Yvonne. She switched to English. "No, Yvonne, as you can see, I'm here, and you are here as well. You don't have to think about that person any more—she got what she deserved." After a pause she said, "The police told me you would never speak again. I'm glad they were wrong."

Her wet brown eyes were clear. "I could always speak, Soleil. I just waited until I thought my words would no longer endanger you. When I saw you on television today, I knew that time had come."

Soleil was touched. She looked over at Camille and said, "This is Yvonne, the woman I told you about." Camille nodded and smiled. Soleil said, "She's my friend."

And then to Yvonne, "When you're healed, that job offer still stands at Tangiere International."

Yvonne smiled. "I'm healed."

So am I, thought Soleil.

It was late.

Max almost missed the small knock on his door. He came out of the bathroom with only a towel around his waist and quickly pulled on the white robe supplied by the hotel.

"Who is it?" he asked in a low voice, switching on the light near the door.

After a few seconds, the answer came softly: "Me."

He opened the door, and she walked quickly into the room and pushed the door closed behind her. She was in a hotel robe as well, which was way too large for her. She had showered and washed her hair, which was now wrapped in a hotel towel. It looked as if she were wearing a floppy white turban.

Her face looked small in all that terrycloth. But it had that radiance that he had fallen in love with in Zurich.

"What's wrong?" There was concern in his voice. They both sat on the couch.

She pulled her feet up under her. "I couldn't sleep."

"And..." he coaxed.

"Just that. Can't sleep."

He got up and went to the minibar. He took out a split of champagne, opened the bottle, and filled two glasses, pausing every half inch so the bubbles wouldn't flow over the edges.

He handed her a glass and sat down at the other end of the couch. They clicked glasses.

"What are we toasting?" Soleil asked.

"Being alive. Being together." Another click, and they each took a sip. Then he asked, "Still mad at me?"

She looked at him with clear eyes and let a number of quiet seconds tick by. "No."

"*Chorosho*. That means 'good.'"

"I know what it means."

She reached up, and in a moment the towel that had wrapped her hair was gone. She shook her head from side to side, and her hair fell over the shoulders of her robe. Max could smell the fresh scent from where he sat.

"S-o-o," he said slowly. "How was your day?"

They both laughed.

She moved over to him and stretched out so her head was on his lap and she could look up at his face. He leaned down to kiss her. She met him halfway.

"*Chorosho*," she said later.

When Camille woke up the next morning, she couldn't find her sister anywhere in the suite.

EPILOGUE

Her voice sounded all choked up, but he was certain it was an act.

"I'm sorry, Kurt. I've been an ass, a real ass."

Kurt Ballas listened without saying anything.

"We can work this out. Since the ball, I realized what a mistake I've been making. You're my husband, the only man I could ever love. I know you feel the same." She paused. Then: "And of course there's the chil—"

"Stop, Amanda," Kurt said suddenly into the phone. "Just stop it."

He felt good, and he felt strong again. He had come to the right decision.

"It's over, Amanda, and that's that. I don't love you, and I'm not going have the kids live in a war zone disguised as a home any more."

"What happened, Kurt?" vitriol suddenly rising in her voice. "You scored big with that Camille woman in New York, and now you're the big Man About Town again, is that it?"

"No."

She continued prattling on. As her voice droned, he slowly raised his head and stared at nothing for a minute. Thoughts of Camille Weston swirled into his head.

"Good bye, Amanda."

In Amanda's hand the receiver went dead.

A black-and-purple flame peeked out from the top of his work shirt.

"I like your new tattoo," she said into the microphone.

There were only one or two visitors today—wives with some time on their hands. Two bored prison guards stood behind her leaning against the wall.

"How's Soleil? I saw her on TV." His dirty blond hair had been cut shorter than usual, and his million-dollar smile was intact.

"She's all right. She says 'hello, Jake.'"

"Well, hello back." He leaned in closer to the clear Lexan barrier.

"Listen, Cami, I'll be out in four months. I was thinking that if you'll be around, maybe we can get together again. You know. Hell, it won't be perfect, never was. But at least it will be better than nothing at all, you know?" The smile.

She looked at her ex-husband. I will say that bad boy *does* still have that smile. But things have changed—now there *is* more than nothing at all, much more.

And she had decided that on the way to Europe, she would stop over in Chicago after all.

"Jake, I'm moving on. I came to say good-bye." She looked at him through the bulletproof glass. Then, mostly to herself, she repeated softly, "I came a long way to say good-bye." She saw the gears grinding in his head but knew how the conversation would end. The "but thises" and the "what ifs" filled the microphone for a few minutes.

Suddenly, in the middle of one of his sentences, she stood up, leaned over the small Formica ledge, put both her hands up against the clear divider, and pursed her lips a few inches from the glass in a pantomime kiss.

She leaned into the mike: "Call me when you get out. Bye, Jake."

He raised a hand, waggled his fingers at her, and smiled the smile.

They made it a point to always keep up with current events.

They had just finished a dinner featuring boiled chicken in noodle soup and were now sitting in the living room in front of the television. Tango had fallen asleep in Izzy's lap, and the old jeweler had a nice hot cup of cocoa balanced on his knee.

Peter Jennings was covering a conference in Geneva. This Russian fellow on TV was making a little speech, and Izzy said, "Look, Brenda, that young woman looks like our Solie. Isn't that something?" Brenda leaned forward in her chair, and her eyes opened wide.

The man was saying, "And its key will now be presented to General Secretary Gorbachev by Ms. Soleil Tangiere, who was instrumental in its recovery…"

It took Brenda a half an hour to get the cocoa stain out of the carpet.

The gray panorama of London spread out before her on the other side of the floor-to-ceiling windows. She gazed at it with intensity as she sat in the large office—her office. There were no chairs, not a one. Visitors can stand, thank you, and I, well, my chair goes with me wherever I go.

She cast a beady and malevolent eye around the starkly modern room. Her eyes and skin had the eerie avian cast of a carrion stork or a turkey vulture: she almost looked like a human mummy.

Silence.

Then Big Ben began to strike:

Bong! The famous sound from the famous bell tower was clear and portentous.

An image had seared itself into her brain: a young girl standing with a powerful man. The man was telling her that she would be protected. Really?

Bong!

The entire Russian army will not protect you. No power on Earth will protect you from *me*, girl.

Bong!

You've destroyed my legacy, my line. Now I want you. And I will get you.

Bong!

She wet her lips with her small reptilian tongue.

"I'm coming for you, Soleil Tangiere."

Her voice was dry as the Sahara.

Bong!

It was hard to hear anything—the noise of the Nevsky plane's engines warming up was an annoying constant.

The Russian corporate jet had been moved away from the gate the previous day to let other scheduled planes up to the terminal.

They stood on the tarmac holding each other.

He looked in her eyes.

"Will you wait for me?" Max asked.

"Maybe."

"Will you miss me?"

"Perhaps."

A quick thought: "You wouldn't come with me now, would you?"

"Of course not."

"Then I must rush back to you, *da?*"

"*Da.*"

They both smiled and hugged fiercely. Men are so dumb. And so many of them are weak. Max has a weakness or two, but not nearly as many as most other men. He saved my life in a bold and clever way, and I think I saved his too. In another way.

He wants to know if I love him but isn't sure how to ask. He doesn't realize that I've already answered that question, just not in words.

She pushed gently away from him, and they stood looking deeply into each other's eyes.

I did what I set out to do: bring Dad's killers to justice. It's taken a few years, and now it's done. That door is closed.

Now another one opens: a new beginning in my life starts now. The mission that's dominated my thoughts and my soul for the last four years is no more. Now I need to sort out the next chapter, find new reasons, new missions.

I love you. I do, Max, and if it's meant to be for us, that would be wonderful.

And I will wait for you.

But don't take too long.

They kissed long and hard, and then Max got on the plane.

Soleil turned and started back to the terminal.

The wind swirled her coat and tousled her hair.

Sapphire eyes flashed.

What's next?

I'll decide.

THE END

ACKNOWLEDGEMENTS

Thanks for your help in production, editing and contributions: Pamela Crotty, Eva and Bill Thomas, Jeannie Merit Bosworth, and Camille Brulè, who taught me that Canadian French is something way different than "French" French.

On a family level I wish to acknowledge the love and influences of my son Alex, my mother and sister on earth and my father and brother in heaven, none of whom appear in this book because I'm smarter than that.

And of course, all my love to my wife Stephanie, the inspiration for Soleil, who endured having a novelist for a husband writing about sexy young women. Now *that's* devotion...

One more thing...Lion's Rock was real and is described as I recall it. It closed in the early 1990's.

www.soleiltangiere.com

Larry Bonner earned degrees in Economics and Political Science from New York University before launching a forty year career in the precious metals and commodities industries. *Soleil Tangiere* is his debut novel.

Bonner currently lives with his wife in Florida and has one son.

Visit Soleil Tangiere at www.SoleilTangiere.com.

25738485R00182

Made in the USA
Charleston, SC
13 January 2014